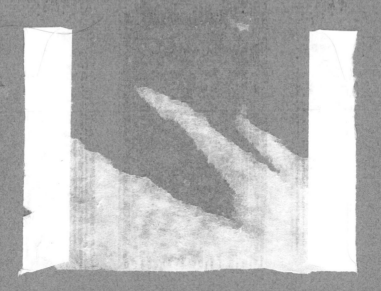

WITHDRAWN FROM
COLLECTION

LOST IN CYBERSPACE

Novels for Young People by
Richard Peck

Don't Look and It Won't Hurt
Dreamland Lake
Through a Brief Darkness
Representing Super Doll
The Ghost Belonged to Me
Are You in the House Alone?
Ghosts I Have Been
Father Figure
Secrets of the Shopping Mall
Close Enough to Touch
The Dreadful Future of Blossom Culp
Remembering the Good Times
Blossom Culp and the Sleep of Death
Princess Ashley
Those Summer Girls I Never Met
Voices After Midnight
Unfinished Portrait of Jessica
Bel-Air Bambi and the Mall Rats
The Last Safe Place on Earth
Lost in Cyberspace

LOST IN CYBERSPACE

Richard Peck

Dial Books for Young Readers

NEW  YORK

Published by Dial Books for Young Readers
A Division of Penguin Books USA Inc.
375 Hudson Street
New York, New York 10014

Text copyright © 1995 by Richard Peck

Designed by Judith M. Lanfredi
Printed in the U.S.A.

First Edition
1 3 5 7 9 10 8 6 4 2

Library of Congress Cataloging in Publication Data
Peck, Richard, date
Lost in cyberspace / by Richard Peck.
p.   cm.
Summary: While dealing with changes at home,
sixth-grader Josh and his friend Aaron use the computers
at their New York City prep school to travel through time,
learning some secrets from the school's past
and improving Josh's home situation.
ISBN 0-8037-1931-0
[1. Time travel—Fiction.   2. Schools—Fiction.
3. Brothers and sisters—Fiction.]
I. Title.
PZ7.P338Lo   1995   [Fic]—dc20   94-48330   CIP   AC

This book is dedicated
with thanks
to Jana Fine and Pat Scales

1
The Mesozoic Era

After the separation, Dad moved to Chicago, and Mom decided to go back to work, so she was practicing getting up early. She'd bought some new outfits. Heather and I were dressed for school. I go to the Huckley School for Boys, so I was in dress code:

black blazer
blue-and-white Huckley tie
big shirt
gray flannel pants
any shoes but sneakers

Heather goes to the Pence School for Girls:

white blouse, choice of style, with collar
Pence plaid skirt
any shoes but sneakers

Heather's shoe statement was lace-up black blobs with stainless steel eyelets and tire-tread soles. Each of her shoes weighed an easy six pounds.

"There are children with tragic foot deformities who have to wear corrective shoes much better looking than those," Mom often said to Heather. "And cheaper."

This morning Mom had some news for us. It was about somebody named Fenella, who was coming from England to live with us. Mom had found Fenella on an Internet link-up called "Au Pair Exchange."

"And what's an O Pear supposed to be?" Heather was tearing open a Pop-Tart and examining its insides, which is a thing she does. "It sounds like a baby-sitter who never leaves. Who needs her? I'm virtually thirteen and emotionally fourteen. I missed the Gifted and Talented Program by *this much*. I can sit myself. I'll O Pear Josh."

She jerked a thumb at me. And I'm only one grade behind her. "I'll be the O Pear who never leaves," Heather said.

I slid out of my chair and checked out the window for the school bus. We live twelve floors above Fifth Avenue. The trees over in Central Park were bare branches with wrinkled balloons left over from summer. The Huckley bus was held up at the light on the corner. It's a Chrysler minivan with a blue-and-white paint job. Heather's Pence bus was in the distance behind a tie-up.

"Buses," I said.

"Don't think of Fenella as a baby-sitter," Mom said.

"I'm not thinking about her at all," Heather said. "She's the farthest thing from my mind. And where are we going to put her? We use the maid's room for storage."

"And don't think of her as a maid," Mom said. "Au pairs are not baby-sitters. And they aren't servants. They're English girls from very nice backgrounds. They come over here to help out with families and to see American life. They're here to expand their horizons, and ours."

Heather said, "My horizons are already—"

But Mom said, "Whoa," because I was heading for the door. She had new glasses with giant lenses for her upcoming career. She looked me over. Standing, I'm as tall as she is sitting. "How did you learn to tie a tie that well?" She peered at me. "It even has a little dimple under the knot. That's professional work."

"Practice," I said.

"Is the day coming when you won't need your old ma for anything?"

"Not right away," I said.

"I have the final interview today," Mom said, "at Barnes Ogleby."

"B.O.," Heather said.

"I'll be home before you two are unless they let school out early again. Why can't schools run the full day anymore?"

"Because we're pressured enough." Heather clutched her forehead. "We need a lot more time off than we get."

"All the more reason for Fenella. I don't want you turning into a couple of latchkey kids," Mom said. "Wet or dry?" she said to me.

"Dry as possible."

She planted a careful kiss on my cheek. It was hardly damp, and she didn't have her lipgloss on yet.

I didn't give Fenella any more thought. I mainly think about what's happening now. When I left the apartment for school, Heather was still popping her tart. We try not to take the same elevator.

Aaron Zimmer was on it, coming down from the penthouse. He's in my year at Huckley, but shorter. We call him the A-to-Z man because of his name and because he knows everything from A to Z. Some of what he knows is actual fact. Some of it is just stuff he says.

"Yo," we said. I stick my homework into whatever book. Everybody but Aaron carries gear to school in a backpack. He carries a briefcase-style laptop computer with a certain amount of software. Even without storing it electronically, he has a lot of signal compression in his biological memory bank. He's what they used to call a smart kid.

"Six hundred and sixty-five more class periods till summer," he said. "I estimate that at seven classes a day, five days a week, allowing for holidays, spring break, and field trips."

"What about—"

"I've factored in fire drills. The field trip today is dinosaurs."

4

The Huckley School catalogue tells parents that all its students are to be interactively computer literate for the challenges of twenty-first century corporate competition.

This means they've walled off one end of the media center and have a couple of terminals in there. I'm not that much into it. Also, I spell better in real life than on the keyboard. Aaron has named the computer room the Black Hole. That's his personal name for it, possibly because it doesn't have natural light. He's in there most of the day. You can sign out of classes and go there if you can get a teacher to cover for you.

They tell us that in the future we won't have to leave our screens for global video-conferencing across the information superhighway. All we'll need is a mouse and a modem and we'll never need to go outdoors.

But we get out quite a bit for field trips. So we were looking at another day at the Natural History Museum. You can get all this edutainment on CD-ROM. But in the winter we have two field trips a week to keep the restlessness down.

At the museum, they threw our class in with the fourth and fifth grades. The fourth graders aren't even in middle school yet, but we integrate with them for field trips to get them ready for us. Even the fourth graders have been coming to see the dinosaurs for years.

"All they do is stand around like dorks," said a fifth grader, meaning the dinosaurs. "What this place needs is some electronic manipulation. They could use some digital film techniques."

"Kids," Aaron said, shaking his head.

We passed up the headphones. Aaron had the whole dinosaur evolution stored and was happy to display his own personal version of it.

"The jury is still hung about whether dinosaurs were hot-blooded or cold like your contemporary reptiles," he remarked. "The speed of their movements argues for hot blood."

We moved into the Hall of Mongolian Vertebrates.

"In Asian deserts fossilized nestlings have been uncovered along with clutches of eggs. This means dinosaurs conducted family life. To defend against the meat-eaters, the larger herbivores developed a herd mentality."

A herd of fourth graders were hanging around us by now. Aaron talked them right through to the extinction of dinosaurs, touching lightly on the giant asteroid theory.

They listened, but some of them were still confused by "fossilized nestlings."

"Say hello to the baluchitheres," he said in passing, "ancient cousins of your modern rhino."

Then he summed up by saying, "The only certain fact about dinosaurs is that no species was ever purple and named Barney."

The fourth graders stared.

Now the museum cafeteria was in sight. A huge, long-necked, small-headed shadow fell over us.

It was Mr. Headbloom, the teacher in charge. He has us for homeroom, and he's our reading teacher. He calls the reading class Linear Decoding. You'd think teachers would be impressed by Aaron. He has all this knowl-edge he doesn't even have to call up on a screen. But with teachers he's not that popular. Mr. Headbloom is glad to sign him out of class to go to the Black Hole anytime Aaron wants.

"Zimmer," Mr. Headbloom said, "knock off the voice-over and let the fourth graders interface with the exhibits as units."

As the old Huckley teachers like Mr. L. T. Thaw die off, they're replaced by mouse potatoes like Mr. Head-bloom who talk like this. We went in and did lunch.

2

The Ultimate Computer

Aaron had goat cheese on seven-grain bread, being a vegetarian—herbivore. I had the beef burrito.

"I don't know," I said. "Dinosaurs just don't do it for me anymore. I mean, they're all dead and gone, right? Who'd want them around anyway? Hitting a deer on the highway is bad enough."

Aaron had his laptop on the lunch table. He was idly punching up something on it with his left hand, then squinting at his screen.

"Look, the past is over," I said. "It's okay for museums, but we've got enough problems without digging up the old days. Am I right or what?"

Aaron dug a grain out from between his teeth. "I have a theory." He has a lot of them. "And I think modern cybernetics will bear me out sooner or later. As we know, science is slow."

His left hand was still playing his laptop like a piano. He can think out of at least two compartments of his brain at the same time.

"As I see it, there are a couple of ways to approach the past. You can dig it up, like dinosaurs, which is basically pre-electronic."

"There's cloning too," I said. "DNA and like that."

"Forget cloning. That's not experiencing the past. That's reproducing it."

"There's virtual reality," I said.

"That's show business," Aaron said.

"Or you can get into your time machine," which was my last idea.

Aaron sighed. "Josh, I can read your mind. Time machine to you means this thing made out of sheet metal with ten-speed gears, flashing lights, and little puffs of smoke coming out of a tailpipe. A contraption."

"With seat belts," I said.

"Forget it," he said. "Grow up." Sometimes he can look at you just like a teacher.

"You can dig up the past. Or you can really test the electronic limits and actually be there. It's a question of dialing into the cosmic internet. The past isn't necessarily over. It's just piping in on a parallel plane." Aaron ran a finger around his collar, which is a thing he does. I think his mom still ties his tie. "Do you follow me?"

"Sure," I said.

"No, you don't. You're like this in class. You're breathing steady. Your eyes are open. But nobody's home. Your modem's unplugged. Let me try it another

9

way." He tapped the table with a finger covered in goat-cheese crumbs.

"We're looking ahead to maybe five hundred TV channels available to the general viewing public."

"So?"

"So how about five hundred and one?"

"You mean the five hundred and first channel is the real past if you could just find a way of calling it up?"

"You're scanning in the right direction," Aaron said, "but I know how you think. You picture yourself sitting in front of a screen viewing the past like an old movie, with a bottle of Snapple in your hand."

"But big screen," I said, "and better than VHS quality."

Aaron rolled his eyes, so I said, "What you're saying is that the past is still happening if you know where to look?"

"Cyberspatially," said the A-to-Z man. "Or in layman's terms, yes."

"Just how many people are going to be able to channel-surf into another time?" I try not to swallow all Aaron's theories. I try to be skeptical.

He shrugged. "Who can say? Maybe we're already doing it and don't notice. We sleep a third of the time. Teenagers sleep more than that. Who knows where you are when you're asleep? Not all your circuitry is shut down. Think about dreams."

"I dream a lot about falling."

"Who doesn't? That's the first fear babies have. We haven't been babies for ten years. Dreams are strange, and the whole world's strange to a baby, right? And scary. Maybe dreams aren't memories. Maybe they're happening."

"Then you wake up and you're back to real time?" I said.

"Both times are real," Aaron said. "The forward-movement idea of time is a pretech human way of explaining the unknown. It's a primitive invention, like the rotary-dial phone."

"And I have this dream where we're taking a test at school, except it isn't exactly Huckley. And if I fail this test, I'm in deep—"

"Perfect example," Aaron said. "That could be something from a hundred years ago when flunking a test was serious. You could be living the experience of a kid in a really strict school, in England or somewhere. I mean it's not about now, right? Buster Brewster has flunked every test since preschool. And does Huckley throw him out or keep him back a year or beat him with paddles? No such luck. Not as long as his parents keep paying tuition."

Aaron shouldn't even have mentioned Buster Brewster, because Buster himself appeared at our table. We don't have bullies at Huckley. We call them hyperactive. Buster was the main one in our grade.

He whacked the back of Aaron's head and reached across him for our salt shaker. Buster was going from table to table, loosening the tops of the salt shakers like he does in the school cafeteria. There's nothing too original about his thinking. He wrenched ours loose with his mighty fist. Salt rained all over the table.

"Don't even think about tightening that," he said.

Buster's voice hasn't changed yet, but it's lower than ours. "Make my day, wusses." Then he lumbered on to the next table.

"Be nice if Buster Brewster entered another time frame and forgot to come back," I said, but quietly. "Seriously, though, do you think it's possible to make contact with other times, outside of dreams?"

"Josh," Aaron said, making shapes in the salt, "we've already got video beamed over phone wire. We've got phone calls digitized over TV cable. We've got data-based interactivity going in every direction. We're talking information explosion. We're talking new windows of opportunity. Or in layman's terms, anything's possible."

I'd polished off my burrito. Aaron was picking up scattered grains on his plastic plate with a wet, salty finger. Somehow this annoyed me.

"Like you're fine-tuning yourself, right?" I said to him. "Like you could be time-warped into another age, right?"

"I'm in early stages with it," Aaron said. "And remember, generally speaking, technology is way behind concept.

"And remember this too, Josh." He stared across the table at me like a red-headed owl. "Artificial intelligence is the buzzword of the age and the wave of the future. But the human brain is the ultimate computer."

All this talk about time and distance reminded me of Fenella for some reason.

"We're getting an O Pear."

Aaron pushed back his tray and ran a hand through his hair. Being carrot-red, it suits a vegetarian.

"Tell me about it, Josh." Sometimes he sounds like a guidance counselor.

I hadn't meant to tell him a thing. I hadn't even mentioned that my mom and dad were separated. Dad had only been gone three months and a week, and usually called Sunday nights. I hadn't gotten around to mentioning it to anybody. I didn't even like mentioning it to myself.

"Your mom's getting some help around the house now your dad's left and she's going back to work at Barnes Ogleby?"

I stared. "Aaron, how do you know my dad's—not around? How do you have access to all this personal data about my family?"

"Vince. The doorman. Day shift. Doormen know it all. Who's there. Who's not. What we eat, because they see the grocery deliveries. Your mom's not having the groceries delivered anymore. She's cutting down expenses by carrying them home. Doormen read our mail."

"They read our mail?"

"The envelopes. How else could they sort them? Your dad's writing from a 60611 zip code. Chicago, right? You people ought to get E-mail."

"It's just a trial separation," I said, though I wasn't too sure about that. Maybe I should ask Vince.

"Is it a French au pair or a German one?" Aaron asked. "Because they'll try to teach you the language.

Bonjour, mes enfants; Guten Tag, Kinder—that kind of thing."

"English," I said, "but our apartment is filling up with women."

I didn't have to say I wanted Dad back. Aaron could figure that out. His dad and mom are together. But his mom is his dad's third wife, so you never know.

The field trip shot the day. We only went back to Huckley to catch our buses home. Mom was already there when I came in.

"I got the job," she said. She was in jeans and a sweatshirt, clearing everything out of Dad's old den. He hadn't taken much but his computer and fax. I thought that was a good sign. But now Mom was sweeping clean. She was dusting Dad's empty shelves.

"What a long face," she said, fingering my chin. "It's just for now, Josh. Really. I'm tidying things away so we can put Fenella in here. We've always used it as a guest room anyway. Think of Fenella as a—helpful guest. She'll be good for Heather. Heather needs a . . . role model."

So Fenella was nearer than I knew.

I dreamed that night, big-time and nonstop. It was about Aaron and me at the Natural History Museum. It was us, but it wasn't exactly the museum. It was actual Mesozoic times. We weren't wearing anything except blue-and-white Huckley ties, which is typical of my dreams. As we trudged along through the swamp, mud and twigs seeped between our toes.

"Primeval ooze," the dream Aaron said.

Volcanoes were erupting in the distance. Some really scary things were flying around on webbed wings. All my dreams are colorized. Aaron was eating a carrot. When he clutched my dream arm, we took cover under a plant with giant leaves.

A huge, long-necked, small-headed shadow fell over us. It blotted out the sky. Aaron and I grabbed each other. The leaf we were hiding under turned transparent. And this dinosaur spotted us. Its head wasn't so small anymore. A snaky neck coiled, and it was coming down at us, and it was all teeth.

"Tyrannosaurus Regina," Aaron whispered. "Cretaceous period. Meat-eater."

Now its eyes were zeroing in on me. And its face was changing. Now it was half-human with big brown eyes.

"My name is Fenella," it said. "Think of me as a helpful guest." Then its jaws opened wide.

That was enough to knock me out of bed. I fought my way up toward being awake. It's a long way from the Mesozoic Era. But I was nearly there. I could feel the sheet twisted under me. And I had on my pajamas, which is more than I was wearing in the dream.

I wasn't alone, though. Somehow Heather had horned in on my dream. But I was moving faster than she was. Her shoes were slowing her down.

3

The Club Scene

"Let's put our best feet forward," Mom said. She'd rounded up Heather and me to meet Fenella at the airport. She even hinted we might wear our school clothes.

"No way," Heather said. "We're only inmates during the day." She wanted to stay home because she said Camilla Van Allen might call. Heather says Camilla Van Allen is her best friend. But we hadn't seen anything of her.

"She'll leave a message for you on the machine," Mom told Heather. "If she calls."

Heather looked sulky in her parachute silk puffy jacket, jeans, and her biggest shoes. I wore the Bulls warm-up jacket Dad sent me from Chicago after one of the Sunday nights when he didn't call. We cabbed out to JFK Airport in the middle of the evening rush. Then

Fenella's flight was two hours late because snow was blowing. Only one runway was open.

That gave Mom time to run over the Au Pair Exchange printout. Fenella was seventeen, a recent "school leaver," whose interests included

reading
field hockey
gardening
needlework
flower-arranging
and gourmet cooking

Her career aspirations were in the areas of

teaching
editing children's books
or interior design

Halfway through the printout Heather wandered off to browse the airport arcade shops.

There was a fuzzy Xerox picture of Fenella in a school uniform and straw hat. It didn't look too recent and could have been anybody.

The contract said Fenella could be expected to "assist with light household work, food preparation, and child care, no more than twenty hours a week, with opportunities for extended travel experience in the United States." She had a right to her own room.

"Do we pay her, or does she pay us?"

"We pay her," Mom said.

Heather came back and said, "Let's eat." We went to

the Skyteria until they announced that the London plane was on the ground.

Passengers came pouring out through the Customs doors, pushing their luggage on carts. Mom kept the picture handy and was watching everybody. "Let's be very careful about our speech patterns," she said. "English people speak so beautifully."

I lost count after a hundred and eighty people. Aaron would have had his calculator with him. "Maybe she's not coming," Heather said, perking up. The waiting crowd was pretty much just us by now. Most of the people coming out were flight attendants. "When we see the pilot," Heather said, "let's leave."

Then the door banged open, and this girl appeared, dragging a giant laundry bag with tags. She was fairly giant herself, dressed in total, recycled black. Several layers over a black body stocking and big elf boots below.

But what you really noticed was her face. It was a large pale moon with black lips, three nose rings, and a small spider tattooed on her right cheekbone. The hat on top was hard to miss too. It had a big floppy brim pinned back by a bunch of black plastic flowers.

Heather blinked. "Beyond grunge," she said.

Mom was still looking for somebody to match the picture. But the girl came toward us, getting bigger and bigger. We weren't hard to spot. We were the only people left.

"Fenella here," she said, gazing over our heads with big sleepy brown eyes.

"Oh," Mom said. "Oh. I'm . . . Mrs. Lewis."

"I'm Josh," I said, staggering back because Fenella had dropped her laundry bag on me.

"I'm like amazed," Heather said, staring.

The snow was blowing out to sea, and the air was crisp and clear. You get a great look at Manhattan on a night like that: all the twinkling towers and the chains of lights on the bridges. Mom wanted to show Fenella the view. But she slept through it. She was zonked right to our door. We had to wake her up to get out of the cab.

"Jet lag," Mom said in a hushed voice. "It's just temporary. But I wonder if that spider is permanent."

Then Fenella dozed off in the elevator, slumped against the wall with her hat tipped down to her nose rings. She snored.

She slept for nineteen hours. By then it was Saturday evening. Mom was getting nervous. For one thing, she was going out that night. Behind a door, I heard her and Heather.

"It's not a date," Mom was saying. "Stop calling it a date. It's dinner and the theater with Mr. Ogleby, Jr. It's business. He's head of the accounting department, and he's welcoming me into the firm. He's just showing me professional courtesy. Should I wear my drop earrings, or are they too much?"

"It's a date," Heather said when she caught me listening outside the door. "Mom's dating again. We better get Fenella on her feet or Mom won't leave. She'll cancel Mr. Ogleby, Jr., and stay home with us. She'll want to pop popcorn and rerun *Honey, I Shrunk the Kids.*"

We cracked the door of Dad's den. The sofa folds out into a bed. There was a large lump in the middle of it. Fenella's hat was on Dad's desk, covering most of it.

"Hey, Fenella," Heather said. The lump moved. "It's like a whole different day. In fact, it's night again. Get up."

Fenella seemed to be on her hands and knees now, shaking her head. "Crikey," she said, or something like that.

Mom was dressed in her best and beginning to pace when Fenella came into the living room. She filled up the whole door. She'd taken off some of her black layers and left on the rest. We hadn't caught a good look at her with her hat off before. Hair sprang up like a stiff mop all around her head, and it was between maroon and purple. On her right cheekbone was a small human skull with a dagger through its eye socket. So the spider wasn't permanent.

"Oh," Mom said. "Feeling rested?"

"Feelin' like I just been jumped by a bunch of skinheads," Fenella said. "Feelin' like I was just kicked in the—"

The buzzer rang, and it was Mr. Ogleby, Jr. Mom had to go. "Maybe I should call when we get to the theater," she said at the door. She didn't feel any too good about leaving us.

"It's cool, Mom," Heather said. "We'll O Pear Fenella. She'll be fine." Then Heather gave me a look which she usually doesn't do.

After that we showed Fenella the kitchen. She stood in front of the refrigerator, making a few selections.

"Do you want to do some gourmet cooking?" Heather inquired, testing her.

"Some wot?" Fenella said. "You got Big Macs in this country yet?"

It wouldn't have surprised me if Fenella had wanted to call it a day and go back to bed. She didn't move fast even in her thinking. And I'll tell you this. She never did figure out what our names were. We followed as she roamed around the apartment, ending up at the living room windows. "Oy," she said or something like that. "It's night."

"I tried to tell you," Heather said.

"So let's go," Fenella said, beginning to stir.

Heather blinked. We're talking New York here, so we don't go out at night a lot. On the other hand, Heather began to see some possibilities. Anyway, maybe Fenella would be protection enough.

"Like where?" Heather said carefully.

"Like outta here is flippin' where," Fenella said. "Clubs and such."

"Clubs?" Heather had heard of them, but didn't know where they were.

"Clubs, raves, venues," Fenella said. She was waking up now. "I got some addresses. Downtown."

To us, downtown is anywhere south of Saks, and we don't go there. A strange, eager look came over Heather's face. "I don't think Josh can get in," she said, still carefully. "Of course, we could leave him at home."

"*You* couldn't get in like that." Fenella looked down

21

at Heather in her peach cableknit cardigan and then at me in my Bulls warm-up jacket, which I'm always wearing when I'm not wearing something else.

"You, Tiny Tim," Fenella said to me. "You got a school uniform? Coat and tie, something like that?" I nodded. "Go put it on. They'll think you're a midget." This could have been Fenella's little joke. But I didn't want to get left behind, so I went to change. Fenella pointed Heather to her room and followed her in.

In fifteen minutes the three of us were out in the hall, waiting for the elevator. I was in blazer and Huckley tie.

Fenella didn't look too different. She had her hat on, a major statement. She'd freshened the black on her lips and added a ring or two to her nose. From her laundry bag she'd come up with a long black cape. She looked like a cross between a vampire and a graduating senior.

Underneath, she had on a really micro-skirt, also black, with fishnet stockings. The stockings had holes in them with a lot of Fenella showing through.

But Heather was the center of attention, which she likes. Fenella had done her over. In fact, Heather had on Fenella's face. Her lips were coal-black. Fenella had even drawn in nose rings with her eyebrow pencil, along with a small coiled rattlesnake with fangs on Heather's cheek. Heather's hair is pale and preppy. But Fenella had wrapped it in a black scarf, turban-style. Heather's skirt was amazing. It wasn't any wider than a scarf itself. In this light it looked like shiny black leather.

"It's a plastic garbage bag folded and pinned behind," Heather whispered. "Fenella's a genius."

Heather wore her own panty hose, which she'd torn some serious holes in. She already had the right shoes. She looked like Minnie Mouse from Long Island, but older, which thrilled her.

The elevator door opened, and a man and woman were inside. The woman saw us and screamed. The man jammed a button, and the door closed in our faces. We took the next elevator. But the man and woman had been the Zimmers, Aaron's parents.

"Wot come over them?" Fenella wondered. Then we were past the doorman and out on Fifth Avenue. "Which way's downtown?" she asked, and we pointed her south. With her cape billowing behind her, Fenella was like a large pirate ship under full sail. There was a lot of space in that cape. I began to see how all three of us might get into a club.

"It's south of SoHo," said Fenella, who was a little better organized than she seemed. "Do we hoof it or wot?"

I had money, but didn't know what a cab that far downtown would cost. So I aimed us left on 68th Street for the subway entrance.

We rocketed downtown on a train. And I have to say there were some stranger sights on it than Heather and Fenella. Heather kept giving me looks with her new eyes, which had giant lashes painted in. She was pretty excited. We don't do the subway and certainly not after dark.

We got off way downtown in the warehouse district. But Fenella had a good sense of direction when it came to finding clubs. Finally we were walking along a dark street that was all stripped cars and fire escapes with icicles.

Then we were walking past a line of people who seemed to be looking for a Halloween party. Half of them were on Rollerblades. You had punk and post-punk. You had important hair and totally shaved. You had prom dresses with leg warmers. You had more tattoos than a tractor pull. You had everything from biker boots to bikinis. You had stuff you can't believe. At the front of the line two big guys were guarding a metal door.

"Right, you two," Fenella muttered to us, "under the cape and put a sock in it."

"Put a sock in what?" Heather asked.

"Shut your gob," Fenella explained. "Keep quiet."

Suddenly I was sandwiched between Heather and the back part of Fenella under the cape. The world got even darker.

Fenella had planned to talk us straight into the club, no waiting. But the big guys at the door were giving her static.

"Aw right, aw right," she said. "Don't get your knickers in a twist. I come all the flippin' way from Lunnun to get in this club. I get in all the Lunnun clubs. I'm a personal mate of Boy George. Wotcher mean, I'm too dressed down? 'Ere, stand aside, you miserable gits, or I'll have your guts for garters."

When she stamped her big elf boot, she nearly flattened one of my toes. My foot jerked back and caught Heather on the shin: one more hole for her panty hose.

"A right pair of yobbos you lot are," Fenella was telling the door guards. The cape flapped, and I realized she was putting up her fists.

She was about to punch out two bodybuilders of gorilla size. By now Heather had both hands around my neck, holding on. We'd never have gotten in that club anyway, not with all those extra legs under the cape.

Fenella was starting up the steps anyhow, fighting her way in. I tripped, but followed. Then the world shifted. Robo-hands slipped under Fenella's armpits. She was suddenly off the ground. Her big legs windmilled in every direction. Then we all seemed to be airborne and peeling out of the cape.

We hit frozen litter in the gutter between two stripped cars. A cheer went up from the waiting line of Halloweeners.

The next thing I remember is limping down a side street, listening to what Fenella was calling the two bouncers. They were probably pretty bad words in England. "Prats" was one of them, and "wallies" was another. Heather was beginning to trail behind because of her shoes.

No cab would pick us up, so we had to take the subway again.

Since we hadn't been out that long, I thought we might be home free. But Mom opened the door. She'd called from the theater, and her own voice answered her on the machine. She panicked and came home.

Now she was looking at us. Fenella's hat was still knocked sideways, with the skull on her cheek showing.

Her cape was crusty with gutter slush. Heather's turban was unwinding. But her drawn-on nose rings were hanging tough, and you could practically hear her snake rattle. She'd lost the pin, so she was holding what looked a lot like a narrow garbage bag around her waist. And she wouldn't get another wearing out of those panty hose. We looked like we'd been in a wreck, but not serious enough to feel sorry for. I was wearing school dress code, which made me look responsible, though I wasn't.

4

The Last of Fenella

We took Fenella out to JFK for her flight back to London the next day.

"As a single parent, I see I'm going to have to make a lot of split-second decisions," Mom said. "Fenella goes."

Frankly, Fenella didn't seem that surprised. This may have happened to her before in other countries.

Coming back into the city, I wanted to sit up front with the cabby. He didn't speak English. I thought that might be better than what Mom had to say. But they don't let you sit up front. You could be armed.

Mom sighed. "Fenella had no more judgment than you two." I was on one side of her, and Heather was on the other, staring out the window and trying not to be involved.

We'd been over everything last night. Now we had to go over it again. "All right, Josh," Mom said. "Who should be out at night in New York?"

"Adults," I mumbled, "in cars or cabs. Aboveground."

"And where should they be?"

"Well-lighted neighborhoods. Uptown, East Side preferably, except in the immediate Lincoln Center area."

But Mom couldn't let it go. "Planet Hollywood, I could understand," she said. "The Hard Rock Cafe maybe. Even the Harley-Davidson Cafe in a pinch."

"You could look at it as kind of a field trip," I said.

"Field trip, my foot," Mom said. "The only reason Fenella came over here is to go to so-called clubs in Tribeca and other battle zones that sell drugs to New Jersey teenagers."

Heather sighed. She was waiting for Mom to say "disco," which is a word out of Mom's past she uses sometimes.

"You could see at a glance Fenella was a night person," Mom said. "All she wanted to do was go to discos."

Heather looked around her at me.

"And don't think she wanted the two of you along. She only took you because it was her first night. Later, she'd have dumped you. I wouldn't know who was in charge of you or where you were."

"Mo-om, you don't need to know where I am all the time," Heather whined. "I'm virtually thirteen and emotionally—"

"If you were half as mature as you think you are," Mom said, "you wouldn't have walked past the door-man last night, twice, wearing nothing but a rag on your head, a snake on your face, and a Hefty bag."

"The Zimmers saw us too," I mentioned.

Mom slumped. "You don't mean to tell me that the Zimmers saw you."

"Put a sock in it, Josh," Heather said.

5

Muggers to the Fourth Power

The first field trip that next week was to the Museum of the City of New York. This is probably the most low-tech museum in town. But it's worth a trip, though probably not twice a semester. They had us in with the fourth and fifth grades again.

Most of what they've got in this museum is either under glass or roped off. But you have to watch the fourth and fifth graders. You've got to watch Buster Brewster like a hawk. Three teachers had to pry him loose from a scale model of the Empire State Building. Buster was being King Kong.

After that we had to walk with a teacher according to grade. Mr. Headbloom ran us through the history of the city: dioramas and room settings like "A Dutch Kitchen in Old Nieuw Amsterdam."

Somewhere after "Washington Inaugurated in Wall Street," I missed Aaron. He hadn't been giving his own voice-over because we were too close to Mr. Headbloom. One minute Aaron was there. The next he wasn't. I may have seen him darting up to the second floor. I may not have. Then we were gridlocked behind fourth graders who were hung up at "The Evolution of Hook and Ladder Companies."

Upstairs they've got complete rooms from historic houses. We were coming up on John D. Rockefeller's bedroom (1880). He was a rich tycoon who gave away dimes to show he was generous.

Heavy curtains, gas fixtures, many rugs, and a big bed, all in dim, old-fashioned light. The younger kids moved past the doorway at their top speed. We would have too, except Mr. Headbloom glanced into the bedroom and stopped cold. Sixth graders walked up his heels.

Mr. Rockefeller was in his bed. He died in 1937 at the age of ninety-eight. It says so on a plaque out in the hall. But there was a lump in his bed. I thought of Fenella, but it wasn't that large. What size Rockefeller was, I didn't know. By now he probably wouldn't be too big. The covers were pulled up. But the pillow was dented like there might be a head up there.

Mr. Headbloom looked around for Buster. But for once, he was with the rest of us. The lump in the bed moved. You had to be watching, but it did. "Is this real or multimedia?" somebody said.

Mr. Headbloom scanned up and down the hall,

checking for a museum guard. Then he took a quick, giant scissor-step over the rope across the door. "You," he said to Buster, who was about to go with him, "back."

We watched Mr. Headbloom tiptoe across the oriental carpets. It was cool because this was almost breaking and entering. How often do you see a teacher do that?

He got closer and closer to the bed. He reached down and pulled back the covers. Another rule broken.

There was a flash of red hair, and Aaron sat up in Mr. Rockefeller's bed. His laptop was in his lap.

"Where am I?" he said, looking everywhere except at Mr. Headbloom.

He snatched Aaron out and tried to remake the bed with a few quick moves of one hand. It was the best part of the whole field trip. Mr. Headbloom sprinted out of the exhibit and high-jumped the rope. He had Aaron by one arm. The laptop was swinging from Aaron's other hand. They both cleared the rope like champions. When they lit out in the hall, Mr. Headbloom was breathing hard.

This museum has no cafeteria. We had box lunches in an area with tables. I couldn't interface with Aaron because he had to sit next to Mr. Headbloom.

"I am still shocked, Zimmer," he said, "profoundly shocked."

"It was a project," Aaron said in a small, mouselike voice. "I was doing an I.S." Meaning Independent Study.

"Zimmer, we don't do I.S. until upper school. What you did was infantile. Preliterate. You were acting like . . ."

He was acting like Buster Brewster is what Mr. Headbloom meant. But teachers don't mention Buster's name lightly. Checking around for Buster myself, I saw him in the distance. He had a fourth grader up against a wall and was going through his backpack.

"Profoundly shocked," Mr. Headbloom said to Aaron again. But we were over the worst. At Huckley they don't call your parents unless you're in the actual hands of the law.

We decided to bypass the school bus and walk home that afternoon. We live thirty-some blocks south on Fifth. And it was a fairly mild day, January thaw or whatever.

Aaron strolled along, as normal as he gets.

"Zimmer, I'm shocked," I said. "Profoundly shocked."

"Knock it off, Josh. It was an independent study, like I told Headbloom."

"You were doing an independent study of Rockefeller's bed?" At the Eighty-sixth Street intersection I had to play crossing guard to keep Aaron from walking out into the traffic.

He sighed. "Look, I'm in early stages, but I'll try to explain."

"Do that."

"And I'll try to keep it simple."

"Appreciate it."

"You familiar with dark fiber?"

"Sure. What is it?"

"It's the part of fiber-optic cabling that isn't being used yet," Aaron said. "The data being beamed over fiber-optic networks is rising exponentially."

"What's that mean?"

"We're beaming a whole lot more data every minute. But only point one percent of fiber capacity is being used."

"Right."

"The rest is dark fiber."

"Okay."

"There's a strand in there somewhere that'll beam present-day people into the past. And probably back. I think it must be cellular reorganization."

"Says who?"

"It's my own theory. Hit the right digital frequency, and you'll experience physical translation."

"When do we get to Rockefeller's bed?"

"I've got my theory reduced to numbers that I'm satisfied with. And I've worked up some graphs. Did you know that the computer printer at school can do transparencies?"

"Hadn't noticed that," I said.

We strolled on down Fifth Avenue. And I wondered if Aaron was too weird to know. The elastic on one of his socks had given out. The sock drooped down over his shoe.

"It's more than an equation. It's all part of a larger internet," he said. "I haven't got it fine-tuned yet. It's like I'm one number off. It's like I'm shy one dark fiber. It's like I'm one channel away. It's like—"

"Okay, okay," I said. "I get your point."

"You know what I'm missing?" He elbowed my side. "It's something like the will or the need." He made a fist and looked at it. It was about half the size of Buster's. "I want it, but I don't want it enough. Something like that."

"Which means what?"

"The Emotional Component."

Emotional Component?

"It's not just what you know," Aaron said, "it's what you want. Maybe you can only get to the past if you really need to a lot."

Then it happened.

Four guys came out of Central Park a half block ahead. They were held up by a wagon train of city buses. Then they were crossing Fifth Avenue, giving cabs the finger.

Ball caps on backward. Black leather jackets. T-shirts down to their knees. Ripped Levi's. Two-hundred-dollar gym shoes. And eighth grade if not older. Trouble.

I was trying to remember what you're supposed to do. You're supposed to run out into traffic and take your chances against vehicles. But this bunch was already out there.

Then they spotted us. Aaron was still in his dream world of dark fiber and Emotional Component. I was screaming inside.

We were right in the middle of a block. No side street, nothing. There were a few people on the sidewalk. But they were all don't-get-involved types. Local people, and you're really safer with tourists.

The fearsome foursome was in the middle of Fifth Avenue and angling our way. They'd spotted us, and they'd talked us over. They'd probably even voted. Now they were heading for us, and they had public school written all over them. We were sitting ducks in Huckley dress code and still eleven blocks from home. Dead meat. You can count on your doorman, but not other people's.

I nudged Aaron, and for once this alerted him. "Yikes," he said. "Muggers to the fourth power."

Then he must have freaked out. He lifted one knee to balance his laptop. He flipped it open and started to type up something, an equation or formula or whatever. I had about ten seconds left to look cool. Then I had ball caps on all sides of me.

"Yo, preppy," a ball cap said in an already-changed voice.

I was worried about boxcutters. But all I saw now were big bunches of knuckles. The whole world turned black leather. And the first punch connecting with my head really unplugged my modem.

6

Aaron Up a Tree

When I came to, I felt a wet nose in my ear. At first I had thought it was my own nose. I thought maybe my face had been that rearranged. But out of the swelling eye on that side, I saw it was a French poodle in a plaid jacket. Its owner pulled it away and continued on uptown.

I was stretched on cold concrete. I hadn't been this flat-out since Fenella got us thrown out of that club. At least this was Fifth Avenue. My backpack had broken my fall, more or less. I could feel the shapes of books still in it. Somehow the killer quartet hadn't been too interested in books.

I only had about an eye and a half. Trying to move set off car alarms in my head. Aaron was crouching over me. "You okay?" he said.

"I been better. What did they get?"

"What did you have?"

"About four dollars and change."

"That's what they got. They didn't want your watch. They had Rolexes. You feel like moving?"

He was talking to me, but he was gazing around at Fifth Avenue. Maybe he was worried that the gang would circle back and zero in on us again.

My backpack weighed a ton, but I sat up. My nose was bleeding slightly on my shirt. When I looked down, I saw I had only half a Huckley tie left. It was sliced off just under the knot right through the dimple. So they did have boxcutters.

"You got a handkerchief?" I said.

"You kidding? Use your sleeve. This is an emergency." But still he kept gazing over his shoulder at the street, which was nothing but cabs racing to make the light. He wouldn't look me in the eye, and I only had one eye. I began to wonder about this. I looked him over. He had two eyes and a complete necktie, with traces of goat cheese.

"What did they get off you?"

"Nothing," he mumbled.

"Hey," I said, "why me?"

He shrugged.

"You telling me that they walked right past you to get me? You're smaller. They'd have gone right for you."

"They didn't see me," Aaron muttered.

"You're not that little."

"I wasn't here," he said, almost whispering.

"You didn't run," I said. They'd have brought him down in three paces.

"Not exactly. Let's see if you can stand up."

I had to make two trips, but I got there. I found my feet while heavy metal played in my head. My eye on the poodle side was now swollen shut. Aaron just stood there. He was sneaking peeks at the street, or across the street at the park.

"Let's go home," I said. "I can make it."

"In a minute." Now he was edging away, out to the curb.

"If you want a cab," I said, "you're paying."

But he wasn't looking for a cab. He was looking across at the trees in the park. He was so cyberspaced I thought about limping home by myself. Then he came back and gave me one of his owl looks.

"I was over there," he said, "up that tree, the third one down from the trash can."

"You were up in that tree while I was being pounded on?"

"In a sense."

"Wrong. You didn't have time to get there. You'd have to shoot across three lanes of traffic and two parking lanes before you even squirreled up a tree. You'd have been flattened."

"The traffic was already stopped before I even started across. They'd all hit their brakes. It was deafening."

"They'd stopped for my mugging?"

"No. There'd been sort of an accident down there, just past that manhole cover."

It made me look, one-eyed, out at Fifth. The cabs were flying by. There was no accident out there.

I told him that. "Aaron, *I'm* the accident. Do you see an accident out there?"

"Not now," he mumbled. "Not today."

My left eye felt like a paperweight. A bunch of people were line dancing in my head.

"It worked, Josh."

"What worked?"

"My equation. My formula." He held up his laptop. "It combined spontaneously with my need to escape. I was dark fibered into another time frame."

"And up a tree?"

"I've got some of my numbers wrong. Or something."

"Let's have this in layman's terms," I said. "You turned invisible to get away from that gang and, pow, you're up a tree and back in time?"

"Not exactly. I didn't turn invisible. I just suddenly wasn't here."

"I was. They nearly beat the—"

"And you weren't here either. I looked over from my tree, and you weren't here. Neither was the gang. And another thing. I didn't go back in time."

"Aaron, trust me. I never thought you could."

"I went forward."

My eye bored into him. "You went forward? Like into the future?"

He nodded. "I'm off on my numbers. I shouldn't even be trying anything like this on a laptop. It's going to need a new battery pack, at least."

"How far into the future do you think you went? Were there spaceships? Were there people here from other planets? Was the whole city climate-controlled under a dome? Was there trash collection?"

Aaron's eyes looked shifty. I may have looked bad, but he didn't look so good himself. Under the red hair his face was so pale that he looked like a radish. "Not that far," he said. "Maybe just a matter of days. A week or so."

"You mean everything looked the same?"

"More or less. It was still winter. You weren't here. You were probably someplace else that day. I probably was too. I didn't see us."

"Then how do you know it wasn't a few days *ago* instead of a few days *from now*?"

Aaron looked really worried. "Because of the accident."

I try to be skeptical. "Accidents happen every day on Fifth," I said. "Yesterday, today, tomorrow."

"Not this accident," he muttered.

"Like it was really bad? A big pileup or something?"

"It wasn't cars. It wasn't that kind of accident. Anyway, I wasn't there long enough. I was only gone about ninety seconds. What do you want from that, a miniseries?"

This was weird talk, even from Aaron. "So how'd you get back?"

"Well, I still had my laptop with me. I wedged it into that fork in the tree over there. I punched up my formula in reverse. Then I had these shooting pains all over my body. I'd had them before on the way out. That could have been my cells falling into place. Then I was right here on the sidewalk again, and you had a poodle in your ear."

"Aaron—"

"But I don't want to talk about it anymore now. I don't feel so good."

"*You* don't feel good? I probably need stitches."

He was already walking off down Fifth. I caught up with him and kept him in my good eye. At Seventy-ninth Street I had to hold him back to keep him from walking against the light. I'm still bleeding down my front, but I have to monitor him. If I hadn't been hurting so bad, I'd have been mad.

"Look, Aaron, I want to be on the record about something. I don't believe one word you—"

"I'm not going into the future anymore," he said. "It's too big a responsibility."

When I got home, the apartment felt empty. Aaron had gone on up to the penthouse. He had some major data-mining to do. He has a state-of-the-art, stand-alone microsystem workstation in his bedroom.

Mom wasn't home from Barnes Ogleby, and I kind of wished she was. I wanted to show her my eye and my nose and maybe cry a little.

Edging out of my backpack, I headed off to my

bathroom. At the door I heard a whirring sound. But my head was still whirring anyway. I opened the bathroom door. There was a piercing scream from inside.

Heather. In a bath towel. She'd been standing at my sink. In my mirror she caught a glimpse of my face. She whirled around and dropped her hair dryer, which stopped whirring. "What *happened* to you?"

"Why are you in my bathroom?" I said. "Why aren't you in your bathroom?"

"I always wash my hair in your bathroom. I don't want to get hair in my drain."

"Why didn't I know this?"

"You weren't supposed to. It's my business. What *happened* to you?"

"Mugged."

"What—getting off the school bus?"

"We didn't take the bus. We walked."

"You walked? What do you think the bus is *for*?" Heather smacked her forehead. "You are so immature. What happened to Pencil-Neck?"

Pencil-Neck is her name for Aaron. Don't ask me why.

"He . . . got away."

Heather tightened her towel and started wringing her hands. "Come on," she said. "We've got to clean you up before Mom gets home. Let me see that eye. Yewww. I'll get ice. You start washing. What happened to your tie?"

"Boxcutter."

I peeled out of my blazer and untied my stubby tie. Then I took a chance and looked in the mirror. I was pretty scary. My eye looked like it belonged to a giant frog. My nose had stopped bleeding, but there was a big clot on my lip. I grinned to see if I had all my teeth. I did. The blood came off, but the eye was looking worse. I dabbed around it with a soapy washcloth.

Heather was back with a bowl of ice. "Here, slap some of this on your eye."

"I'm not slapping anything near that eye."

"Give me that washcloth." She folded some cubes into it. "Take off your shirt. I'll soak it before the blood sets. Do I have to do everything? This is so typical of you, Josh. You never think a minute ahead. The future is a big blank space to you. What if Mom comes home and sees you like this? Think about it. You know how she overreacts. She'll start carrying on about how we're latchkey kids and need supervision. She'll be all over us. She thinks we're about four years old anyway. She'll want us in *day care*. And all because you're dumb enough to wander around getting mugged. She'll call Dad."

I hadn't thought about that.

"She'll lay a major guilt trip on him. He'll probably fly back here from Chicago." Now she was shaking a bloody shirt in my face.

"That would be okay," I said.

Heather sighed. "Josh, they've just separated. It's not time for a reconciliation. It's—*premature*. Don't you know anything about relationships? Don't you ever watch *Oprah*?"

She was running water to soak my shirt. "Oh, great," she said. "Your drain's clogged.

"And another thing. You know how Mom and Dad will see this, don't you? They'll think you managed this mugging as a cry for help."

"I didn't cry for help," I said. "They beat me senseless before I could open my mouth."

"Not that. They'll think you made this happen because of the separation. Like you're acting out because you're being single-parented. Mom'll take you for counseling. She'll take *me*. That eye is so gross."

Then Heather was gone. But she told me not to move. I wouldn't have minded an aspirin. But I just stood there. Then she was back with a bunch of stuff from Mom's makeup table.

"What's that for?"

"Your eye looks like an Easter egg. It won't heal for ages. I'm going to touch it up a little."

"Don't even think about coming near that eye."

"It's just a little Max Factor Erace creamy coverup. It's just a little pressed powder I can brush on."

But there was still some fight in me, and I fought her off.

That's when Mom appeared in the bathroom door. It took her a moment to see everything. The bloody shirt floating in the sink. The busted hair dryer on the floor. Heather bath toweled with half-dried hair. Me shirtless and fighting her off as she tried to revise my face with Mom's own Max Factor and Estée Lauder products.

Then she got a good view of my Easter-egg eye. Mom's hand clamped over her mouth to stifle a scream.

7

No Seat, No Hands

"All right," Mom sighed, "let's try to put our best feet forward."

We were in a cab again, heading out to JFK Airport. Mom was giving Au Pair Exchange another shot, and we had another plane to meet.

"I can't be in two places," Mom said, "and there can't be two Fenellas."

A week had passed. Now I just had a black eye. Mom could look at me without bursting into tears.

"Okay," Heather moaned. "Who's it going to be this time?"

"Feona," Mom said, trying to sound confident.

According to the Au Pair Exchange printout, Feona was seventeen, a recent "school leaver," whose interests were

reading
field hockey
gardening
needlework
flower arranging
gourmet cooking
and equitation

"What's equitation supposed to be?" Heather asked. "Horseback riding," Mom said.

There was a dim Xerox picture of Feona in a school uniform and straw hat. It didn't look too recent and could have been anybody.

There was the usual business about Feona assisting with light household work, food preparation, and child care, twenty hours a week tops.

"I don't like her already," Heather said as we pulled up to the British Air terminal. "And if her plane's late, I'm going home in a cab by myself. Camilla Van Allen might call."

"She's never called yet," I muttered.

"Mo-om," Heather said, "make Josh put a sock in it or I'll have to go to boarding school."

When they announced the flight from London, the first passenger out of the Customs door was this girl. She was pretty tall, with long red cheeks and plenty of teeth. Her hair was pulled back in a ponytail. She was wearing a tweed jacket, riding pants, and spit-shined high boots. You couldn't miss her. She was carrying a saddle.

"Who's this?" Heather said. "My friend Flicka?"

"Feona?" Mom said, because the girl was looking around, maybe for a horse.

"Actually, yes," Feona said. "Brilliant to meet you." She propped her saddle under one arm to shake hands with all three of us. "Absolutely brill." She had a bone-crusher grip.

"You'd make a super jockey," she said down to me, "if you don't get any bigger."

"I'm Josh," I said in a short voice. "Want me to carry your saddle?" I hoped not. It was bigger than I was.

"Thanks awfully. I'm never without it. But you're an absolute poppet to ask," Feona said.

Fenella had called me Tiny Tim. Feona called me a poppet. It was like a whole different language.

She turned to Heather. Expecting another Fenella, Heather had punked out. She was in total black except her lips, which Mom wouldn't let her do.

"Feona, actually," Feona said. She lifted Heather's hand from her side and gave it a bone-crusher. "How's your seat?"

"My *what?*" Heather said.

"No seat, no hands, Daddy always says," Feona said to Mom.

"Ah," Mom said. "And what would that mean . . . actually?"

Feona stared. "If you don't sit a horse well, you'll never handle the reins well. No seat, no hands."

"Ah," Mom said.

"I've got a pain in my seat," Heather muttered. "And I know who's caused it."

Outside, Heather and I were the last ones into the cab. Heather turned back to me. "She even smells weird. Do you know what it is?"

"Horse," I said.

"That's the first syllable," Heather said.

The saddle had to go into the trunk, which Feona wasn't too happy about. The four of us were bunched in the backseat. I was practically on the floor. It was dark, but you could see that every time Feona moved, her ponytail swatted Heather in the face. Heather was bobbing and weaving, trying to keep hair out of her mouth.

". . . I hope you'll be—comfortable with us," Mom said. I could read her mind. At least Feona wasn't another Fenella.

"Oh, I'm quite comfortable anywhere," Feona said. "My school didn't have heat."

"Ah," Mom said. "I suppose that would be boarding school?"

Feona twitched her tail. "We go away to school when we're seven. It's super, really. You meet such a lot of jolly girls. And it lets your parents get on with their marriage."

"Ah," Mom said.

"Actually, at school, I slept most nights with Cheeky Bob in the stables."

"Cheeky Bob?" Mom said doubtfully.

"My horse, of course. We're about to put him out at stud. All the mares are mad for him."

Heather looked around her at me.

"I'm really just a bumper in the saddle," Feona confided. "And I'm better on the flat than at the fence. But I'm dead keen. And it's brill being here. I'm only missing the first of the point-to-points. Absolutely riveting, but filthy weather for it."

"Point-to-point?" Mom said.

Feona stared again. "It's a race like a steeplechase. But the jumps are six inches lower. Surely you have them? Mummy brings a hamper and we have picnics. Absolutely br—"

"Then it's not a hunt," Mom said. "You don't kill animals."

"No," Feona explained. "That's later in the season."

Now the whole cab smelled like a stable. Up front, the cabby was spraying his area with an aerosol can.

We gunned along the expressway. It was another one of those nights when you get that great view of the city. Twinkling towers, chains of lights on the bridges. That type of thing.

Feona leaned forward, whisking leather. "Whatever is that?" She pointed through the bullet-proof Plexiglas and over the cabby's shoulder.

"That's Manhattan," I told her. "The Big Apple."

Feona blinked. "But whyever is it getting nearer and nearer?"

"We *live* there," Heather said.

Feona fell back in the seat. "There's been some mistake," she said to Mom. "Au Pair Exchange said you lived in the country. They said you kept horses. They said you were deeply committed to stalking and shooting. They said you had some jolly good coverts."

"Coverts?" Mom murmured.

Feona sighed. "Places where the fox hides."

"There's a lot of stalking and shooting in Manhattan," I said. "But we don't do it."

Mom was tensing up. "Au Pair Exchange said you liked flower arranging," she said to Feona.

"Me? You mean weeds and grasses in pots? Mummy does that."

Mom clutched her purse with both hands. "I'll kill those Au Pair Exchange people," she said. "I'll find out who they are. I'll get a gun. I'll track them down. I'll flush them out of their coverts. And I'll kill them."

8

Alone in the Black Hole

School's not that much fun without your best friend. Aaron had made himself scarce ever since my mugging day. For over a week he'd been signing himself out of classes to work at the terminals in the Black Hole. He went in early and stayed after school, so I didn't see him on the bus. He was in there at lunch.

Then, whenever I did run into him, he'd say, "I'm still diddling my data." And he'd be off to the Black Hole again like he didn't have time for me.

At first I thought he might be mad. He knew I didn't believe he'd time-warped himself up a tree for my mugging. I try to be skeptical, but this time it might have hurt his feelings.

Then one day in the school lunchroom I was down at the end of a table eating a lonely burrito. Aaron comes in, scanning around to see where I am.

Huckley School is built in a row of four old houses put together. They flattened one roof and fenced it in for the lower-school playground. Otherwise they've tried to keep the houses pretty much the way they were. They even named them for the families who lived in them years ago. The lunchroom is the old dining room of Havemeyer House. It's decorated with hockey sticks and pictures of past lacrosse teams and old Havemeyers.

Aaron spotted me. He worked his way through the crowd, carrying a lunch off the salad bar. He dropped down beside me.

"Getting there," he said like the old Aaron. So maybe he wasn't mad at me. He probably wasn't. "Like I said, I was off on my numbers. Also, I can do better work on the terminals here at school. How far did I think I was going to get on a one-chip laptop? And at school I can work on two computers. This could be the evolutionary reason why we have two hands. With two on-line databases, you can practically conduct a symphony."

So it was definitely the old Aaron.

"I'm making progress," he said, "but it's not all a matter of direct data entry."

"Wouldn't be," I said.

"There's the Emotional Component."

"After all, the human brain is the ultimate computer," I reminded him.

"But if it means scaring myself into some other time," Aaron said, "I'm up for it. I'll jump that fence when I come to it."

54

Jumping fences reminded me of horses. Horses reminded me of you know who.

"We've got another O Pear," I said.

But Aaron wasn't listening. For once he didn't have his one-chip laptop with him. But the fingers of his left hand were punching up something on the bare wood of the lunch table. Once in a while his fork would come up, and he'd stuff lettuce in his mouth. But his eyes were unfocused, and his mind was way off somewhere. There was a blob of Thousand Island dressing on his nose.

This began to make me mad. It happens a lot. Right after you think your best friend is mad at you, and then you find he isn't, you get mad at him. Aaron was taking himself too seriously. He was getting weirder. He was beginning to buy his own theories. I thought about turning him in to the counseling office. He wouldn't even notice if I got up and walked away.

Then he got up and walked away. He wandered through the lunchroom crowd, returned his empty salad bowl, and left in the direction of the media center.

I had a little bit of burrito left but didn't even feel like eating it.

After school I was getting on the bus with the rest of the backpackers. I was going with the flow. Then I turned around and went back into school. Having to find a new best friend at my age is just too big a deal.

The media center is in Vanderwhitney House, a couple of buildings over from Havemeyer House. It was probably the personal library of the Vanderwhitney family in the olden days. Some of the shelves are real wood built into the walls.

The front part of it still has some books. Mrs. Newbery, the media specialist, was giving a story hour there to a bunch of preschoolers in miniature dress code. The back part is walled off with a door in it, and that's the Black Hole where the computer workstations are.

Aaron was in there, positioned between two terminals. He was keeping them busy with both hands. All the compartments of his brain were fully engaged.

I just stood there. What are you going to do with a kid like that? I couldn't see his face, but I knew his lips were moving. Then I got this idea. It was a spur-of-the-moment thing. If Aaron's so sure he can be scared into another time frame, let's find out.

I closed the door behind me to keep Mrs. Newbery from being involved. Then I made a dead run for Aaron. I came pounding up on his blind side.

"Aaron, look out! Buster Brewster's got a gun, and he's heading this way!"

Aaron froze. Then he yelled, "Yikes!" His hands flew up. He was surrendering or something. Then his hands dropped down on both keyboards. His fingers flew. The entire Black Hole seemed to give out a glow. It was like a power surge.

Then the scariest thing that ever happened, happened.

Something was happening to Aaron. He was beginning to . . . dim. He was like somebody fading into the distance, except he was right here—a reach away. I didn't know whether to touch him or not, but I put one hand out on his bony shoulder. It was changing under my hand. It felt like a Baggie full of bees. This could have been his cells reorganizing themselves. I think I even heard buzzing, but that could have been the terminals.

Then my hand was just there, hanging in space. I was standing behind an empty chair. Aaron was lost in cyberspace.

I panicked. Who wouldn't? I checked under the terminals, in the corners, even. But I was alone in the Black Hole. Through the wall I could hear the drone of Mrs. Newbery's voice, summing up a story.

If Aaron will just get his tail back here, I'll never doubt him again, I was screaming inside. Did he have his laptop with him? Could he program himself back from wherever? Will I be held responsible for this? I looked at both screens. They were blank.

Time passed. I don't know how long. Something had gone wrong with time. The door opened behind me. If it had been Buster Brewster with a gun, I'd have had it coming. It was Mrs. Newbery.

"Oh, Josh," she said. "I thought it was Aaron in here. It usually is. Brushing up on your computer literacy?"

But then she looked over my shoulder at the terminals. Across both blank screens words were spelling themselves out:

HARD DRIVE FAILURE

9
Aaron Zimmer Is Missing

I had to leave. Mrs. Newbery was closing up for the night, and what could I tell her? Then I was drifting down Fifth Avenue in a fog all my own. I even walked right past my mugging site without flinching.

What was I supposed to do, call the police to put out an all-points for Aaron? They'd drag the rivers, and I was almost a hundred percent sure he wasn't there. Was I supposed to put up laser printouts on lampposts?

AARON ZIMMER IS MISSING
Undersized crazed redhead in Huckley dress code
swallowed by two hostile computers

Please.

Then I was home, fighting my way out of my backpack. Then I went into action. In my room I punched up the Zimmer penthouse on my phone. Nobody knows the native language of the Zimmers' housekeeper. But she speaks four words of English: "hello," "say what?" and "okay."

"Hello," she said.

"This is Josh down on twelve. Aaron is . . . here. He wants to spend the night. We're . . . going to put up a tent and camp out in the living room."

Nobody older than third grade would do that. But it was all I could think of. "Can Aaron sleep over?"

"Say what?"

I repeated the message. "This is Josh down on twelve. Aaron is . . ." etc.

The housekeeper said, "Okay," and hung up.

This bought me some time. But so what? Maybe Aaron wouldn't be back. Maybe he wasn't . . . bidirectional. I didn't even want to think about going to school tomorrow. But then, I mainly think about what's happening now. I'd jump that fence when I got to it.

I was just collapsing my phone aerial when my bedroom door burst open.

Heather.

She shrieked and clutched her head. "Get off that phone!"

"Why should I? It's mine. Use your own phone."

"But I give out your number." She snatched the phone out of my hand.

"Give out your own number," I said.

"I do. I give out both. I might be getting two calls."

"We have call waiting."

"I know that. But giving out two numbers makes our apartment sound bigger."

"Why didn't I know you were giving out my number?"

"You weren't supposed to. It's my business." She was patting my phone like a Barbie doll. Now she was in my face, whispering. "You'll never guess who's here."

"Feona?"

"Of course Feona's here. Guess who else."

But I was out of guesses.

"Camilla Van Allen." Heather can squeal and whisper at the same time.

"Great," I said. "So you're in the peer group finally?"

Heather did a dance with my phone as her partner. "It's like a miracle."

"So if Camilla Van Allen is here—"

"She is. She's right in this apartment. As we speak. In the living room with Feona. We're having English tea. With cucumber sandwiches. Camilla loves it. Her grandmother is English."

"Great. So if Camilla's here, why do I have to keep off my phone?"

"Josh, you are so immature. Think. Now that I'm in with Camilla, everybody will be calling." Heather did six more dance steps toward the door and left, taking my phone.

Then she was back, handing me my phone.

"Listen, if I get a call, take a message. Stay in your room. You don't need to meet Camilla. I don't want anything to go wrong. Are there any questions?"

"Look, Heather, I've got a lot on my mind," I said. "Maybe you could just tell me why Camilla Van Allen is here and what it has to do with Feona. Keep it short. I thought you didn't like Feona. You said she smelled like horse—"

"But I remembered that Camilla Van Allen's family has a horse farm in Far Hills. Feona's on Camilla's social level, but English. She rides. She's going to teach me to ride. I'm going to get a good seat. Camilla will invite me to Far Hills. What am I going to wear? I happened to mention Feona in school where Camilla could hear. I didn't say Feona was an O Pear, for heaven's sake. I said she was like related to us. Do you know what her last name is?"

"Didn't catch it."

"Foxworthy," Heather breathed.

Feona Foxworthy?

"The Foxworthys are practically royalty. Their name rang a bell with Camilla. Feona's family lives in two places: London and their country estate."

"Our mom and dad live in two places. New York and Chi—"

"Not like that."

"I thought Feona wasn't staying. She thought we had stables and horses. She thought we stalk and shoot."

"But we've got Central Park. Camilla's telling her how you can rent horses from a stable over on West Eighty-ninth Street."

"Great," I said. "Brill." But Heather was out the door.

When I was sure she was gone, I punched the Zimmer penthouse number again, just to be on the safe side. I told their housekeeper that Aaron and I would leave from here for school tomorrow. I'd loan him a clean shirt and underwear.

"Say what?" she said. I repeated myself. She said okay.

When I signed off, the phone rang. "Hello," said this voice. "This is Muffie MacInteer. Is Camilla Van Allen there?"

I took a message. The next day I had to go back to school. And Aaron wasn't going to be on the bus.

10

To Horse and Away

Feona was an early riser. I had a quick breakfast with her. She wore her velvet riding hard hat at the table and was reading a magazine called *Horse and Hound*. She sort of fed and watered herself.

I was at school by seven-thirty. The media center in Vanderwhitney House wasn't officially open yet, but it was unlocked. I crept past the books back to the Black Hole. That door was locked.

The situation looked hopeless. My head hurt from worrying. I rested it against the door.

A voice spoke from the other side. "Mrs. Newbery?" A familiar voice.

"Aaron?"

"Josh?"

Now I was annoyed. I practically hadn't slept all night. Now this.

"Get the key," the small voice said. "It's in Mrs. Newbery's top left-hand desk drawer. Under her bottle of Maalox."

I went for it and got lucky. Mrs. Newbery didn't come in to find me rifling through her desk. She was due any minute.

When I opened the door, Aaron was standing there in yesterday's clothes. Red rims circled his eyes. He was eating an apple. He looked around me.

"You were just kidding about Buster Brewster and a gun, right?"

I sighed. "Aaron—"

He put up a small hand. "Josh, it's too late for skeptical. You were there. And then I wasn't. Right? You can't deny it."

"But I didn't see anything. You were gone. And where did you get that apple anyway?"

"It was in a big silver bowl of fruit over there on a table."

"Aaron, I don't see a big silver bowl of fruit. I don't see a table."

"Not now," he said. "Then."

He strolled over to the terminals. He'd shut them down. They were blank-screened and cold. "Let me show you how I did it. Two keyboards helped. I entered half the formula on this one, half on that one. It set up a real matrix."

"So what is this formula anyway?" I said.

His red eyes peered up at me. "It's a forty-eight-character combination of numbers and letters, clustered. With some visuals."

"Ah," I said. "Right."

"Josh, why tell it to you? It took you till third grade to remember your zip code."

"Rub it in," I said.

"And I'm not writing it down," he said. "This could be dangerous information in the wrong hands. I'm keeping it up here." He tapped his temple. "The human brain—"

"Is the ultimate computer," I said. "Aaron, I'm doing my best, but I still can't buy in. Numbers on a screen, clustered. Visuals. The whole forty-eight-character ball of wax. But how does it get you . . . there?"

Aaron looked a little worn, like a teacher after seventh period.

"Let me give you a metaphor, Josh. It's the best I can do. You can fax a letter, right? You can fax a document, right? You can fax a photo, right?" He dropped his voice even lower. "Josh, you can fax yourself."

I stared.

"You helped," he said. "You scared me about Buster. You gave me the boost. Adrenaline is a definite factor. I just lined up my numbers with my need and . . . went."

"But you didn't have your laptop with you. How did you get back without entering your formula or whatever?"

"Good point," Aaron said. "Important point. I didn't have to. I hadn't needed it the other day up that tree in Central Park. Cellular reorganization is a temporary condition. In layman's terms, when your time's up, you're back. It's fairly painful both ways."

"So you're—"

"That's right," Aaron said. "I'm bidirectional."

I stood there, trying to stare him down, trying to see into his quirky brain. Skeptical dies hard.

"How long were you gone?"

"Not long," he said. "Minutes. Then I was back. But I was locked in here for the night. I had to sleep on the floor."

"I covered for you," I said. "I told your housekeeper you were sleeping over. I told her we were putting up a tent in my living room."

"Nobody older than third grade does that," he said. "Couldn't you think of anything better?"

Which was the thanks I got.

"Okay, Aaron. Let's get down to basics. Where did you go?"

His eyes shifted away from mine. He'd nibbled his apple down to the core. Also, he probably had to go to the bathroom. "Zero distance," he muttered.

"Meaning you weren't up a tree again?"

"I was right here in this room. But it was then, not now. Way back then."

"Aaron. When?"

"Put it this way," he said. "I've just eaten an apple that I estimate to be about seventy-five years old." He showed me the core.

A shadow fell over us. A voice spoke. "Are you boys losing track of time?"

It was Mrs. Newbery in the doorway. We jumped. "You've practically missed Mr. Headbloom's homeroom," she said. "If you don't cut along, you'll be late for Linear Decoding." We started to cut along.

"I'll take my key if you don't mind." Mrs. Newbery put her hand out. Then she said to Aaron, "Better tidy up before you go to class. You look like you've slept in those clothes."

In Linear Decoding, Aaron was sitting across the room from me. We were reading *The Time Machine* by H. G. Wells, a dead English writer. I didn't see Aaron in Science or Gym. I didn't see him at lunch. He'd be diddling his data again.

This gave me time to get skeptical again. True, he'd vanished before my eyes. But it could have been an . . . optical illusion. He could have been messing with my mind.

After school he turned up and said, "Let's walk home."

"What about muggers?"

"Muggers, shmuggers," Aaron said. "I haven't been outdoors since yesterday morning. I could use some air."

As we turned down Fifth Avenue, I decided not to ask him anything. If this whole thing was a scam, I didn't want to fall for it. Then I couldn't think of anything to talk about. We trudged along for a few blocks. Aaron sticks his feet out funny when he walks.

At the Eighty-sixth Street light I said, "We've got another O Pear."

"Tell me about it, Josh." But he was listening with only half an ear.

"She's different from Fenella. Way different. Her name's Feona Foxworthy. She's okay, I guess. The funny thing is, Heather likes her."

Aaron froze. "Heather?" He doesn't have that much of a relationship with Heather. And she calls him Pencil-Neck.

"Feona got Heather into Camilla Van Allen's peer group, so Heather likes her. Feona's horsey."

Aaron quivered. He pulled on his chin in a thoughtful, weird way. "Tall girl? Long face? Plenty of teeth? Ponytail? Riding hat?"

"That's her. You see her on the elevator or someplace?"

"Someplace," he said. "Where are they now?" His hand was closing over my arm.

"Heather and Feona?" I said. "Who knows?"

"Yikes," Aaron said. "This could be the *day*." He was so hyper, he was almost doing a dance.

He started running down Fifth, dragging me along. I didn't know he could move that fast. He should go out for track instead of always signing himself out of Gym.

"Where are we going?" I gasped. But he was saving his breath. We almost vaulted the hood of a cab at Eighty-second.

"Whoa," I said at the light on Seventy-ninth, which has traffic both ways. But he was jogging in place and breathing hard. He was stretching his neck to see down Fifth Avenue.

He wouldn't wait for the light to change. He made an end run around a crosstown bus, stopping a van in its tracks. Then we were streaking down the sidewalk again, coming up on my mugging site. Yellow cabs flowed south, and we almost kept up with them.

Then it was like the world stopped. All the cabs screeched to a halt. So did Aaron. So did I. Cabbies leaned on their horns. Metal crunched from a couple of fender-benders behind us. The cabbies were rolling down their windows and yelling in every language but English.

"Too late," Aaron said. "And we were *this close.*"

The cabs weren't going anywhere now. He darted out and sprinted between them down Fifth Avenue. Then we got there.

Two horses—big ones—were in the middle of the street. One was reared up with its hooves fighting the air. Our O Pear, Feona Foxworthy, was on it. One of her boots was out of the stirrup. Her riding hat was slipping off. She'd lost the reins and had the horse's neck in a death grip. "Daddy!" Feona shrieked. "Mummy!"

The other horse was stamping on Fifth Avenue pavement, and its eyes were rolling. Connected to it by a rein was Heather. She was stretched out in the middle of the street in a new top-of-the-line riding outfit: velvet hard hat, tweed coat, riding pants, and boots. Some gray snow was sticking to her, so she must have been thrown off in the park and dragged here into traffic. You could tell the horse didn't like her.

A cop and a couple of cabbies were trying to talk Feona's horse down. And they were getting between Heather and her horse to keep it from kicking her in the head.

Heather was gazing glassy-eyed into the winter sky with one arm up because of the rein. The cop and the cabbies were trying to untangle her. But she must have been stunned because she yelled, " 'Ere, stand aside, you miserable gits." Then just as Aaron and I got up to her, she fainted, or seemed to.

"Too late," Aaron said again. "This is the future I saw from my tree the other day when my numbers were a little off. This was the accident."

"Whoa, Aaron," I said. Heather's horse looked at me.

"But I guess we couldn't have headed off the accident anyway." Aaron gave a helpless shrug. "I couldn't even believe it was Heather at the time. That riding outfit's new, right? She'd never been on a horse before, right?"

"This looks like her first lesson," I said.

"This was the future I cellular-reorganized into, Josh. I saw all this happen more than a week ago. I was up that tree." He pointed into bare branches.

"You're not up there."

"Not now. I left before we got here. I left while Heather's horse was just dragging her over the curb into traffic. I didn't know who the other girl was."

"Mummy!" Feona was still shrieking as she slid down the side of her horse, or its flank or whatever. "Daddy!"

"Aaron—"

"I'm not going into the future anymore," he said. "Like I said, it's too big a responsibility. I'm going to stick with going back into the past."

11

A Tasteful Private Residence

Mom said, "Feona goes," and she went, that night.

The last we saw of her, she was lugging her saddle onto a British Air flight. She looked back and gave us a big toothy smile from under her velvet hard hat. "Do write!" she called out. Then she galloped onto the plane.

In the cab back to the city Mom sat with her eyes closed for a while.

"I am getting very near the end of my rope," she said.

I knew we were going to have to go over it again, even though we'd been over everything already. Heather stared out the window.

"Fenella tried to smuggle you into that *crack house* club where you might have been drugged for life or arrested. Or both. And the two of you followed along like a pair of geese. And Feona was worse. She was practically homicidal. Heather, what was your first mistake?" Mom waited.

"The riding clothes," Heather said in a sulky, mouselike voice. "On your credit card."

"I haven't even had my first paycheck from Barnes Ogleby," Mom said. "And you can't take them back to the store, not after that wild horse—that mustang— dragged you over half of Manhattan Island. *And* you cut school."

"Feona said it was the same as school," Heather mumbled. "At her school, riding lessons are part of the curriculum."

"That awful girl was all talk. She could have used a few more riding lessons herself. She must have fallen off her horse too often. On her head," Mom said. *"How's your seat,* my foot. I've come to the conclusion that Au Pair Exchange is a criminal outfit. I'm thinking about reporting them to the Better Business Bureau. I blame myself there."

If Heather was taking most of the heat and Mom blamed herself, I figured I could relax.

"And by the way, Josh," Mom said. "I ran into Mrs. Zimmer in the lobby. She wanted to thank us for having Aaron sleep over. I really didn't know what to say since I don't recall Aaron sleeping over. When you can come up with a good explanation for that, I'll be glad to hear it."

I sank lower in the seat and passed up that great nighttime view of Manhattan: twinkling towers, lit-up bridges. But I had a lot on my mind. Usually I think about now. But I was hung up between the future and the past that night. Way hung up.

At school the next day Aaron was in and out of class all morning. He's usually in business for himself, but today he was really hustling. He was late for Mr. Headbloom's Linear Decoding. Swinging past my desk, he dropped a sheet of paper on my copy of *The Time Machine*. It was a Xeroxed page from an old *New York Times*. It was black and white and blotchy, but I could read it.

A dim picture showed the Vanderwhitney House part of the school when it was brand-new:

Tasteful Residence of
the Osgood Vanderwhitneys
Distinctive New Home
for Distinguished Old Family

Architects acclaim this residence of Mr. and Mrs. Osgood Vanderwhitney as the most tasteful private domicile to be built in the city during 1921. It features thirty rooms lavishly paneled and commodious accommodations for servants under a bronze dormer.

The house, only steps from the Central Park, is the last to be built in a street already home to such prominent families as the Havemeyers, the Van Allens, and the Huckleys.

After summering at Tuxedo Park, the Osgood Vanderwhitneys will reside here, along with their

two small sons, Cuthbert Henry, aged seven, and
Lysander Theodore, aged three.

Cuthbert Henry and Lysander Theodore?
At the bottom of the sheet Aaron had written:

*House looked new when I was there but
not this new.*

This must mean he thought he'd cellular-reorganized
back to the early days of the Vanderwhitneys' house. I
missed him at lunch. He was late again for History.
When he bustled in, he dropped another Xerox copy on
me on the way to his desk.

"Zimmer. Freeze," Mr. Thaw said. He's Huckley's
hardest teacher and the oldest. He should have retired
long ago and gone to the Old Teachers' Home. "Number one," he said to Aaron, "you're late. Number two,
you're passing notes. These are both misdemeanors in
this class."

Aaron blinked.

"I'm doing an independent study," he squeaked.

"Zimmer, we don't do I.S. until—"

"I know," Aaron said, "but this is about the history
of the school. Josh Lewis and I are putting together a
program on it for Parents' Night."

This was quick thinking. But why drag me into it?

Huckley teachers are pretty careful about parents. Even
crusty old Mr. L. T. Thaw. He stroked his straggly beard.

"Very well, Zimmer," he said, after giving it some
thought. "I'll follow up to make sure that you and

75

young Lewis make a presentation on Parents' Night. And make it good. The grades of both of you will depend upon it."

Thanks a lot, Aaron, I thought.

Mr. Thaw went back to the lesson. We were reading up on the presidents of the United States. At least Mr. Thaw was. He could probably remember most of them personally.

I had time to glance over Aaron's latest Xerox copy. It was a clipping from a 1923 *New York Times*:

Hook and Ladder Company Called to Fashionable Address

The fire brigade answered an alarm from the home of the Osgood Vanderwhitneys on the smart Upper East Side at 3:30 P.M. yesterday. A fire of unknown origin in the library of the palatial townhouse threatened the lives of the two Vanderwhitney children, Cuthbert, aged nine, and Lysander, aged five.

When New York's stalwart fire fighters arrived, the blaze had been extinguished. Damage was limited to a scorched bookshelf and the collected speeches of President Buchanan. Mr. Vanderwhitney was summoned from his Wall Street office. Mrs. Vanderwhitney is said to be en route from the family's Tuxedo Park country address.

" 'All's Well That Ends Well,' " Mr. Vanderwhitney remarked, quoting Shakespeare.

Underneath, Aaron had put in a giant exclamation mark and a message:

*Meet me after school in the Black Hole.
I'm going back. I've got enough Emotional
Component to send myself to the moon.*

Nobody was around as I slipped through the media center. There were afternoon shadows everywhere. At first I thought Aaron wasn't in the Black Hole. The only thing I noticed was a big metal frame where they store manuals, floppy disks, and back issues of *Byte*. It was pulled out from the wall.

Down in the corner I saw a flash of red. Aaron stood up. "Shut the door behind you and come over here, Josh." Behind the metal frame were the original built-in shelves of the Vanderwhitney family's library. They were carved all around with wooden flowers, way too fragile to stand up to school use. "Look right there."

Some of the wood was darker than the rest, like flames might have licked up it long ago.

"Like the newspaper said."

"But it doesn't prove you went back there, Aaron."

"No, but I did. And it was around that time. About 1923. It could have been before the fire, or after. But I was there."

"Okay, what was this room like?" I said. "We've already heard about the table with the silver fruit bowl."

"It was where the terminals are now. The wall between here and the media center wasn't there, of course. It was one long room. It was nice. Polished wood floors, not this crummy tile. Big vases of flowers were standing around."

"Did they have electricity?"

"Of course they had electricity. It was 1923. And they were rich. But the lights weren't on. It was this time of day, more or less. Afternoon light was coming in that window."

"What window?"

"It was right there. They must have bricked it up when that big apartment building was built between here and Fifth Avenue." His voice trailed away.

"That's it?"

"I was only there for a few minutes. What do you want from that, a mini—"

"Was anybody in the room?"

He looked shifty and worried. "A couple of people," he murmured. "They were kissing. It was kind of embarrassing."

Kissing?

"Kissing each other?"

"Of course they were kissing each other. What else? She'd been crying. She took a handkerchief out of her sleeve and dabbed her eyes. The guy kept looking over his shoulder. They were both worried, like they might get caught. He had his arms around her, and they were whispering and kissing."

"That's it?"

"The girl reached inside the collar of her dress and pulled up a gold chain with a ring on it. Maybe he'd given her the ring, and she was wearing it around her neck, hiding it."

"Did they see you? Were you visible?"

"I don't know. They were kind of busy."

"Then what?" I was watching him closely.

"I stood there a while, just hanging around. Then I wanted to see if I could pick up an apple. I could. I was really there. Then I felt myself coming back. I was kind of embarrassed by all that kissing. So then I had shooting pains, that type of thing, and left."

The Black Hole was quiet. I wanted to go home now. "Aaron, it wouldn't hold up in court."

"I've got some more work to do on my formula. I'm still flying blind. I want some more control."

"Well," I said, "these things take—time."

Aaron had me about half-psyched again. And I was really ready to go home. We'd missed the bus, but we could walk. We both needed the air. Muggers, shmuggers.

But he was going into action mode again. Now he positioned himself between the two terminals. "You stand behind me, Josh. Put your hands on my shoulders so I'll know you're right there. I'm going to try to go back without Emotional Component, so don't try to scare me or anything. Just be there."

Already his hands were reaching for the keyboards.

"Wait a minute, Aaron."

"What for? I said I was going back, and I am. I'm going to try the same formula again. Later I'll diddle my data and fiddle my figures. For now I want you here. Mrs. Newbery is liable to turn up any minute."

"Let's say she finds me here in the room alone," I said. "She'll throw me out and lock up as usual."

"Then find a way of getting back in to spring me," Aaron said. "Use your initiative."

"But what if you don't—"

"Enough talk," Aaron said. His fingers splayed out over the two keyboards. Both my hands dropped on his bony shoulders. Maybe I could even hold him back. The formula unfurled like a flag of hot letters across both screens.

But Aaron's shoulders didn't feel like a Baggie full of bees this time, though I heard buzzing. Instead, pain like I'd never felt raced up my fingers, and along my arms, and burst like a blown fuse in my brain.

My mind raged and reorganized. I realized Aaron was entering the past. And I was going with him.

12

Thousands of Afternoons Ago

We whirled through time without moving. I smelled something frying and hoped it wasn't us. The whole experience hurt worse than my mugging. Then we fell over backward. Me being there probably threw us off balance. We landed on a polished wood floor.

We were behind a carved table. The first thing I saw was the ceiling. It had fancy plasterwork now—then. And a tinkling chandelier.

I was still clinging like a monkey to Aaron's back. He jerked around. "What are you *doing* here?"

I blinked.

"You must have been in my force field," he muttered.

Then we heard screaming.

We scrambled up in a crouch and peered over the table past a silver fruit bowl. There were two kids there: boys.

One was about nine or an overweight eight. He was wearing a full Indian costume: buckskin breeches, war paint over his freckles, feather headdress, and beaded moccasins. He had a tomahawk in his hand, and it looked like the real thing.

He was doing a war dance around a chair in the middle of the room. A smaller kid was tied to the chair by a lot of rope. Half the screams were his. The other half were the big one's war whoops.

"That is one hyperactive Native American," Aaron said.

It must have been Cuthbert in costume. Lysander was trussed up like a turkey in the chair and screaming his head off. Then I noticed the crumpled-up newspaper around the chair legs.

My head was aching anyway, and the screaming and whooping didn't help. I still had Aaron in a near-death grip.

Then Cuthbert dropped his tomahawk, reached down into his buckskin breeches, and came up with a box of matches. Before you could think, he struck a light. You could smell sulfur. A breeze from the window that was there then sent the lace curtains billowing. The flame jumped onto them. But Cuthbert was too focused to notice. He leaned down and set the crumpled paper on fire under Lysander's kicking feet.

Flames licked up the curtains. More flames started licking Lysander's feet. Luckily he was wearing buttoned-up high-tops.

Aaron and I leaped up and skidded around the table.

Little oriental rugs skittered under our feet. Cuthbert went on with his authentic war dance, waving his tomahawk around. Smoke drifted around the room, and Lysander was really yowling.

I didn't know what to do. "Quick," Aaron said. "Get a vase." There were flowers in glass vases around the long room. He grabbed one off a reading table, dumping out the flowers. Then he doused the burning paper under Lysander.

"Hey, no fair," Cuthbert said. We were visible, and he was annoyed. But he didn't seem that surprised to see us. He was probably used to having a lot of servants around. And by the way, where were they?

The lace curtains were going up like dry weeds. There was a fireplace on that wall. Two vases of flowers were up on the mantel. I went for one and could just reach it. I dumped the flowers and ran over to the window. The curtains were gone, but the flames had jumped to the bookcase. When the fire hit shellac, it went wild and spread over the books. I let fly with a vase full of water. Aaron came up with another. We were both breathing hard. I wasn't sure the bookcase was doused, but we were out of vases. Flowers were everywhere.

"Who do you think you are?" came Cuthbert's voice behind us.

"Untie me at once!" Lysander howled in a higher voice. But he was all tied up and too busy screaming to notice us.

Aaron and I stood there panting. Then we heard footsteps running down a hall that isn't there now. A big double door began to open. We whirled around, but I was having shooting pains all over like you can't believe. I reached out for Aaron, and his shoulder felt like a Baggie full of bees. We heard buzzing and a voice, but I blacked out for a moment. Hard fluorescent light hit us.

"What in the world!" Mrs. Newbery was standing there with her hands on her hips. "I didn't see you two at first. Have you been in this room all along?"

"Yep," Aaron said, lightning-quick.

"Well, cut along home," Mrs. Newbery said, "and let me lock up. And shut down the computers."

I was ready to pull their plugs permanently.

We filed out. My head felt like a melon. You can get jet lag from this kind of behavior. We were walking out over the crummy tile floors of the Vanderwhitney part of school. Outside, raw winter weather hit us. There was some snow in the air, and the last buses had gone. We turned toward Fifth Avenue, trudging, silent.

"Anyway, now we know who extinguished the blaze before the hook and ladder company got there," Aaron said.

"Us," I said, totally psyched.

"How you got to go along, Josh, I can't figure at all," he said. "You were standing too close or something."

"Aaron, please," I said. "I've got a headache the size of Lincoln Center."

"No pain, no gain," he said. "Josh, we both did it. We cellular-reorganized back like seventy-five years.

We're not talking information superhighway here. We're talking a toll-free ten-lane expressway. And we're on it—in both directions. Talk about interactive."

I let him rattle on. What choice did I have? He tried to walk out into traffic at the Eighty-sixth Street intersection. Part of me was still back in the Vanderwhitneys' library all those thousands and thousands of afternoons ago. I thought I could smell smoke in my dress code, under the Bulls warm-up jacket.

"Kids." Aaron shook his head. "If that was Cuthbert's idea of playing, thank heaven for *Wolfenstein* and *Sim City 2000*. When you get right down to it, there's nothing safer and more user-friendly than a video game."

But I couldn't get my mind away from where we'd been. "If we hadn't put out that fire, the room would have gone up like a torch. Curtains, rugs, polish on everything—that room was totally   "

"Combustible," Aaron said.

The whole idea that we saved Cuthbert and Lysander Vanderwhitney's lives, especially Lysander's, all those years before we were even born was still a hard concept for me. Now Aaron was quiet.

"There's more to this process than I thought," he said after a while.

"Meaning?"

"Well, I've made three trips, right? The first time I saw Heather practically wiped out on a horse in traffic. The second time, when I went backward, I saw that girl and that guy doing all that worried kissing. They were like really furtive. This time it was a kid trying to bar-becue his brother. Think about it."

"Like they're all connected?"

"I'm afraid so. I never seem to run into anybody just reading a book or taking a nap. People sleep a third of the time, you know."

"I know. So?"

"It looks like my formula depends on Emotional Component at the other end."

"You mean—"

"Right. Every time I get there, somebody's upset about something. Turning up just in time for trouble could be a problem. I've got mega-diddling to do."

We continued trudging home. When I got off the el-evator on twelve, Aaron's lips were moving, but his mind was somewhere else.

Even though I'd taken a really long way home, Mom wasn't there yet. Without an O Pear, Heather and I were turning into a couple of latchkey kids. The apart-ment was all shadowy. But when I went into my room, all the lights were on.

A girl was sitting on my bed. She was in dress code: white blouse with collar, Pence plaid skirt. But she wasn't Heather. She was sitting on my bed in big shoes, legs crossed, making herself at home and talking on my phone.

When she saw me, her pale eyebrows jumped up high on her pale forehead. She slapped her hand over the phone. "Who do you think you are?"

"I think I'm Josh. I think this is my room."

"Josh who?"

"I live here."

"You're like Heather's brother?" Boy, was she annoyed.

I nodded.

"Heather never mentioned she had a brother."

"Figures," I said. "Who are you?" But I had a pretty good idea.

Her eyebrows shot up even higher. "Camilla Van Allen, of course. Just shut up a minute. I'm on the phone."

Then she went back to her conversation. "Oh, Junior," she said in a whole new voice, "I'm sorry. I was interrupted by some little creep in a Huckley tie. Heather's brother or somebody. I'd love to come to the party Friday night. Heather too. We'd bring her cousin, Feona Foxworthy, but Feona had to fly back to England for a point-to-point. What? Of course we can come. What do you think we are, seventh graders?"

It went on like that. Finally Camilla signed off.

"But you are seventh graders," I said.

"In our case it doesn't count," Camilla said. "Heather's emotionally fourteen, and I'm a Van Allen. That was Junior Saltonstall. He's having a party at his place Friday night, late. His parents are in the Caribbean. It'll be wall-to-wall upper-school boys. Junior goes to boarding school."

"Then what's he doing home?"

"He was expelled. Isn't it thrilling?"

But then Camilla realized she was talking to somebody's little brother. She stood up, straightened her Pence plaid pleats, propped her hair behind her ears, and headed for my door.

"Heather's in her room on her phone. We have high-profile plans to make about Friday night." Camilla gave me a hard look from the door. "Forget everything you've heard here. If Heather misses this party, I'll hold you responsible." She sucked in her cheeks. "I have influence, Jake."

"Josh," I said.

"You say," she said, and left.

I get hardly any privacy.

I dreamed that night, big time and nonstop. I was falling, of course, plastered to my mattress and falling through time and space. Then I was walking along a street with antique cobblestones. Aaron was there in a Huckley tie. At least this time we had clothes on. It was an eerie street. Everybody was in black—black horses with black feathers on their heads pulling black buggies, funeral wreaths on doors. It was this city of death.

Next to me the dream Aaron said, "Every time I get there, somebody's upset about something. Turning up just in time for trouble could be a problem."

We went around a dark corner. In the distance was the half-finished dome of the U.S. Capitol against a black sky. So this must be Washington, D.C. "I make it the mid-1860's," Aaron said.

"Right," said a man in a beard and a big hat, brushing past us. I think it was Mr. Thaw, our old history teacher.

A large, tear-stained lady in a black bonnet and hoop skirt ran up to us. "Where have you two been?" she shrieked, reaching out and giving Aaron and me a couple of shakes. "You could have saved him!"

"Oh, great," Aaron said hopelessly. "It's Mrs. Lincoln."

I woke up in a sweat, tireder than when I went to bed, and still jet-lagged. But it was a school day.

13

Possible Breakthrough

Aaron was signed out of his morning classes. He was nowhere around at lunch and late for History. You don't sign out of History because the teacher is Mr. L. T. Thaw.

When Aaron came in, I almost didn't know him. His eyes were all baggy, and his red hair was standing up in uncombed clumps. He looked a lot worse than usual.

"Late, Zimmer," Mr. Thaw said. "In this class, that's a—"

"I know." Aaron stood slumped in the doorway. "A misdemeanor." He was fighting a yawn.

"And what progress have you to report on your historical presentation for Parents' Night? Next Tuesday is practically upon us."

"A certain amount," Aaron mumbled. "For one

thing, there was a fire in the Vanderwhitney House part of school. Quite a while back."

Mr. Thaw stared hard at Aaron over the heads of the class. He pulled on his beard. For once everybody was listening.

"Not a major conflagration, I take it?" Mr. Thaw said carefully. He bored holes in Aaron through rimless glasses.

"Not too major," Aaron said.

"Then I don't suppose that event will be of . . . consuming interest to the parents, do you?"

Aaron shrugged. He trudged past my desk on the way to his. Class went on as usual. But his mind sure wasn't on the administration of U. S. Grant.

When the bell finally rang, he veered past me and said, "Meet me at the Black Hole right after school. We're talking possible breakthrough."

I strolled past Mrs. Newbery's desk after school. When I got to the Black Hole door, there was a sign on it:

BOTH COMPUTERS DOWN

The door was open a crack. Aaron's baggy eye peered through at me. He opened the door, yanked me inside, and closed it.

He was really excited and worn out. Not a good combination. "Possible breakthrough. I've got some figures together that might send me where I want to go when I want—"

"Aaron, I don't want to hear about it. I'm trying

to block everything that happened yesterday. For one thing, it gave me a really bad dream."

"It wasn't about the Great Chicago Fire of 1871, was it?"

"No."

"Mine was," he said, "though I didn't get that much sleep. I was up all night, did—"

"Aaron, spare me. Anyway, the computers are down. It says so on the sign."

"No, they aren't. I put up that sign. A fifth grader came in here at lunch to play *Civilization* or something. We don't want to be interrupted."

He was really beginning to treat the Black Hole like his own personal property.

"I've done serious editing on my formula," he said, taking me by the arm. "Now I need you to—"

"Wrong, Aaron," I said. "I'm staying away from those terminals. They could be hazardous to my health. How much reorganization do you think my cells are going to put up with?"

"I'm probably not going anywhere," he said. "I'm only fine-tuning. I want you here just as backup. I don't want you in my force field."

"Just how big is your force field anyway, Aaron?" I said. "You don't know."

"Just stand here by the door. If I happen to be gone for a while, and Mrs. Newbery—"

"I know, I know." I decided I'd better stay and let him play Mad Computer Nerd one more time. "But this is it for me, Aaron. I'm not coming in here anymore.

I'm going to do something else with my life. I'm going to . . . join the chess club or something."

But he was already over between the two glowing screens. His hands were splaying out over the keyboards. I positioned myself against the door with one hand behind me on the knob.

He entered five or six digits. Then it happened. Both screens lit up like Las Vegas. Full-color supergraphics surged. All the air in the Black Hole was charged. I smelled everything—smoke, flowers, furniture polish. My hand gripped the doorknob. I blinked.

When I looked again, Aaron was still there. But somebody else was in the room, standing between us. One second she wasn't there. The next she was.

It was a girl, older than we were, almost a grown-up. I wasn't sure. Whatever she was wearing, a costume or a uniform, made her look older. She had something in her hand: a feather duster. She seemed to be trying to dust the back of Aaron's head. Then she dropped the feather duster, clutched her head, and screamed.

"Don't!" I said, plastering myself against the door. "This is a boys' school!"

14

The Past People

Aaron whirled around. He was almost standing on her feet. She wore high-heeled lace-up shoes with toes that came to points. Her dress was as black as last night's dream. Both her hands clutched her cheeks. She was really quivering.

"Back to the drawing board," Aaron said quietly.

"Who do you think you are?" she said to us, finding her voice.

"Aaron, who do you think she is?" I said.

He knew. He pointed a small finger at her. "You'd be the girl kissing that guy. You'd been crying," he said in a spooky voice. "You wear a ring on a little chain around your neck inside your dress."

Her hands drew down her face. She was pretty. "Attend to your own business," she said very strict. "And

what have you done with the library? What Mrs. Vanderwhitney will say about this, I shouldn't like to think,
I'm sure."

She was English. You could hear it in her voice. And
really upset. Talk about Emotional Component.

"I was running a feather duster over the library table.
It isn't my responsibility. But the other servants are
American, so you don't get a full day's work out of
them."

"Were you like upset about something at the time?"
Aaron asked carefully. "Like emotional?"

There were tears in her lashes. But then her cells had
just been reorganized, and that hurts.

She shot him a look. "Servants are not expected to
have emotions," she said. "I was merely going about
my business, dusting the library table. Then suddenly it
was replaced by these objects."

She pointed to the glowing computer screens. She
looked down. "And what have you done with the
floors?" She turned to the blank wall. "The window!
Where is it? And we had just replaced the curtains with
best Brussels lace."

She wrung her hands. She really was pretty, and very
neat. Her dark hair was smoothed back and parted in
the center. "And who are you two?"

"I'm Josh," I said. "This is Aaron. Everything's his
fault."

"Am I being held for ransom?" Her chin went up.
"You might better have abducted Cuthbert. Indeed,
you're welcome to him."

Aaron put up a hand. "Let me explain," he said, though there was something hopeless in his voice. He kicked off by telling her what year it is.

Her eyes got big. They were a nice shade of blue and now huge.

"The Vanderwhitneys don't . . . live here anymore," Aaron told her. "They probably sold their house to the school. The school's called Huckley."

"Huckley?" the girl said. "Poppycock. The Huckleys live two doors along, just before the Havemeyers."

"Havemeyer House is where we have lunch," I said.

"And what of the Van Allens next door?" she said, softer. Her hand came up and touched the gold chain inside her collar.

"Van Allen House is part of the school too. It's mostly classrooms."

She stood quiet, thinking hard. She glanced past Aaron at the terminals. "And those devices?"

"That's a little harder to explain," Aaron said. "We're into artificial intelligence here and chronological flow charts. We're—"

"Are they time machines?" she said.

We stared.

"Basically," Aaron said. "In layman's terms."

"I've read Mr. H. G. Wells," she said. "I am an educated girl, you know. I am not a common servant. I was brought to this country as governess to Cuthbert and Lysander. Of course they aren't ready for a governess. I was forced to be nursery maid, even to that great lump of an overgrown boy, Cuthbert."

Aaron nodded. "You're overeducated and underemployed in a prefeminist time frame."

She gave us both a look as stern as Mr. L. T. Thaw's. I thought Aaron and I were too old to be governessed, but she was a take-charge type of girl.

"The pair of you have been in my—time. You were there the day of the fire, weren't you? I knew someone had been in the room. I caught a glimpse of you. Cuthbert took credit for putting out the flames. But no one would take Cuthbert for a hero."

"We were there," Aaron admitted.

"Then you may send me straight back, and we'll say no more about it," she said. "And look sharp. I haven't got all day. If I go missing, Mrs. Vanderwhitney will dock my pay. She is a well-known skinflint. And I have . . . personal matters to attend to."

She was geared up to go. She smoothed down her hair and straightened her uniform skirt. She reached down for her feather duster. "Where do you want me?"

Aaron looked as worried as I'd ever seen him. He didn't look like he even knew how he'd gotten her here. He sure didn't know how to get her back.

"When Josh and I were in your time," he said, stalling, "we just came back when our . . . time was up."

"Well, I shan't wait for that, if you don't mind," she said very brisk.

"Okay," he mumbled. "I'll give it a shot, but it's a needle in a haystack. You can stand right there. I guess."

When he turned to the keyboards, he looked

shrunken and unsure. His hands splayed out, but came back. He tried again. I was hanging on the doorknob, afraid to blink. He entered digits. He zeroized and tried some more.

No power surge. Nothing. The figures glowed dim on the screens. He pushed the Escape button, but nobody did. Time passed. But it was just regular, now-type time. I could read Aaron's mind through the back of his head. His own personal memory bank was a dead letter box.

He turned around. "I'll use my original formula, pre-diddled," he said, trying to sound certain. "I'll try to go back and take you with me," he told the girl. "Stand right behind me and put both your hands on my shoulders."

She propped her feather duster under her arm and dropped her hands on his bony shoulders. His hands went out. Digits unfurled. The room lurched. I hung on the knob. But the formula misfired. We were all still there.

Over Aaron's shoulders I could read the word pulsing on both screens:

ERROR   ERROR

He turned and put up his hands. "This could take some time," he said without a glimmer of hope. "A few days . . . a few nights . . ."

"How very inconvenient," the girl said.

"I can't help it," said the A-to-Z man. "I'm only eleven."

I moaned.

"Aaron, you better come up with the formula of your life. Maybe she isn't ever going to go back on her own. Maybe what worked for us doesn't work for . . . the past people. Maybe she isn't bidirectional."

"I'll get her back," he said in his mouse voice.

"You say," I said. "And what do we do with her in the meantime? Hide her in here, bring her food, and put papers down? She isn't a puppy."

"Kindly don't speak of me as if I weren't here," the girl said. "I am."

"The janitor comes in here at night and sort of sweeps around. He'll find her. He'll throw her out. She'll be homeless. It's winter. She doesn't have a warm coat."

"Josh, do I have to think of everything?" Aaron whined. "It's your turn. Use your initiative."

When my brain goes on overload, I think in every direction. My head throbbed. *I am not a common servant*, the girl had said. That rang a bell. And I was desperate.

"I don't believe I caught your name," I said, trying for polite.

"Phoebe," she said.

Phoebe? First, Fenella. Next, Feona. Then . . .

"Phoebe," I said, "are you familiar with the term 'O Pear'?"

15
Cabbages and Kings

We pulled up three chairs, and I tried to put Phoebe in the picture. I started with what O Pears are.

"They're English girls from very nice backgrounds," I said. "They come over here to help out with families and to see American life. They're here to expand their horizons, and ours."

"But don't they take jobs away from governesses and nannies and nursery maids?" Phoebe looked concerned.

"We don't have too many governesses and nannies and nursery maids anymore," I said. "Now it's mostly baby-sitters, the occasional Mr. Mom, day care, and *Sesame Street*."

Phoebe had pulled a lace handkerchief out of her sleeve and sat there twisting it in both hands.

"My dad's in Chicago, and my mom works," I said,

starting to explain my family and easing up to Heather.
"Heather's going to sneak out to a party Friday night.
But don't worry about her. She comes. She goes." The
explanation took me a while. Finally Aaron tapped his
watch. It was quarter till five. It was time to leave if we
were going.

And Phoebe was still with us.

"You want to give it one more try?" Aaron's eyes
were begging her. "You want to try to—think yourself
back? Really put your mind to it."

She closed her eyes and gripped her handkerchief. But
Emotional Component didn't seem to do her any good.
Maybe in her heart she wasn't that anxious to get back
to Cuthbert and Lysander.

"Okay," Aaron said finally. "Let's take her to your
place, Josh. It'll just be . . . temporary. I'll be doing
some heavy-duty collating and really taking a hard look
at my formula. You'll be back to 1923 in no time,
Phoebe. One way or another. Until then, you can just
O Pear at Josh's house. It'll be—cool."

Easy for him to say.

"What choice have I?" Phoebe reached for her feather
duster. "I trust I can be a useful servant in any household."

"Don't think of yourself as a servant," I told her.
"Think of yourself as a helpful guest."

We cracked the door and peered out at the empty
media center. Mrs. Newbery was long gone. Some
nights she locks up. Some nights she just gives up.
Down the dark hall through Van Allen House we

moved like shadows. But I knew Phoebe was real. You could hear the sharp sound of her high heels on the crummy tile.

The front door of Huckley House was in sight when a figure loomed out of a classroom. We pulled back into a stairwell. It was Mr. Thaw, always the last teacher to leave. He swept out ahead of us with his tweed coat flapping behind him.

"That's our old history teacher," I told Phoebe. "He's making us do a report for Parents' Night next Tuesday." I thought I'd just fill her in as we went along.

Outside, a sleety wind was blowing. Phoebe didn't have a coat, so Aaron and I pooled our money to see if we had enough for a cab. We did. Aaron nodded at the drugstore on the Madison Avenue corner. "We better drop in there first, then catch a cab. Phoebe will need a toothbrush."

Aaron was okay on details, but he was sure leaving the big picture to me. When we got out of the cab at our building, he handed over three dollars and a dollar tip.

"Outrageous," Phoebe said. "Highway robbery. That was a fifty-cent trip and a dime tip. It wasn't even a proper cab. And certainly not a proper driver. He didn't even get out to open the door for us. What has the world come to?"

I had a bad feeling that Phoebe was in for worse shocks than that. Heather, for one.

When the elevator got to twelve, Aaron stayed on for the penthouse. He said his job was to collate, diddle, and fiddle all night. I jammed the elevator door open with a foot. "Aaron, you're leaving me with the hard part. If I'm going to turn Phoebe into an O Pear, I'll have to tell a lot of lies to my mom, because she certainly isn't going to buy the truth. I'm going to have to convince Heather. I'm in deep—"

"You'll be fine," he said, but his mind was already upstairs at his workstation. His foot nudged mine out of the door, and it closed between us.

Nobody was home yet. Camilla Van Allen wasn't even on my phone. I showed Phoebe around, pointing out Dad's den where she'd sleep. She observed everything and checked a flat surface for dust. In the kitchen I talked her through the electric can opener and the microwave.

"Have you a cook?" she asked.

"Just us, when we get around to it. We mainly defrost things." I showed her the freezer compartment at the top of the refrigerator.

"Upstairs maid?" Phoebe's eyebrows could get kind of high on her forehead, like Camilla's.

"We don't have an upstairs," I said.

"Butler?"

"We only have a doorman, Vince. But he's downstairs. He doesn't—buttle."

"Who cleans your grates?"

"What are they?"

"The hearths. Fireplaces."

"We don't have any. We have central heat, central air."

"How very sad," Phoebe said, "not to have a cheery fire to sit before in the evenings and let your mind drift."

"We have TV for that," I said. We were in the living room, and I was trying to explain TV when the front door banged open. Heather. I know her bang.

She appeared in the living room doorway on the way to her phone. She'd been shopping since school was out. She had three or four Bloomingdale's bags.

"Is Mom home yet?" she said. "Because I've got to get these things I'm wearing to Junior Saltonstall's party hidden before she—"

Heather caught her first glimpse of Phoebe. Phoebe folded her hands in front of her and lined up the points of her lace-up shoes. She had excellent posture.

Heather blinked.

I was beginning to get used to Phoebe, but she came as a surprise to Heather. Heather stared, starting with Phoebe's feet. She seemed to approve of the shoes, which were retro-funky now. She wondered about the white stockings. I guess they were stockings. They probably wouldn't be panty hose. Heather's stare hung around Phoebe's waistline for a while. She nodded cautiously at the starchy lace collar—more retro. Phoebe's face was pretty, so doubt filled Heather's. She ended up at Phoebe's smooth hair pulled back in a knot behind.

"Who—"

The front door opened behind Heather, and she jumped. Mom.

"Heather," Mom sighed behind her. "Is my Bloomingdale's charge card anywhere on your person?"

"Look," Heather said, pointing toward the living room.

Mom came in in her Adidas, unwinding a long scarf from around her neck. Her nose was nipped red because she'd walked home from Barnes Ogleby. She saw Phoebe. Sometimes I can read Mom's mind. This time it was blank.

"Mom," I said in a funny, high voice, "this is Phoebe. Au Pair Exchange sent her. They called up, and they— said she was coming. She might be a little jet-lagged. Au Pair Exchange said they were really sorry that Fenella and Feona didn't work out. So they sent Phoebe. She's like a—bonus. British Air lost her luggage. All she's got is a toothbrush."

Phoebe had parked her feather duster in the front hall. "And a feather duster." I'd been on a roll. Now I began to run down.

Mom gazed at both of us. She was really dubious.

"Phoebe," I said in a screechy soprano like Lysander's, "this is my mom, Mrs. Lewis. This is my sister, Heather."

"Good evening, madam," Phoebe said. "Good evening, miss."

Heather gawked. Mom couldn't take her eyes off Phoebe's hands cupped together in front of her waist.

"You're English?" Mom said.

"I am indeed, madam," Phoebe said. "A loyal subject of His Majesty, good King George the Fifth."

Mom wondered. Heather swayed. Phoebe was such a jump from Fenella and Feona, Heather didn't know what to think.

"We've had our difficulties with Au Pair Exchange," Mom said.

"I hope I shall give satisfaction, madam." Phoebe's eyes skated down to Mom's running shoes, which she didn't understand. "I have most recently been in the employ of Mrs. Van—"

"Phoebe's O Peared a lot, Mom. Au Pair Exchange is sending a printout all about her. It's in the mail. She's seventeen and a recent . . . school leaver."

"Thank you for sharing, Josh," Mom said. Her mind was a mixture of suspicion and surprise.

"We hope you'll—make yourself at home, Phoebe," she said. "I don't know what we have for dinner. I could defrost—"

"I shall see to it, madam, as you are rather short of staff at the moment." Hands still cupped, Phoebe walked poker-straight out of the living room, heading for the kitchen.

The three of us looked at each other. My face was blank.

"At least you won't be going to any discos on horseback with this one," Mom said to Heather. "And Josh, you either know more about Phoebe than you're telling, or less. When you can come up with a good explanation for your part in this, I'll be glad to hear it."

I was in my room when my phone rang. For once it was for me.

Aaron. "Is Phoebe still there?"

"She's here," I said. "And get to work. If she—vanishes, I'll let you know. Don't be calling every five minutes."

After a long time a strange smell began to seep in under my door. I couldn't place it. It wasn't anything burning. It was worse than that.

I went out into the hall. Mom and Heather were already there. "Gross me out," Heather said. "What *is* that?"

"Cabbage," Mom said. "I'd bought a head of cabbage for coleslaw. Phoebe's boiling it."

"I'll order a pizza and have it in my room," Heather said. "I've got a conference call coming in from Camilla anyway."

"You'll be at the dinner table with the rest of us, young lady," Mom said. "If we have to eat it, you have to eat it. Josh, drop by the kitchen and see if you can do anything."

The boiling cabbage smell about knocked me out when I opened the kitchen door. Phoebe had found an apron. "Oh, Josh, did you say this microwave machine will cook anything in minutes?" She wiped her shiny forehead with a floury arm.

"Sure."

"Then would you fire it up?"

I opened the microwave door. A dish was inside with mashed potatoes on top. It didn't look too bad. I gave it a few minutes full power.

"Shepherd's pie," Phoebe said, "made from bits and bobs I discovered in the icebox."

"Refrigerator," I said.

"I'm a dab hand with pastry," she said, whatever that meant. "I'll do a proper job of baking tomorrow. If I am still here. I'll do you a nice jam roly-poly for pudding."

"Sounds . . . great," I said. But the boiling cabbage smell was really cutting my eyes. "About the cabbage—"

"An excellent winter vegetable," she said. "I knew you'd like it." She was still somewhat stunned by being here, but her training was taking over. She leaned nearer me. "Aaron seems to think I might go back suddenly, all on my own."

"He hopes," I said.

"But supposing I did? Wouldn't your mother think it odd if I suddenly vanished?"

"Don't worry about that," I said. "The other O Pears vanished pretty quick too. But there could be another problem—about you being a loyal subject of good King George Whatever."

Phoebe listened.

"Heather wouldn't have picked up on it, but Mom wondered. You English people have a queen now. Good Queen Elizabeth the Second."

Phoebe's eyes widened. "You mean . . . the king—"

"I'm afraid that king's been gone quite a while. Aaron would know when."

Phoebe's blue eyes filled.

"Phoebe, you've got to remember. Things change."

The microwave bell rang. She stood up ramrod stiff

and blinked away her tears. Mom was there in the kitchen door behind me.

"Dinner is served, madam," Phoebe said.

When I woke up the next morning, hints of last night's cabbage were still hanging around. But the smell of frying bacon was seeping in too. Which might also mean eggs. On my bedside table was a steaming cup of tea with milk already added. So Phoebe was still with us.

Mom and Heather were out in the hall with cups of tea in their hands.

"Some service," Mom said. She was still in her robe, but she had her face on.

"Wait till Camilla hears," Heather said. "The Van Allens have a whole staff of servants, of course."

"Don't think of Phoebe as a servant," Mom said. But her heart wasn't in it.

16

A Question of Time

Aaron and I took the bus that Friday morning. "Is Phoebe—"

"She's still here," I told him. "You up all night?"

"Most of it," he said. "How are things at your place?"

"Not too bad. Mom's suspicious."

"Moms are," Aaron said.

"Who was the King of England in Phoebe's time?"

"George the Fifth," Aaron said.

"That's him. He's dead, right?"

"1936."

"I figured. Phoebe was upset about that. And she's not too pleased about sitting at the table with us for meals. She says it isn't proper. But cabbage tastes better than it smells. A little. Phoebe cooks. For tonight she's fixing toad-in-the-hole."

Aaron looked up. "Actual toad?"

"That's what we were afraid of. But toad-in-the-hole is just an English term for sausages in a batter, microwaved. We're having jam roly-poly for dessert."

"Sounds like a month's worth of calories," Aaron the herbivore said. "But hang in there. I'll sign out of my morning classes. Mr. Headbloom will cover for me. By noon I might have some solid progress to report."

As soon as we got to school, Aaron headed toward the media center. "Come on," he said. "We've got some time before homeroom."

"Aaron, read my lips. I told you I wasn't going near the Black Hole again."

"You want Phoebe to get back?" he said. "Your mom's going to figure out Au Pair Exchange didn't send her. It's just a question of time. And the Vanderwhitneys are going to wonder where she is. She could lose her job at that end, you know. Besides, I've got a lot on my mind and too many digits in my head. We're in this together, Josh."

"Aaron, you don't even remember those digits you entered when Phoebe suddenly turned up. You were winging it, right?"

"I'm closing in on a breakthrough," he said, not answering. "I'm on the brink of finding a bidirectional fiber. I'm on the threshold of pinpointing a foolproof three-dimensional fax. You've heard of multicultural? I'm about to be multichronological. I'm—"

"Aaron, your problem is you can get us into trouble, but you can't get us out."

We were strolling past Mrs. Newbery's desk. She was

already at it. "Just a moment, Aaron," she said. We froze.

She handed over a Xeroxed sheet. "This is the last reference to the Vanderwhitney family I can find for you in the 1920's *New York Times Index*," she said, "except for an obituary, which is a real downer."

"Appreciate it, Mrs. Newbery," Aaron said, cool as a cucumber. "This will be a big help for our Parents' Night report next week." We strolled on toward the Black Hole, taking our time. The BOTH COMPUTERS DOWN sign was still on it.

Inside, we looked over the sheet. You could see the date on this one—November 1929:

Palatial Home of Late Osgood Vanderwhitney to Serve as Wing of New Huckley School

The Huckley School that has already acquired the properties of the Havemeyer, Huckley, and Van Allen families is proposing to purchase the home of Osgood Vanderwhitney from his estate.

The house, called the most tasteful built in the city during 1921, has recently been the residence of Osgood Vanderwhitney and his son Cuthbert, aged fifteen and now at boarding school. Osgood Vanderwhitney's tragic death has shaken the social and financial communities. See obituary for details of his leap from the window of his Wall Street office following the recent Market Crash.

"What's all this?" I said.

"Osgood Vanderwhitney took a dive," Aaron said.

"I see that. But why had he been living in this house with just Cuthbert? That would make anybody jump out a window. What happened to Mrs. Vanderwhitney? What about Lysander? You don't suppose Cuthbert . . ."

The Black Hole was dead silent. We glanced around. "Maybe little Lysander vanished without a trace," Aaron said in a spooky voice.

"Phoebe—"

"Phoebe wouldn't know yet. It would have happened after she . . . came here." Aaron gazed down at the floor like there could be a small body buried there. Bones now.

"A rich kid disappearing would have made *The New York Times*," I pointed out.

"Not necessarily." Aaron's imagination was really on the move now. "The Vanderwhitneys might have covered up the crime to save Cuthbert and their reputation. They could have said Lysander went off to boarding school. Why not? He was probably way smarter than Cuthbert."

"Knock it off, Aaron." When you get right down to it, he's really safer working at the computers than when his mind starts wandering. The bell for homeroom went, and so did I.

"Skip lunch and be here," Aaron said.

At noon I swung by the Havemeyer House lunchroom and bought us a couple of tuna salads on pita bread and some Snapple.

When I passed through the BOTH COMPUTERS DOWN door, Aaron was hard at work. "I'm practically there.

I've got a lock on that time Phoebe came from. My technology is really beginning to catch up with concept."

I gave him a tuna pita, but he didn't have time for it. "Look, yesterday I entered these digits, combined them with a graphic, and—"

"You zeroized."

"That didn't get me anywhere. If I change that last digit to this—"

It was like the room imploded. Fire flashed. Both computers wobbled. Snapple went everywhere. I grabbed for Aaron, but he stayed where he was. All his red hair was standing up. Air seeped back into the room.

But we weren't alone.

"You two again," a high voice barked. "Who do you think you are?"

Aaron and I spun around.

Cuthbert Vanderwhitney was standing there. We'd only seen him with his feather headdress. His hair was cut in a Dutch boy style. His pudgy fists were on his knickered hips. His freckles glowed in full color, and his lower lip was out a mile.

Aaron's head dropped on his chest.

"What have you done with Lysander?" I said, because Aaron had me totally psyched.

Cuthbert scowled. "I beat him up regularly. It keeps him in line."

"But—"

But it wasn't near 1929 yet. Cuthbert looked the

same as the last time we saw him. He'd still be about fourth grade, though he was as big as me, bigger than Aaron.

His eyes crackled. His feet in high-top shoes were planted wide. He wore long argyle socks, corduroy knickers, and a weird velvet-looking jacket with gold buttons and a big white collar. A wide tie circled his bulging neck.

"You're trespassing. And it's not your first offense. My papa will have you thrown out." He noticed Aaron's tuna pita. He grabbed it up and smelled it. "I don't eat this," he said, and threw it against the wall.

The pita stuck where it hit. The wall hadn't been there in his time. Cuthbert stared. "What have you done with my house? We're Vanderwhitneys, you know."

Aaron was recovering. "Let me put it in a nutshell for you, Cuthbert," he said. "You've cellular-reorganized three-quarters of a century ahead of your time. Your family's house is a school now."

Cuthbert trained mean, beady eyes on Aaron. "Liar, liar, pants on fire," he said.

Which was probably his favorite saying.

"It's true," Aaron said. "Believe it." With Cuthbert you have to be firm.

"Aaron, for pete's sake," I muttered, "send him back."

"If it's a school," Cuthbert said, working this out, "who's in charge?"

"You mean like the headmaster?" I said.

"Buster Brewster," Aaron said, and he had a point.

"Harrison K. 'Blackjack' Brewster from Ninety-second Street?" Cuthbert's eyes narrowed.

"No, Buster's probably his grandson or something. Maybe a great-great nephew. Who knows?" Aaron said. "Just stand right there, Cuthbert."

Aaron turned to the computers and started entering digits. Four, five . . . I was braced. But I looked around at Cuthbert because I really wanted to see him dissolve.

He was already gone.

"Aaron."

He looked around. "Hey, I didn't even—"

The Black Hole door was open. Cuthbert had walked out. He was at large in Huckley School. The bell rang, so lunch was over, and it was time for History. You can't sign out of that because Mr. Thaw's the teacher.

Aaron and I ran into each other. Then we ran out the door. We streaked past Mrs. Newbery, but so had Cuthbert. The hallway outside was full of middle-school guys in Huckley dress code.

"It won't be hard to spot him," Aaron said. "He's dressed like Little Lord Fauntleroy."

"And what if we don't?" I said. "He was trouble enough in his own time."

"We'll get him," Aaron said, looking everywhere.

"Before History?" I said. "Because I don't think so."

Aaron skidded to a stop at the door of Mr. L. T. Thaw's classroom. "It's hopeless with all the halls full of people."

"What if some teacher finds him before we do?" I said. "Some adult. Then what?"

"Look," Aaron said, "do you feel like cutting History?"

"No way," I said. We slid into our seats a second before the bell rang.

"Ah, Zimmer," Mr. Thaw said from the front of the room. "An unexpected pleasure to see you here on time." We were up to James A. Garfield, twentieth president of the United States, assassinated in 1881.

The time dragged worse than usual. I tried to pretend that Cuthbert was a bad dream. What Aaron was thinking was anybody's guess. Fifteen minutes, twenty, we were almost halfway through the period.

The door opened. Mr. Thaw looked at it and froze. You'd think he was seeing President Garfield being shot right out there in the hall.

Cuthbert strolled in.

His hands were on his hips. His necktie was tied in a large bow, and there were gold buttons down his front.

Everybody stared because he looked like an exhibit from the Museum of the City of New York. They thought Cuthbert might be curriculum.

"Awright," he said in his piping roar, "keep your seats. Is Buster Brewster in here?"

Mr. Thaw swayed.

"Who wants him?" Buster reared up out of his desk in the middle row.

Buster got a good look at Cuthbert right down to his knickers. The Dutch boy hair. The white collar. The big perky bow tie. The velvet jacket.

"What a wuss," Buster said.

Cuthbert stalked down the aisle. Now he and Buster were nose to nose. Both their necks bulged.

Up at his desk, Mr. Thaw was turning to stone.

Buster couldn't figure out Cuthbert, so he was off guard. "Who do you think you are?" Cuthbert bawled in Buster's big face.

People were getting under their desks. You don't talk to Buster like that. "You're not so tough," Cuthbert bellowed. "And I was here first."

Buster's mighty fists were clenching.

But Cuthbert brought up a powerhouse uppercut and flattened Buster's nose. Cuthbert's left hook had come out of nowhere. Buster went over backward, sprawling across the desk of the kid behind him. Frederick "Fishface" Pierrepont sits behind Buster. But Fishface was already under his desk.

Buster was flat on his back with his legs in the air. Blood was splattered all over his dress code. But he made a comeback. He lunged at Cuthbert. Grabbing for his neck, he got a handful of big white collar instead.

But Buster was off balance before he began. Up came Cuthbert's right fist, also out of nowhere. The sound of knuckles against nose practically echoed. And Buster's face was rearranged one more time.

Buster crumpled.

By then we'd made a big circle around them. Six or eight desks were on their sides. Mr. Thaw unfroze. He's not too steady on his pins anyway. Now he was shaking like a leaf.

Buster was lolling there on Fishface's desk, and you

could see his tongue. Cuthbert with his collar on sideways was reaching for Buster's throat.

"Cuthbert!" Mr. Thaw howled in an ancient voice. "Unhand him at once!"

It was too much for Mr. Thaw. His old knees gave out, and he slumped to the floor. It looked like our history teacher might be—history. He was out cold at least.

The whole room was up for grabs. A boys' school is always about *this close* to a riot anyway. Fists went up all over the room. Quite a few people were beginning to settle old scores. More desks went over. Fishface Pierrepont burrowed out from under his. "I'm calling 911," he piped, and rocketed out of the room.

Aaron rose up. Cuthbert was staring down at Mr. Thaw's sprawled shape. Aaron got Cuthbert under an arm and ran him out of the room and down the hall. Classroom doors were beginning to open all the way to the media center. Inside we got lucky because Mrs. Newbery was at lunch. The three of us raced into the Black Hole and banged the door shut.

The tuna pita was still on the wall. The floor was sticky with Snapple.

"Never laid a finger on me," Cuthbert said. He was blowing on his skinned knuckles. "Those Brewsters always were yellow."

"Aaron," I said, breathing hard. "Send Cuthbert back. Like now. Whatever it takes."

Aaron moved over to the computers, ready to give it a try.

17

Phoebe's Question

Both screens began to fill up with formula. Aaron took his time. Then he was doing some fancy finger work on the keyboard. The screens glowed and pulsed. The ceiling lights dimmed, then surged. One of the fluorescent tubes up there burned out.

But I never took my eyes off Cuthbert. His hands were on his hips, and his high-tops were planted on the floor. Then between one nanosecond and the next, he was nothing but air space. I was looking straight through where he'd been at the tuna pita on the wall.

The room sizzled and fell silent.

"Aaron," I whispered, "you did it."

He turned around to the room with only us in it. He was radish-pale. You never saw so much relief on a human face. He went back to the keyboards.

MISSION

he entered on one screen.

ACCOMPLISHED

he entered on the other.
Then he jumped out of his chair. "YESSSSSS!" he shrieked, and did a complete war dance around the Black Hole without the tomahawk.

"You want to know how I did it?" he said after he'd calmed down a little. "I took my original formula, pre-diddled, and re-expressed it tomographically."

"Ah," I said.

"You know tomography?"

"No."

"It's diagnostic imaging that directs X rays axially around the human body. In layman's terms."

"Would be."

"Then I got lucky with some random digits. That's what brought both Phoebe and Cuthbert here. To get rid of him, I re-expressed my formula with complements. You know complements?"

"You mean like, 'You look marvelous'?" I said.

"Not that kind of compliment," Aaron said. "A complement is a number representing the negative of a given number. You get it by subtracting each digit of the number from the number representing its base, and in the case of two's complement and ten's, you add unity to the last significant digit. Or in layman's terms, I threw Cuthbert in reverse and sent him on his way."

"Oh," I said. "Or maybe Cuthbert was just ready to go. He'd cleaned Buster's clock. Now he's going back to clean Lysander's."

"Maybe," Aaron said. "But I've got the bugs out, so I can do it again. Bidirectionally. Maybe we can go anywhere in the past we want to, anytime. My formula's still a primitive device. It's covered wagon. But we're looking at Skylab. We're—"

"Have you got enough bugs out of it so people from the past don't keep popping up here? Because I don't think this school can take another dose of Cuthbert."

"I've got some more fiddling to do," Aaron said. "No question about that, but—"

"Aaron," I said. "Let's go home."

He looked around, dazed. His red hair was still on end. His Huckley tie was around under one ear. I wondered if he was too weird to know. "Is school out?" he said.

"Close enough," I said. "The only thing left is math class. I don't think it would do me any good. And I don't think you need it."

He shut down the computers. I peeled the tuna pita off the wall. I hadn't eaten mine either. I dropped them in Mrs. Newbery's wastebasket on our way out. She wasn't back from lunch, but no wonder. School was still in an uproar.

People were milling around out on the sidewalk too. A paramedic van was at the curb to pick up Buster Brewster and Mr. Thaw. Big uniformed guys with rubber gloves were leading Buster into the back of the van. He was holding a bloody towel over his nose. They had Mr. Thaw on a stretcher. He was thrashing around and talking out of his head. So he was alive and kicking, but this looked like his last day of school.

"Now we'll have a sub," Aaron said, "who won't know Warren G. Harding from a hole in the ground."

We walked home.

"Let's go get Phoebe, bring her to school, and send her back to her time," he said. "Mrs. Vanderwhitney will only dock her a day's pay."

That made sense, more or less. "But I wish she'd clear up some things before she goes. Like what happened to Lysander and Mrs. Vanderwhitney. Like why Osgood Vanderwhitney and Cuthbert were living alone in the house by 1929."

"But she won't know," Aaron said. "She's come to us from 1923. That was still all in the future then."

"We could tell her."

"Tell her Osgood Vanderwhitney is going to jump out of a window in Wall Street?" Aaron said. "I don't think so. That would be too creepy for her to know ahead of time. She was upset about King George the Fifth dying, and she didn't even know him."

But she might have an idea about what happened to the Vanderwhitneys. I didn't think little Lysander was buried under the floor of the media center. But you never know.

Aaron was still with me when I slipped the key into our door at home. It opened before I could unlock it.

Phoebe. Mom and Heather had loaned her some clothes, but she was still in her black uniform and starchy collar.

"Great news, Phoebe. Defining moment," Aaron said. "You can—"

"You two young gentlemen had better wash your hands and tidy up a bit. There's cocoa in the kitchen for you afterward."

We filed off and washed.

The kitchen was full of good baking smells. The floor looked like a mirror. "I gave it a good scrub and a coat of wax," Phoebe said. "It was in a shocking state."

Baking, scrubbing, polishing. Even toad-in-the-hole. "I don't think O Pears are supposed to have to do all those things," I told her.

"They sound like useless creatures to me," Phoebe said. "I've run an iron over Miss Heather's new party dress. Clothes are very poor quality these days."

"You've been busy, Phoebe."

"Idle hands are the devil's workshop," she said.

"Are we alone?" I said. "Is Miss—is Heather home yet?"

"She is not," Phoebe said. "And if she is late coming from school, I shall have to speak to madam about it."

"Do that," I said. "And listen to this. We . . . ran into Cuthbert today." Phoebe had been standing over us with her hands cupped. She staggered.

"Right," Aaron said. The mug of cocoa had given him a brown mustache. "My formula went a little haywire and cellular-reorganized Cuthbert. But I think I've got the bugs out of it. We sent him back, and we can send you—"

"Cuthbert?" Phoebe said. "Here?"

"And he isn't all bad," I said. "He beat Buster Brewster to a pulp before he left. But what I want to know is, can you think of anything that might take Mrs. Vanderwhitney and little Lysander . . . away from the family?"

Phoebe's hand crept up to her cheek. She looked away. "It isn't for me to say, I'm sure," she said.

"She suspects something," I said to Aaron. "Even in 1923."

"Kindly don't speak of me as if I weren't here," she said. "As a matter of fact, Mr. and Mrs. Vanderwhitney are not happy in their marriage. They live apart for much of the time."

Phoebe pursed her lips.

"They're going to separate," I said to Aaron.

"Mrs. Vanderwhitney is going to leave Osgood," Aaron said, "and take little Lysander with her. He isn't buried under the floor."

"Certainly not," Phoebe said. "The pair of you gossip worse than servants. But in fact, Mrs. Vanderwhitney has an admirer."

An admirer?

"She is not a bad-looking woman in her way, you know," Phoebe said. "And wealthy in her own right. I fear she's going to run away with a certain gentleman of her acquaintance. Indeed, I've seen a letter or two that has passed between them." Phoebe flushed. "When I was dusting her dressing-table drawers."

"So Mrs. Vanderwhitney is going to take a hike," Aaron said, "and leave Cuthbert behind with Osgood. It fits."

Phoebe nodded sadly. "Yes, I expect any time now that Mrs. Vanderwhitney is going to divorce Mr. Vanderwhitney and marry Mr. Thaw."

Mr. Thaw?

"Mr. Thaw?" Aaron said. Cocoa went everywhere.

"Mr. Thaw?" I said. "You mean she's going to marry our old history teacher?"

Phoebe looked uncertain.

Aaron's head dropped onto the kitchen table. "Josh, you goofball," he said, "her Mr. Thaw would be long gone. Don't you get it?"

"Get what?"

"Mrs. Vanderwhitney married Mr. Thaw. And Mr. Thaw adopted Lysander."

"I still don't get it."

"Josh," Aaron said, "our history teacher, Mr. L. T. Thaw, is Lysander. Lysander Theodore Thaw."

Aaron looked up from the table. We stared at each other.

"Couldn't be," I said.

"Is," Aaron said. "Think about this afternoon. Mr. Thaw yelled out Cuthbert's name."

I remembered that.

"How would he know it?" Aaron said. "And the shock of seeing Cuthbert just the way he'd been way back when Cuthbert was beating him up regularly and trying to barbecue him—it knocked Mr. Thaw out."

My head was pounding, and Phoebe looked puzzled. "Of course he would be a very old man now," she said.

"He is," I said. "He should have retired a long time ago. But he probably thinks he owns the place. He was that old geezer who came out of the classroom last night with his coat flapping. You saw him, Phoebe."

"Little Lysander," she said softly, "after all this time." Her blue eyes had a lot of long distance in them.

"And if he is still here," she said, "am I?"

18

Midnight on the Nose

Phoebe's question hung over the kitchen.

Aaron didn't ask her if she wanted to go back to 1923 this afternoon. She didn't seem that anxious to leave yet. She had things on her mind. And she couldn't stop reaching for the gold chain inside her collar.

The front door banged. You know who.

Heather's head appeared around the kitchen door. "Yo, Pencil-Neck," she said to Aaron, overlooking me. "Listen, Phoebe, I have this friend coming over probably. We have vital plans to make. How about some cucumber sandwiches?" Then she was gone.

Phoebe tinkled a little laugh, the first we'd heard. "Imagine cucumbers in the market at this time of year," she said. "She and her friend will have to settle for hot buttered scones and strawberry jam."

"Actually, cucumbers are in the market this time of year these days," I said. "Everything is."

"How sad," she said. "Is there nothing left to look forward to anymore, not even long summer afternoons and cucumber sandwiches for tea?"

Then Mom appeared in the kitchen in her business suit and Adidas. "What good smells," she said. Her eyes popped. The floor you could see your face in. Everything dusted to death. Phoebe was taking a long pan of scones out of the oven.

"Pinch me," Mom murmured. "This is too good to be true." She saw Aaron and me. We'd finished off the cocoa and were trying to look like a couple of innocent kids.

"I better be getting home," Aaron said.

"Tea, madam," Phoebe said, holding out the pan of scones. "In the drawing room."

I walked Aaron to the elevator. "Listen," he said, "when Phoebe's ready to go back, let me know."

"It's Friday night," I said. "What are we supposed to do, break into school over the weekend? You can't send her back from your home microsystem workstation, can you?"

"Too risky," he said. "Better use two terminals. We can't do much till Monday. But keep me informed."

"Keep yourself informed," I said. "You're always running out on me and leaving me with the hard stuff." The elevator door closed between us.

Heather and Mom and Phoebe were in the living

room with our best teacups. Heather was restless because Camilla hadn't shown. Mom had buttered herself a hot scone. Phoebe was perched on the edge of a chair because Mom had told her to sit down with us. I eased in.

"Phoebe," she said, "these scones absolutely melt in the mouth. You're a real treasure."

"Thank you, madam." Phoebe's hands made a little nest of themselves in her lap.

"But we don't know very much about you," Mom said in a firm voice. "Your family, for instance."

"Oh," Phoebe said, "the Vander—"

"Mom means your own family, Phoebe," I said. "Back home in England."

"I haven't any parents, madam," Phoebe said. "My brother and I are orphans. We grew up in the asylum. Then he emigrated to New Zealand after the Great War."

"Desert Storm," I said. "Right?"

"If you say so," Phoebe murmured. "Of course, all English people have the royal family," she said carefully. "Good Queen Elizabeth the Second." Phoebe beamed. She was proud of herself for that, but I thought we were about one more question from big trouble.

Phoebe thought so too. She stood up. "But I mustn't sit here chatting. I had better see to my toad-in-the-hole." She did her good-posture walk out of the room.

"There's something about that girl I can't quite put my finger on," Mom said. I just sat there, picking some raisins out of my scone. But I could feel Mom's gaze.

"So what?" Heather said. "She makes my bed."

"Well, don't get too used to it, young lady," Mom said. "I have the feeling Phoebe won't be with us for long."

I jumped. Raisins went everywhere.

"Mo-om," Heather said. "You're not going to send her back to England *too*."

"Not on your life." There was a small smile on Mom's face and scone crumbs around her mouth. She was looking into the bottom of her teacup. "But Phoebe's in love."

"Mom," Heather said, "how would you know *that*?"

"I've been in love," Mom said. "I know the signs. It's always a secret you can't keep. And what's that on the chain she wears around her neck? I'll bet it's an engagement ring. Phoebe has a young man. Somewhere."

But Heather was beginning to pace. Camilla hadn't shown. And they had major plans to make about Junior Saltonstall's late-night party. Since it was tonight, Heather was practically down to the wire. She had her dress. But she was going to have to get out of the apartment in the middle of the night. I can read Heather's mind. Basically, it's not that complicated.

We had toad-in-the-hole for dinner and jam roly-poly for dessert. Not a bad meal, but it was like trying to digest a giant hockey puck. We all turned in early, especially Heather. But I was up and down most of the night.

Also, I was monitoring Heather.

At eleven by my digital clock, she was out of bed and

bumping quietly around her room. I had my ear to my door. By eleven-fifteen I was back in bed pretending to be asleep because Heather was heading down the hall and might be planning to use my bathroom. Her bathroom is right next to Mom's room.

Heather cracked my door. This must have been eleven-sixteen. I was breathing steady. She crept across the room to my bathroom. I heard her new dress rustle and smelled Mom's perfume. Heather didn't turn the light on in my bathroom till she'd closed the door.

I slid out of bed and put an ear to the keyhole. Heather was whispering. She'd brought her phone.

"I'm dressed," she said. "I'm like ready to rock. No, I can't talk louder. I'm in Josh's bathroom. Who is he? He's my little brother. I'm wearing heels. Are you wearing heels? How high? I'm wearing blush. Are you wearing . . ."

It went on like that. Then she said, "Okay, but when you get here, knock softly. I'll be waiting by the door. Come in with your shoes off. You can change in my room. We can take a cab from here." Then she signed off.

I had time to get back into bed because she was doing something at my sink and probably looking at herself in my mirror. Then the bathroom door cracked. She was pretty quiet. I'll give her credit for that. I let her get right by my bed.

Then I said, "How's Camilla getting out?"

My voice came out of the dark, so it probably sounded louder than it was. Heather stifled a scream. I flipped on my lamp.

There she stood with her hand clapped over her mouth. Her eyes were huge and all made up. Her hair was practically standing up from shock. But she'd done something funny and new with it anyway. She had on her new party dress. Black, of course. The skirt was so short it reminded me of the Hefty bag she wore downtown to Fenella's club. She was carrying her shoes and her phone.

"If you rat on me, I'll have your guts for garters," she barked in a loud whisper.

I eased up on my pillow. "Hey, I'm sound asleep. But how's Camilla getting out? Just curious."

Heather sighed. "She told her parents she was spending the night with her grandmother who lives around the corner on Seventy-second. Getting out of her grandmother's place is a piece of cake. Her grandmother's real old. She goes to bed early. But she's a light sleeper, so Camilla's going to get dressed here. Josh, if I miss this party, my life's over. It's that simple. So put a sock—"

"I'm fast asleep." I laced my fingers under my chin and closed my eyes. But I was still sitting up and the light was on. Heather crept out of the room.

I turned out the light. Sometimes you can hear better in the dark. Around eleven-thirty I was drifting off when I heard a quiet knock on the front door. Then some rustling. I dozed, but something brought me around. My clock said eleven-fifty. It must have been the front door closing behind Heather and Camilla. They'd be out by the elevator now, putting on their shoes. I drifted off again.

A sharp rap knocked me awake at eleven-fifty-four. Somebody was outside Mom's door.

"Madam," Phoebe said.

I rolled out of bed and cracked my door. Phoebe was still in her uniform. She even had her apron on, tied behind. She was still knocking.

Mom mumbled. She works a full day, so she's tireder at night than Heather.

Phoebe opened Mom's door. The light went on, and I could see a section of Mom trying to sit up. Her hair was in a big tangle.

"Oh, madam, I thought you might require help dressing," Phoebe said.

"I'm dressed," Mom said in a fuzzy voice. "For bed."

"But, madam, I thought you'd be attending the party. Miss Heather has already left." My jaw dropped. Mom bolted up.

"What party?"

"At a Mr. Junior Saltonstall's, I believe," Phoebe said.

Mom was grabbing around for her robe. "Wake up Josh," she said.

I made a run for my bed, dived in, and got the covers up. The room flooded with light. I was breathing steady.

"Josh," Mom said.

I put one eye over the cover and squinted. Mom was standing over me, knotting her robe belt. Phoebe was there, her hands cupped. "But, madam," she said, "I merely assumed you'd be going to the party as well, to chaperone. Surely young girls don't go to parties without their mothers."

She sounded innocent, even a little bewildered. But there was something sly in her eye.

"Josh, what do you know about this?"

"Who, me?"

"Talk to me," Mom said in her firm voice.

"Heather said if I told, she'd have my guts for—"

"I'm listening, Josh," Mom said.

"Junior Saltonstall is having a party at his house, with upper-school guys. Heather has a new dress. She went."

"The Elise and Howard Saltonstalls?" Mom asked.

"I should think so, madam," Phoebe said. "I took the liberty of looking them up in the telephone directory. They are the only Saltonstalls. On Sixty-fifth Street."

"I thought they were in the Caribbean," Mom said.

"They are," I said. "That's why Junior's having a party."

I can read Mom's mind. It was full of drugs, alcohol, and upper-school guys breaking the Saltonstalls' furniture.

"And Heather's out by herself in the middle of the night, heading for that—"

"She's not by herself," I said. "Camilla's with her."

"Camilla?" Phoebe said. She put a hand out on the end of my bed.

"Camilla told her parents she was staying at her grandmother's on Seventy-second. When her grandmother went to sleep, Camilla came over here to change clothes. It was an airtight plan." I checked my clock. "They've only been gone about ten minutes." It was midnight on the nose.

Mom stared away at my ceiling. "This single parenting is a twenty-four-hour-a-day deal," she said. She's thirty-eight, so around then I guess you start talking to yourself.

"All right, Josh," she said. "Get up and get dressed. You and I are going to a party."

"Mom, if Heather finds out I—"

"Up, Josh. We're going to bring Heather home. I want you to see this so-called party for yourself in case you ever think of having one."

Mom stalked out of the room, running hands through her hair.

But Phoebe stayed stone-still at the foot of my bed. "Miss Camilla," she said softly. "Is she a Van Allen?"

I nodded. "And she really lets you know it."

"The Van Allen family live just next door to the Vanderwhitneys, you know. They used to."

"Right," I said. "Now it's all classrooms."

"Mrs. Van Allen, the Mrs. Van Allen of that time, was named Camilla too," Phoebe said, her mind going years back. "But of course that was all long ago, wasn't it?"

And her hand slipped into the collar of her dress.

19
Phoebe

Mom was more or less dressed, and I was in my Bulls warm-up jacket. We were zooming down Fifth Avenue in a cab. It was a cold night, but Mom was hot under the collar. She'd actually told the cabby to step on it.

Then we were on our way up in the elevator in the Saltonstalls' building. You could hear the party from here. When the elevator door opened, the party had already spilled out into the hall. Girls and guys all over the place. And enough smoke to pollute your lungs permanently. Everybody had drinks in their hands, and they weren't Snapple.

Some silence fell when Mom and I got off the elevator. I was too young, and she was way too old. She had my hand in a death grip. But I was looking around. After all, this was my first party.

The front door of the Saltonstalls' apartment was open. Inside, it was wall-to-wall preppies and pounding heavy-metal sound. Some people were kind of dancing, but there wasn't a lot of room. When they saw us, they cleared a little path, and Mom kept walking. She had parent written all over her.

"Hey, Junior," somebody said. "Looks like you've got a couple of gate-crashers."

Out of the crowd a guy loomed up, a big sixteen in a damp shirt. He was wearing the official necktie of a well-known boarding school as a belt. And he had a six-pack in each hand. His face was blurred. Junior Saltonstall. "Who do you think—"

Mom shoved him aside.

The living room was a real mob scene. I didn't know you could get that many people into one apartment. The light wasn't too good. The smoke was terrible. Almost everybody was in black, and preppies look a lot alike anyway. The pictures were still on the wall, but the night was young.

Then we saw them. Heather and Camilla were over against a wall, kind of clinging to each other. They were pretty young for this crowd. Their dresses fitted in better than they did. They didn't look like they were having that great a time. I couldn't see how anybody could be having a great time. With the noise and the smell and the crowds, it was like the subway.

"Heather," Mom said.

Heather's made-up eyes enlarged and began to melt. She tried to turn invisible, but her back was to the wall.

"Who *are* those people?" Camilla said. Her pale eyebrows shot up. "Omigosh, it looks like your mother and Jake. Oh, how embarrassing for you, Heather. Couldn't you just die?"

"Mom," Heather said, completely confused. "What am I doing here?"

The next thing I remember, we were in a cab, zooming back uptown. Mom had Heather on one side of her and Camilla on the other. I was practically on the floor.

Heather was getting over the shock and beginning to sulk. Camilla was trying for cool. "Terribly sweet of you to give me a ride home, Mrs. Lewis. But honestly I'll be fine. Grannie knows all about the party. She doesn't expect me back for ages."

"In a pig's eye," Mom said.

We pulled up at Camilla's grandmother's place and got out. She lives in that building on Seventy-second that looks like a cathedral. Tall pointed stained-glass windows and a big, dim lobby with polished wood. The doorman was seven feet tall and had gold braid on his shoulders.

"I am afraid, madam," he said down to Mom, "that Mrs. Van Allen has retired for the evening."

"Wake her up. I'm delivering her granddaughter to her," Mom said brief and firm. "In person."

"Mrs. Van Allen's maid will have retired too, madam," the doorman said. He was also firm. "And she is hard of hearing."

"That's right," Camilla said. "Gladys is as hearing-impaired as a post. She's lots deafer than Grannie. She won't hear a thing. I'll just say good night to you here and—"

"Don't budge, young lady," Mom said to Camilla. "Keep ringing till somebody answers," she told the doorman.

"On your head be it, madam," he said. But he dialed the house phone.

After a lot of rings he was saying, "Mrs. Van Allen, I have a lady in the lobby who wishes to return your granddaughter." He gave us a glance. "No, Camilla is not in her bed. She's in the lobby and dressed for a night on the town."

Camilla propped her hair behind her ears and looked into space.

"Very good, Mrs. Van Allen. I'll instruct them to wait." He hung up. "Mrs. Van Allen will see you in ten minutes exactly. You may take a seat."

It was a long carved bench. Heather wouldn't sit next to me because I'd ratted on her. Mom wouldn't let Heather and Camilla sit together. So it was Heather, then Mom, then Camilla, then me. Heather and Camilla's feet were killing them in those high heels. But nobody spoke. It was one in the morning. I thought being out this late was interesting.

Then the doorman gave us a nod and walked us to the elevator. Camilla was all out of small talk. Heather was still sulking. Her black eyeliner was sliding down her blush. The elevator rose to the Van Allen floor.

Camilla led the way to her grandmother's door, but

she was in no hurry. "I forgot my key," she said in a small voice. But the door was opening anyway.

At first her grandmother was just a dark shape. You could only see her hand. It was real old, just a bunch of bones and veins. An old-fashioned wedding ring and engagement ring were loose on one finger. She was clutching a cane.

The cane came up and aimed at Camilla. "You, young miss," said an ancient voice. "Into your room at once. You will be dealt with later."

Camilla scampered inside, and the apartment swallowed her up. Mrs. Van Allen was still just a dark shape. She saw the three of us out in the hall. Her hand shook. The cane nearly got away from her, but she gripped it.

"Mrs. Lewis?" she said to Mom.

Mrs. Van Allen's gaze swept over us. Her glasses were like nickels winking in the dark. She wore something long and black like a shroud. But it could have been her robe.

"We don't like to disturb you," Mom said, "but I wanted to deliver Camilla to you safe and . . . sound."

"Very kind of you, I'm sure," Mrs. Van Allen said. "But then, you always were." There was the ghost of an English accent in her voice. "Come into the drawing room for a moment. It is so gloomy out here, and I see so dimly now."

She turned around and expected us to follow. Heather hung back, but we did. Mrs. Van Allen needed her cane, but her back was straight. In the dimness her hair glowed white. It was smooth against her old head with a knot behind.

Her drawing room was vast and full of interesting stuff, like the Museum of the City of New York. Marble busts, high-backed furniture, old-time lamps glowing, pictures all over the walls.

She was looking away from us and aiming her cane at the picture of a man over the big stone fireplace. "That is Camilla's late grandfather," she said, "my husband, Gilburtus Van Allen, the handsomest man you ever set eyes on. We defied the world to marry."

She pivoted slowly on her cane. I was standing there. She leaned nearer and examined me. "I married the boy next door," she explained, "and we lived happily ever after."

She looked past me at Mom and Heather. "I won't keep you. But I get so little company these days. Of course, I treasure my privacy. And memories are the best companions. But you must come again soon. To tea. Cucumber sandwiches, I should think, and hot buttered scones with strawberry jam."

They didn't know her. How could they? Her face was all webbed with wrinkles, and her glasses hid her eyes. But I knew who she was. I couldn't believe it. But I knew. She was Phoebe.

20

Parents' Night

It was really late when we got home. Mom was worn out. Heather was still sulking. I was stunned speechless. We all went straight to bed. So it wasn't till the next morning we realized Phoebe was gone.

When I woke up, no cup of tea was steaming on my bedside table. Instead there was a note. I'd never seen Phoebe's handwriting. She'd had very good penmanship and a steady hand when she was young.

> *Dear Josh,*
> *I have written to your mother to say good-bye.*
> *I am sure she will understand that I am a girl*
> *in love. He is far above my station in life, and*
> *so I thought it hopeless. Perhaps that is how*
> *Aaron was able to bring me to your time. I*
> *had often thought of running away.*

*Please thank him for offering to send me
back with his time machine. But I do believe
my time is drawing to an end anyway, and I
may find my own way back. My brief absence
may just make my beloved's heart grow fonder.
I know now that nothing can keep us apart.*

She didn't sign her name. She might have left before she had the . . . time.

The rest of the weekend was all downhill from there. Heather told me she was never speaking to me again because I'd ratted on her. In fact, she kept on telling me. Mom told Heather that her party dress was going back to Bloomingdale's, but she wasn't going anywhere. She was grounded until she was thirty. Heather told Mom it didn't matter because she was shamed for life. It was as simple as that. Camilla Van Allen would drop her like a hot potato. And we were all lost without Phoebe.

Then on Sunday night, Dad didn't call from Chicago. You wait and wait for weekends, but they're not always that great.

Aaron wasn't on the bus Monday morning, but I found him in the Black Hole before homeroom. I showed him Phoebe's note. After all, it was really for him too. I told him all about Phoebe, then and . . . now.

He was interested, but not that much. He was already word-processing something on one of the computers, and his mind was basically on that. He's always up to something.

"Josh, are you losing total track of time?" he said.

"Tomorrow's Parents' Night. We've got to get our act together about the history of Huckley School. Mr. Thaw will be all over us. He told us our entire grades were riding on this."

"They took Mr. Thaw off to Lenox Hill Hospital," I said. "Remember?"

"But he's back," Aaron said, not looking up from the screen. "He was the first teacher in school this morning. He probably thinks Cuthbert in the classroom was a figment of his imagination or whatever. He probably thinks he was some kid wandering in from public school to clean Buster's clock. Anyway, he's back."

"Is Buster back?"

"I don't know about Buster. He'll probably take the week off. After all, he got punched out with witnesses. What's that going to do for his self-esteem? If he's here, he'll be down with a counselor. Forget that. Concentrate on our report."

His screen was filling up with a report. But he hadn't printed out anything yet.

"So what have we got here?" he said. "Once upon a time there was a row of townhouses just off Central Park, with four families living in them."

"The Havemeyers, the Huckleys, the Van Allens, and the Vanderwhitneys," I said. "We don't know squat about the Havemeyers and the Huckleys."

"We'll get Mrs. Newbery on that," Aaron said. "What are media specialists for anyway? And in 1929 these four townhouses were recycled as Huckley School, right?"

"Works for me," I said.

The bell for homeroom rang. "I hate being inter-rupted by school," Aaron muttered. But then he came out of his chair. "Yessssss!" he said, doing his war dance.

"No, Aaron," I said. "Forget about it. We're not do-ing a demonstration of your cellular-reorganization formula for our history report. We're not doing our vanishing act with witnesses. And what if we got Cuth-bert again?"

"You kidding?" he said. "That's top secret. That's not information you put into the hands of parents and teachers. But we already have somebody from the past—a living legend."

"Not Phoebe," I said. "Not Mrs. Van Allen. She's real old, and she treasures her privacy. It wouldn't be fair."

"Not Phoebe," Aaron said. "Mr. L. T. Thaw. He'll be at the meeting anyway, won't he? Parents' Night isn't required for parents, but it's required for teachers. Am I right? We'll just call on him."

"You call on him," I said. "I'm not calling on him."

"Boys," Mrs. Newbery said from the door, "it's time you cut along for Mr. Headbloom's homeroom. Why do I have to remind you of this every morning of my entire existence?"

Parents' Night was in the auditorium of Huckley House, and there was a good turnout. Aaron's parents were there somewhere in the throng. Mom and Heather came. Heather had plea-bargained to be let out of the apartment for school-related events. By the weekend she'd probably be a free woman. She'd already been on the phone with Camilla. I knew because it was my phone.

Aaron and I had to sit in the front row with the rest of the people taking bows, doing acts, and making reports. Mr. Thaw had made sure we were on the program, and in it:

> Josh Lewis and Aaron Zimmer will present
> a brief report on the colorful and aristocratic
> origins of Huckley School, founded 1929.

The president of the parents' organization and the headmaster sat right behind us. Aaron and I were in freshly pressed dress code. We weren't the first item on the program. There were introductions and rounds of applause while the upper-school squash team, lacrosse team, and hockey team held up their trophies. An all-school string trio sawed out a couple of selections from *Beauty and the Beast*. A chorus of lower-school first graders in ball caps and long shirts did an original rap:

> Huckley be the best
> forget about the rest

The whole lower school seems to be turning into rappers.

"Kids," Aaron said.

We finally got around to middle-school reports. But then Aaron and I still had to sit through a long science-class demonstration with pig embryos. Fishface Pierre-pont gave his lecture on

> Collecting classic comic books for
> fun and your investment portfolio

Then it was time for Aaron and me. It was getting late, and the audience was restless. We speeded up our presentation and charged through it.

"Picture it," Aaron began, looking around the too-tall podium at the audience. "Four high-profile New York families whose fortunes were amassed before confiscatory income tax. Picture them in the 1920's in four hard-to-heat white-elephant houses and about to make the move into the modern, climate-controlled grandeur of new Park Avenue buildings even then rising along their eastern flank."

"The Havemeyers," I said, taking over. Then I gave a rundown on this family from sources Mrs. Newbery looked up for us.

"The Huckleys," I said, "who gave their name and a bunch of money to our school." Then I went over them and moved on to the Van Allens. When we came to the Vanderwhitneys, I let Aaron take over.

"No name rings louder in the annals of American wealth and privilege," Aaron said in a ringing voice, "than the Vanderwhitneys."

He summed up a century or so of their family tree, working up to Mr. and Mrs. Osgood Vanderwhitney.

"Mrs. Vanderwhitney's second husband," Aaron explained, "was the once well-known man about town,

Mr. Thaw. We are honored to have on Huckley School's faculty a man who was born a Vanderwhitney and is the adopted son of Mrs. Vanderwhitney's second husband."

The audience of parents was getting a little confused by this, though there are plenty of second marriages among them too. And in the Zimmers' case, third.

"And so Josh and I introduce to you the last living link between Huckley School and the families who founded it, Mr. Lysander Theodore Thaw, our old— our history teacher. Step up and say a few words, Mr. Thaw." Aaron blinked out into the auditorium. Then he and I filed off the stage and went back to our seats.

From the back of the room came the sound of creaking joints. Then Mr. L. T. Thaw began to stalk down the aisle to a growing wave of polite applause. He limped to the podium.

From behind us, the president of the parents said to the headmaster, "The poor old duffer. We really must find a way to retire him."

Mr. Thaw frowned over the audience like they were history class. But this was his moment, maybe his last. Pulling on his beard, he launched into his boyhood in Vanderwhitney House. He dealt briefly with his mother running off with Mr. Thaw. He left out how his father had taken a dive onto Wall Street. But the more he talked, the more he remembered. He even recalled a pretty nursery maid from England who married the Van Allen boy from next door.

His old hands gripped the podium, and now he had

the audience listening and interested. After all, he's a living legend. Then he was winding down.

"And last but not least," he said, "I remember my dear brother Cuthbert, gone to his reward these many years, but as clear in my mind as if I'd seen him last week. Cuthbert is gone but not forgotten as the fire commissioner of the City of New York."

Mr. Thaw even took a bow. Then he tottered off the stage to more applause.

So that was Parents' Night. Our entire grade in History depended on it. But Aaron and I weren't worried.

"Now I can get back to my formula," he said on our way up the aisle. "We're talking new windows of opportun—" But then his voice broke. He went from high alto to baritone and back again. It was like cracking the sound barrier.

"Yikes," he said. "My voice is beginning to change. What's puberty going to do to my Emotional Component?"

A lot of the dads in the audience had gone to Huckley School. They made a ring around old Mr. Thaw because he'd been their teacher too. They must have forgotten how crusty he is because they were shaking his hand. They seemed to be thanking him. His old pink eyes were moist.

The crowd parted, and I was looking for Mom and Heather. But then I saw Dad. My dad.

He was there beside Mom, and they were kind of looking at each other. Heather was beside them. In fact, she was beside herself. "This is just like *Oprah*," she breathed, practically jumping up and down.

Dad spotted me. I wasn't sure what to do. I thought maybe we should shake hands. But he put out his arms and gave me a big hug. We gave each other a big hug.

"Have you grown?" He looked me over.

"Not an inch," I said.

"Plenty of time," Dad said.

"But how did you even know about Parents' Night?" I asked him. I hadn't told him about it. I didn't think he'd fly in from Chicago.

"I got a phone call late last Friday night. Must have been midnight your time. A young lady called me. She told me you had a report to give for Parents' Night. She told me it was my responsibility to be here. She was pretty definite about it. English too, I think."

Phoebe. I could picture her looking up Dad's number in Mom's address book. I could picture her young finger punching up Dad's area code.

Phoebe, one last time.

The four of us went home together. Mom and Dad, Heather and me. I don't know if Dad's home for good. We'll see. Plenty of time.

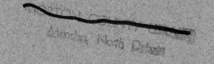

THE
CREATIVE
EXECUTIVE

THE
CREATIVE
EXECUTIVE

How business leaders innovate by stimulating passion, intuition, and creativity.

Granville N. Toogood

Adams Media Corporation
Holbrook, Massachusetts

Published by Adams Media Corporation
260 Center Street, Holbrook, MA 02343

ISBN: 1-58062-199-6

Printed in the United States of America.

J I H G F E D C B

Library of Congress Cataloging-in-Publication Data

Toogood, Granville N.
The creative executive: how business leaders innovate by simulating passion,
intuition, and creativity. / Granville N. Toogood.
p.   cm.
Includes index.
ISBN 1-58062-199-6
1. Executive ability. 2. Executive—Training of. I. Title.
HD38.2 .T63 2000
658.4'092—dc21
99-046805

The interview "The Three Faces of Steve," ©1998 Time Inc. is reprinted by permission.

This book is available at quantity discounts for bulk purchases.
For information, call 1-800-872-5627.

Visit our exciting website at http://www.businesstown.com

"The Creative Executive makes it clear how to think about getting the most out of yourself and others. It's an eye-opening book from a superb executive coach."

"The master coach has done it again. In the tradition of *The Articulate Executive* and *The Inspired Executive*, *The Creative Executive* is the kind of book that can change your life."

"Granville Toogood is not only the best executive coach I know, but *The Creative Executive* is an absolute must for business leaders who want to know how to get the most out of themselves and their people."

"The Creative Executive is the best book of its kind I have ever read—inspiring, motivational and above all enormously useful."

—STUART JANNEY
CHAIRMAN
BESSEMER TRUST CORPORATION

"The Creative Executive is one of the most inspiring business books ever. It should be required reading for every manager."

—BOB SIMMS
CHAIRMAN
SIMMS CAPITAL MANAGEMENT

"Read this book and understand, maybe for the first time, what should be fun and rewarding in your career and life."

—RICHARD L. BALLANTYNE
V.P., GENERAL COUNSEL AND SECRETARY
HARRIS CORPORATION

"Granny Toogood's teaching, coaching and mentoring have taken me to a whole new level of personal and professional vision and achievement."

—Ed Allen
Rear Admiral USN (retired)

"The Creative Executive is a *must* for business leaders who want to better understand and unleash the power of creativity. It is an inspiring book for executives who want to get the most out of themselves and their employees."

—Elizabeth A. Baltz
Senior Vice President
MasterCard International

"Granville Toogood has assembled a treasure trove of examples of creativity that any executive at any level can be guided and inspired by."

—Harvey W. Greisman
VP–Communications
IBM Global Services

Contents

ix

Part two
The Players: How the Game Is Won

Part three
The Rewards: Reaping the Harvest

Dedication

Yet again …

For Pat, Heather and Chase

Has Your Clock Stopped?

Why It's Time to Wind Yourself Back Up

Has your clock stopped?

That's a question we all ought to be asking ourselves—because sometimes the clock is stopped and we don't know it.

For example, have you ever met someone who for all intents and purposes has "died"—but just hasn't been buried yet? Do you know people who have had the light go out of their eyes, who just seem to be going through the motions?

Have we not all at one time or another, if only for an awful sinking moment, been that very person ourselves?

Most of us cannot remember the original discovery of passion. Unadulterated, raw, delirious passion happened way back even before the first toy with wheels or the first Barbie doll. Real passion was like an explosion of the sun or a sudden symphony of color, a rare moment of truth so cataclysmically exquisite that it has naturally been left almost entirely to infants, poets and other innocents. A comparable burst of ecstasy might well give your average grownup a case of serious disorientation.

> Sometimes the clock is stopped and we don't know it.

This passion I'm talking about is a function of discovery. And discovery—with all its stabbing freshness and excitement—is the tap root of creativity. Sometimes discovery is the only thing that can inspire us to greatness. Those lucky enough to be blessed with an entire lifetime of discovery experience one magic moment after another in a daisy chain of personal fulfillment that stretches from cradle to grave.

Every one of us is by nature creative. We're all artists of one kind or another. We all want to make, shape, engineer, design, build, alter, improve, or change things. It's only natural. The business person structuring a deal in Thailand and the sculptor creating sensuous art in Santa Fe are both drinking from the same well. The craftsman who whimsically etches his initials in an engine block at a Ford plant in Dearborn and the neon sculptor in Soho who signs his name in twisted tubes of gas are both singing the same song. The twenty-something trader on Wall Street who fires a funny joke into cyberspace on his workstation is talking the same talk as the fledgling standup comedian who's knocking them dead at an uptown laugh house.

> Every one of us is by nature creative. We're all artists of one kind or another. We all want to make, shape, engineer, design, build, alter, improve, or change things. It's only natural.

Yet most of us fail to recognize our creative potential. If you need proof, you need look no farther than Las Vegas. Las Vegas was created especially to take advantage of our phenomenal capacity for boredom and an almost pathological inability to amuse ourselves. We travel to this great glittering Mecca by the millions, sheepishly foregoing a birthright that could help make us whole.

While Las Vegas has its authentic attractions—sunshine, desert air, and nice scenery to name a few—the gambling casinos of Las

Vegas are a neon testament to the fact that millions of us have (a) come to rely too heavily on outside amusements to substitute for our own lapsed creativity; and (b) our willingness to be distracted by inane pursuits that gobble up precious time better spent finding ways to be creatively useful.

We race through our careers often never recognizing that creativity is as important to business as DNA is to evolution. If we didn't create, nothing would ever get better. If we didn't create, our jobs would stop being fun. If we didn't create, we would never have anything new. Tell a whole population to stop being creative, as has happened in any number of Communist states, and time stops. Visit Havana forty years after Fidel Castro took over and you would think you were still back in the 1950s. Travel to Tirana, Albania, and suddenly you're in a world that disappeared in the 1940s.

> We race through our careers often never recognizing that creativity is as important to business as DNA is to evolution.

Kill creativity in our lives or in our jobs and we might as well all be trying to play poker blindfolded.

When creativity pops up around us, we are often quick to mock it. Corporate cultures the world over talk a good creativity game. But human psychology is a powerful thing. The herd favors mediocrity. We talk up the merits of risk but put it down in real life. We sing the praises of individual effort and leadership, but in reality we embrace the committee or the team at the expense of genius. We advocate innovation but privately cherish the tried and true. We universally acknowledge the need for research and development, but when the budget crunch hits, R&D is the first to get whacked (while the CEO gets another $7.5 million bonus for the year). And when the CEO bails out three years later with his $34 million golden parachute, the first ominous rumblings of the R&D shortfall are just beginning to be felt.

The creative flower cannot flourish, may not even be allowed to bloom, if we fear failure. To understand the full impact of creativity, we've got to turn the clock back years.

> The creative flower cannot flourish, may not even be allowed to bloom, if we fear failure.

Kids can teach us something about risk and fear of failure. Kids will build nine different versions of a sand castle in one day and not stop until something in the design—the engineering or the aesthetics—tells them they finally got it right. Kids will keep improving on a tree house until the whole thing threatens to collapse under its own weight. Kids will paint the same picture of a horse a dozen times, seeking perfection.

Naiveté is a wonderful thing. When I was ten, my friends and I tried to build a car (because no one bothered to tell us we couldn't). We actually wound up making a little wooden two-seater with everything on it but an engine.

Kids I grew up with thought nothing of jumping from a barn loft into a haystack fifteen feet below—without first checking for hidden dangers like pitchforks. (Most of those kids are still alive.)

Parents shudder—remembering their own magical times of growing up with daily adventure and its attendant risks. They cringe trying to imagine (or not to imagine) what their own children are going through right now. We all quake. But if the leaders and innovators of history had all looked before they leaped, we might still be living in caves.

Throughout history, leaders have had to breach the status quo and even make new rules to forge new territory. We are all capable of new territory. But most of us are afraid to fail, so we hesitate. In the end, we don't even bother.

As Sun Microsystems chief Scott McNealy puts it, to ask permission is to invite failure. To merely seek approval is to take one's eye off the ball and miss the point entirely. Early on most of us learn that no matter how hard we try to please, some people are not going to love us—a lesson at first troubling, then actually quite relaxing. Great success breeds resentment. Consistent failure breeds contempt. Mediocrity breeds indifference. (The truth is that most people are neither for us or against us, because they are thinking about themselves.)

We all want a scoring system that tells us when we've piled up enough points to count ourselves successful. But what price success, or lack of it? Let's face it. *Everyone* blows it—once, twice, maybe many times. That's life. But how to learn or grow if we can't err? Even champions falter. As Joe Louis put it, "Everyone has to figure to get beat sometime." The question is, do we collaborate in our own defeat? When we hit a spell of trouble, and we all do, we've got to ask ourselves, what is this unpleasantness trying to teach us. The lessons are not always happy ones, but they just keep coming.

> Early on most of us learn that no matter how hard we try to please, some people are not going to love us—a lesson at first troubling, then actually quite relaxing.

At the end of it all we've got nowhere to run. Among other things, we become addicted to, and crippled by, such obvious disablers as self-pity and resentment. The point at which we become intoxicated with feeling sorry for ourselves and resenting other peoples' good fortune is the point at which we have decided we no longer really want to know ourselves, depend on ourselves, or even live with ourselves. In fact, by middle age most of us are

By middle age most of us are accomplished fugitives from ourselves.

accomplished fugitives from ourselves. Whatever professional or personal path we have chosen, that path is our adventure.

A wise person said that at the end of every road we meet ourselves. Paradoxically, the person at the end of the road should not be unlike the inquisitive, creative, innovative, daring, adventurous kid at the start of the journey. The person at the end of the road should still be jumping into haystacks.

Jump into haystacks and creativity will come to you.

Has your clock stopped?

Read on.

part one

The Wake-Up Call:

Jumping Up to the Next Level

1

Are You the Ripple or the Stone?

The Most Critical Choice
You Will Ever Make

An important first step towards unleashing our innate creativity is simply understanding the difference between action and inaction.

What child has not wondered at the curiously mellifluous effect of a pebble arching through the air then falling with a delicious "plunk" into the molten surface of a still pond? When stone meets water, the stone wins. Water yields, generating concentric circles to mark the exact point of impact.

It is not long before the child observes that even the smallest pebble can send gentle shock waves to the farthest edge of the pond. And perhaps this boy or girl cannot help but wonder where those ripples might end if there were no limits to the pond.

Can a single pebble affect an entire pond? Can a single pebble make itself known even far away?

> An important first step towards unleashing our innate creativity is simply understanding the difference between action and inaction.

3

Watching and pondering these mysteries, some children will begin to focus on the ripples, while others will be drawn to the pebble. One child will watch the ripples spread. Another will delight in the path of the pebble and its splash.

At some point during this private moment of discovery, one child will experience an epiphany. This child will ask himself, is it better to be a ripple or be a stone? And for this child the answer will resonate like a loud bell ringing. The answer for this child is as clear as sunlight filling a room: It is better to be a stone.

Create something—anything—and you become a stone. Any willful act of creation—a plan, a letter, a sketch, a recipe, even a new hairstyle—creates waves, no matter how sublime. By contrast, if you choose to remain fallow and wait for something to happen, you will always be a ripple.

> Any willful act of creation—a plan, a letter, a sketch, a recipe, even a new hairstyle—creates waves, no matter how sublime.

t w o

Turning on the Creative Lights:

How to Hit the "On" Switch That
Can Change Your Life

Winston Churchill liked to paint when he wasn't saving the world from Fascism. I remember reading that a famous CEO liked to raise orchids in his spare time. A Japanese industry giant tends his rock garden. A retired United States General loves origami, the Japanese art of folding paper figures.

The owner of a hugely successful tabloid newspaper was also a train nut who designed and installed one of the world's largest and most spectacular narrow-gauge model railroads in his ample basement where he used to put on a trainman's hat and spend hours playing engineer and conductor.

The head of a large American reinsurance company spends every free

> The owner of a hugely successful tabloid newspaper was also a train nut who designed and installed one of the world's largest and most spectacular narrow-gauge model railroads in his ample basement where he used to put on a trainman's hat and spend hours playing engineer and conductor.

5

minute designing, building, and remodeling houses. (He secretly admits to having missed his true calling as an architect.) A top Wall Street analyst shuns the golf course on weekends in favor of pursuing his greatest passion: photography.

And a senior vice president of a big consumer products company moved to Italy after retirement to pursue the ancient art of glassblowing.

In each of these individuals, creativity bubbled right up through the vocation—helping to make each one successful in his discipline—and then overflowed into avocation. Creative in work, creative in play. The same natural impulse to make something good and beautiful was as effective on the job as off.

In my own case, as a kid I used to love to draw pictures. Later, I turned to writing for a living, then finally wound up running a business. The only business school I ever knew was a naive passion to make something out of nothing. I allowed my instincts to help fashion a little business the same way I might fashion a picture or a story:

1. Start with an idea
2. Figure out the big picture
3. Make a plan
4. Add background and details
5. Work at it until you know you've got it right (this part can take years).

> Millions of people walk through their lives never knowing they are carrying a magic box just waiting to be opened.

I was inexperienced and dumb enough to believe my approach would actually work, and incredibly it did.

But millions of people walk through their lives never knowing they are carrying a magic box just waiting to be opened. Witness the Bird Man of Alcatraz, who had to end up in the slammer before his true calling—a near-mystic affinity with avians—was finally given the opportunity to blossom. Witness the world's acknowledged top genius, British physicist Stephen Hawking, who wrote his bestseller, *A Brief History of Time,* only after a crippling disease confined him to a wheelchair. Witness Grandma Moses, who didn't stumble onto her true talent of primitive landscape painting until she was already well into her seventies.

Millions of other people understand they may have something special to offer but for a lot of different reasons leave their creativity at home when they go to work. Still others recognize their creative gifts but don't know how to apply those gifts to their business.

> Millions of people leave their creativity at home when they go to work.

In his book, *The 9 1/2% Solution,* idea meister, author, and lecturer Bryan Mattimore talks about how geniuses discover their creative source.

When he was just six years old, Albert Einstein pondered the laws of nature governing a simple compass. He was so inspired, he spent the rest of his life trying to figure out the mysteries of the universe.

A light went off in Thomas Edison's head when as a boy he realized he was equal in weight to two bags of grain. From then on, he worked to make one thing equal another: electricity equal to light, electricity equal to sound, and photographs equal to motion (light bulb, phonograph, motion pictures).

Buckminster Fuller never got over the excitement he experienced playing with blocks and geometric shapes as a child, then devoted his entire life to creating geometric spaces for people to live in.

Samuel Colt got such a bang out of explosives as a youngster that he went on to create the world's most famous pistol.

Edgar Bergen, the famous ventriloquist, learned from a dummy named Charlie McCarthy. One day a visitor went to Bergen's backstage dressing room only to find the door open and Bergen and his dummy, with their backs to the door, actually having a private conversation. Incredibly, Bergen was asking Charlie everything from the meaning of life to the structure of the universe. Uncomfortable eavesdropping, the visitor coughed discreetly. Embarrassed, Bergen sheepishly said, "You caught me." He explained to the startled visitor that when he asked Charlie questions, he always got answers—answers that were always unexpected and sometimes profound.

Some people draw inspiration from dreams. The idea for Dr. Jekyll and Mr. Hyde came to Robert Louis Stevenson in a dream. The Russian chemist Mendeleyev "saw" the periodic table of elements in a dream. James Watt got the idea for manufacturing shotgun pellets when he saw them falling like rain in a dream.

To find out which of his clothes absorbed or reflected heat the best, Ben Franklin took swatches of fabric, ranging from white to black and various colors in between, and laid them on the snow on a sunny day. The black fabric, absorbing the most heat, sank the farthest, while the white made hardly a dent. Franklin's conclusions:

wear black in winter, white in summer. Summer hats should be white, and "garden walls intended for fruit should be black."

Opportunity is all around us. One day inventor Stan Mason realized that because more women were working, people were turning to microwave ovens to save time preparing meals. Mason saw that what was needed were special cooking containers to make the job easier and get it done faster. To meet that need he came up with Masonware, which worked a lot better than conventional dishes and bowls.

Walt Disney was one of America's greatest creative minds, a master of illusion who had an uncanny sense of magical detail. For example, when he was touring the Disneyland Pirates of the Caribbean attraction shortly before it opened, he felt strangely dissatisfied. Everything looked great. The boats looked great. The pirates looked great. The effects were great. But something was missing. Disney just couldn't put his finger on it. So he started asking his people what they thought. Everybody said they loved the attraction. But finally one carpenter mentioned that he'd grown up in the south and what Pirates seemed to be missing was lightning bugs. "Yes!" Disney shouted. "That's it!" He then had real lightning bugs brought in until his imagineers could figure out a way to duplicate them mechanically.

Cybercash chairman Dan Lynch, a playful intellect who helped build the Internet and a research pioneer in the computer industry for thirty years, has had fun doing just about everything—and it shows.

Majoring in math was fun.

Designing robots was fun.

Debugging TCP/IP (Transmission Control Protocol/Internet Protocol) was fun.

Helping turn the old Arpanet into the Internet was fun.

Running Cybercash is fun.

As long as he's creative, he's having fun—and he's not having fun unless he's creative.

True creativity needs no justification. But sometimes a bad idea can masquerade as a creative one. And very successfully. Take the curious case of shareholder value.

For a time, prevailing wisdom held that the most enterprising and useful way a CEO could serve his company is by appealing to the investment demands of shareholders. But this approach—once regarded as innovative and far-thinking on the argument that what's good for the shareholders must also be good for the company—has begun to lose appeal. Meeting financial targets and racking up performance points at the expense of research and development and long-term planning is a formula for long-term trouble.

"Managers of U.S. companies should understand two points," says John Kay, director of Oxford University's School of Management Studies. "One is that focusing exclusively on increasing shareholder wealth may preclude you from doing things that would actually be in the long-term interest of the shareholders. The second is that adopting the shareholder priority rule not only may make it harder for you to maximize shareholder value in the long run but may also prevent you from running your business in ways that everyone would agree lead to better results."

This is creative—and contrarian—thinking in our time.

Mayree Clark, head of Global Equity Research at Morgan Stanley Dean Witter, takes a unique approach she calls "The Competitive Edge," which identifies great picks hiding in a sea of stocks.

Restless, energetic, curious, not content with the status quo, Mayree Clark is a good example of the creative mind at work.

The minute she took the job she knew she wanted to try some-thing new. So she and her people set out to comb the world looking for companies big or small, long established or relatively new, which shared a single common characteristic: they had to have a defining competitive edge that put them out in front of their competitors.

A good stock, she says, has got to have something special going for it. That something might be strong management, or the fact that the company is a low cost producer, or has a great brand name, or ter-rific research and development, or a strong balance sheet, or is an undervalued long-term investment, or any combination of the above.

Mayree's team started with 2,000 stocks worldwide. They culled that number down to 250 stocks that definitely had a competitive edge and eventually wound up with 40 favorites.

On that list are a few surprises such as Coca-Cola, an old standby that Mayree says has two competitive edges: a great brand name with two and one-half times the market share of its nearest competitor, and a secret weapon in the form of distribution. And dis-tribution, after all, is the name of the game in beverage marketing. Coca-Cola's bottlers, she says, can put Coke in all sorts of markets all over the world where, for different reasons, competitors like Pepsi can't penetrate. Because of its outstanding distribution, Coke will have the edge for years to come. That's why she finds the stock still a good buy.

Mayree also likes Asia Pulp and Paper, a little-known company in Indonesia, because Asia Pulp and Paper is the lowest-cost pulp producer in the world.

Another top forty selection is Tokyo Electron, a Japanese semi-conductor equipment maker which enjoys outstanding business relationships with Japanese manufacturers, excellent technology, and a huge market share. The stock, Mayree says, is cheap because the Japanese fail to recognize the underlying strengths of this very competitive company in their own back yard.

Mayree must be doing something right because her picks consistently beat the market.

Across town at Credit Suisse First Boston, Mayree's counterpart, Al Jackson, head of research, found yet another way to determine the true value of companies. He tried applying a calculation process called economic value added (EVA) to evaluate corporations and was amazed at what he found.

"We discovered that the old method of using return on investment (ROI) and earnings per share (EPS) did not always tell us the true story," he said. "We found the only way to accurately determine what a company is really worth today and what it will be worth tomorrow is to subject that company to an EVA analysis."

For example, in 1994, Jackson saw that Wal-Mart was headed for trouble—at a time when ROI and EPS were indicating everything looked great. EVA revealed that Wal-Mart had hidden supply and distribution problems that did not turn up in conventional analysis.

EVA also revealed that the Compaq Computer company was really more of a server company than a personal computer maker. Credit Suisse First Boston adjusted its ratings of Compaq accordingly.

For years, the giant food company CPC regarded its European operations—Knorr soups and Hellman's mayonnaise—as its crown jewel. But EVA told a different story. It turned out that Knorr and Hellman's were actually a drag on earnings with hidden problems that would take a lot of fixing.

A quick look at General Mills using conventional analysis would have told you that General Mills was in good shape. But EVA revealed that an underperforming restaurant division was a deadweight on the entire firm. It turned out that several General Mills food divisions had been subsidizing the lackluster restaurant division. From 1989 to 1994, restaurants represented only a quarter of General Mills' profits. But the company was spending almost half of its capital expenditures on restaurants. EVA caught the flaw, and Credit Suisse First Boston alerted its clients. Thanks to Al Jackson, a creative approach is also a profitable approach.

Few people in business appreciate the value of creativity at work as much as Steven Spielberg, Oscar award-winning producer and cofounder of DreamWorks SKG. Spielberg has arcade games all around his office, as well as his home. But not content with things as they are, Spielberg set out to create the ultimate game. He's dreamed up a super arcade extravaganza called "Vertical Reality," in which players are strapped into moving seats as they advance up a giant screen doing battle with evil Cyborgs. The winner gets to free fall twenty-four feet back down to the bottom. Spielberg believes the future of entertainment is interactive, and he's betting a bundle on this and other wowzer ventures.

Talk about ventures, it took just ten years for then Travelers chairman Sandy Weill to transform a handful of lackluster performers into a financial services powerhouse. His creative secret, according to one Travelers director, is that, "he's a genius at running crappy businesses." Or as GE chairman Jack Welch put it: "Sandy's been fantastic. He took air and turned it into this big, successful thing." Weill's strategy is to cut costs to the bone, grow through acquisition, hire top talent, think like an owner, and target one goal: improving shareholder value.

Not everybody can run a company or make millions or be called a genius. But each of us has something special and unique that can change lives for the better.

If Traveler's were an orchestra, Weill would be conducting a symphony that is music to the ears of every Traveler's investor. (Weill went on to co-chair Citigroup, the financial services mega merger of Traveler's and Citicorp.)

Not everybody can run a company or make millions or be called a genius. But each of us has something special and unique that can change lives for the better.

My point is that the creative spark, like the heart, resides naturally within. If our heart stops, life stops. But if we fail to hit the creative "on" switch, we simply live incompletely—without joy, without passion, sometimes even without love. The conscious ignition of the creative light is like answered prayer. We rise up out of the humdrum shadows of daily life into the warmth of the sun. It is in the sun that we meet our potential with other like-minded creative people who have willed themselves to be turned on and lifted up. Things happen here that don't happen back in the shadows.

Given a choice, you don't want to be anywhere else.

> The creative spark, like the heart, resides naturally within. If we fail to hit the creative "on" switch, we simply live incompletely—without joy, without passion, sometimes even without love. The conscious ignition of the creative light is like answered prayer. We rise up out of the humdrum shadows of daily life into the warmth of the sun.

three

The Fifteen Keys to Creativity:

Practical Tips to Generate New Ideas

When fifteen different companies are making the same product you are making (think of computer electronics), and when what you make becomes obsolete in six months rather than six years, you've got to start doing things differently. In other words, you've got to be creative.

If that sounds daunting, or if you feel you are not by nature creative, relax. The fact is that life itself is a constant creative experience. We come into the world vulnerable and defenseless. Compared to other large animals we are weak and clumsy. As a species we could not have come as far as we have without a God-given talent for invention and adaptability.

Every day we solve a thousand little problems at work and at home: how to make changes the boss demanded in the presentation and still be ready on time; how to fix the broken garden hose; how to design the bunk beds in the loft for the

> If you feel you are not by nature creative, relax. The fact is that life itself is a constant creative experience.

kids; how to dress up the dog for the Halloween party; how to, in other words, get through every day and still have a good time.

Even the smallest challenge is an invitation to be creative. When you've got to get to the airport to catch a plane but an accident blocks the road ahead, you try to find an end-run route around the obstacle. When shareholders complain the annual report is too boring, you try to give the same information in more interesting and memorable ways. When you're about to introduce a new gizmo and just a month before launch you hear the competition has come up with a similar and cheaper way to make an even better gizmo, you get all your best people together, put them in a big room, and don't let them out until they come up with a solid market leader.

Perhaps the greatest creative challenge of modern times came with the nearly disastrous moon mission of Apollo 13 in 1970. When an explosion blew a panel off the side of the ship, with power system and life support failing, and emergency backup energy kicking in, the three astronauts on the tiny spacecraft suddenly found themselves facing a life-or-death situation of unusually dramatic proportions.

Within seconds after the initial blast, a host of urgent problems avalanched on the crewmen in the capsule and Mission Control in Houston. The first problem was simply to stay alive. The second problem, with onboard computers down, was to somehow manually guide the ship on a razor-thin trajectory to safe earth orbit. One degree of error too high would send them skipping back into space and on into the black depths of the universe for eternity. One degree too low, and they would plunge into an inferno and burn up. With one crewman sick with possible pneumonia and temperatures sinking towards the freezing mark in the cramped cabin, the astronauts faced bleak odds. While their families began an anguished waiting game and the world held its breath, the hour-by-hour drama unfolded.

First, Mission Control threw their best engineers all together in a room with replicas of every last piece of material the astronauts said they could find on their stricken ship: hoses, metal containers, fillers, duct tape, wires, rubber bands, sheet metal, cellophane, toilet paper, and other odds and ends. The assignment: come up with a workable makeshift scrubber to do temporary duty for the failed carbon dioxide scrubber. A buildup of carbon dioxide was slowly asphyxiating the astronauts and the engineering cowboys on the ground had to work fast. Each engineer had an invisible gun up his nose to not only get it right, but get it right the first time.

We all know the results. Within hours, the crack team of engineers did, in fact, come up with a clumsy but working device that helped save the astronauts' lives.

Once the air on board the ship was stabilized, the astronauts were free to focus their full attention on getting Apollo 13 safely back into earth's atmosphere. With the onboard computers either out or malfunctioning, they had to work as a team—even if one of them was sick—to manually handle the intricate thruster adjustments and calibrations needed to pilot the ship home. Using simple cockpit math and coaching from Mission Control, they defied all the odds and managed to save their lives and the mission and bring Apollo 13 all the way down to a perfect landing. Later, they would look back and marvel at their performance.

Every business has hidden reserves of talent that typically go untapped.

As in NASA, every business has hidden reserves of talent that typically go untapped. The talent I'm talking about is locked up in every person who draws a paycheck. It's talent that can emerge only if allowed to emerge, an unmined treasure of intellectual property that can change poor performance into peak performance.

Challenged, everyone can be creative in countless ways. But people with a special affinity for creativity share certain characteristics: sharp powers of observation, a restless curiosity, relentless questioning of the norm, a penchant for ideas, and a knack for seeing things in new ways.

If you want to prime your creative pump, here's a roundup of advice from a number of experts:

1. *Don't sweat the rejections.* If you're a creative person, or seek to siphon off some of your latent creative energy, you can expect to fail a lot before you succeed. You can also expect people to say no more than yes. Thomas Edison failed more than 1,000 times before he finally figured out how to make the first electric light. Margaret Mitchell had to swallow almost forty rejections before she finally found a publisher smart enough to recognize that *Gone With the Wind* could be a winner. (Outside of the Bible, *Gone With the Wind* is said to be the bestselling book of all time.)

> If you're a creative person, you can expect to fail a lot before you succeed. You can also expect people to say no more than yes.

2. *Be a full-time, not part-time, creative person.* Experts seem to agree that you can't turn the creative process on and off. So as you start to encourage yourself to seek new solutions, or re-engineer processes, or upgrade the design of new products, or reformulate ingredients, also keep that creative third eye wide

open at home when you want to redesign the den or remodel the whole house, put a garden in out back, or when you sign up for that clay or painting or photography class you've always wanted to take.

3. *If you're a boss, tolerate bad ideas.* Bad ideas are often the basis for good ideas. Take a bad idea, talk it over, look at it from different angles, roll it around a while—and maybe you can borrow a part of a bad idea to start assembling a good idea. If you come up completely empty-handed, at least try to have a good laugh. When you've put the bad ideas behind, then you can begin to identify and build on the good ideas.

4. *Look beyond the ordinary.* Creative people see things differently. A glass bead is just a glass bead. But put glass beads in highway markers and you can steer people clear of drifting into oncoming traffic or driving off a cliff at night. A ceramic tile is just a ceramic tile. But put enough of them on the heat shield of a space probe or re-entry vehicle and you've got a firewall that can easily withstand temperatures over 3,000° Fahrenheit. Millennia ago an enterprising person in China contemplated the amazing natural tensile strength of the fiber from a worm's cocoon. The silk industry was born. Today, silk is still a sizable piece of China's export trade.

5. *Hang out with people not like yourself.* Nothing seems to feed the creative mind more than cross-fertilization. People we call "interesting" are interesting in part because they probably exhibit creative thinking. Creative thinking, in turn, is often the product of wide experience, exposure, and education, all of which are available free of charge from people who are not like us. Some of the most interesting people I know happen to be among the most creative. The physicist,

for example, who is also an authority on the ancient Basque game of jai alai; he once dated a Basque model in New York. Or the Special Forces Army Colonel, retired, who practices meditation at home and writes Japanese haiku poetry for recreation (very good, too, I might add); he became an admirer of Japanese culture when stationed in the Orient. Or the dentist who is also an accomplished sculptor; he went to art school after developing an interest in wax modeling in dental school and is today married to a painter. Or the investment banker who is also a world-class collector of pre-Incan art; he once served in the Peace Corps in South America. Result: Deeper well to draw on.

6. *Aim your creative talents at real targets.* Silly or frivolous creativity can be fun for its own sake (like putting a pink urinal on a black wall or leaning a blue light bulb against a brick and calling it art), but creativity can also be useful. Designing a better urinal, for example, can be useful. Or creating a poem for a friend's twentieth wedding anniversary that inspires both tears and laughter can be more useful, say, than poetry of the absurd, which is fun to listen to, and even on occasion intellectually interesting, but in the end leaves us feeling empty (which is also a function of some art, but that's another issue).

7. *Pay attention to small ideas.* That's where lots of big ideas begin. Global satellite communications is arguably descended from two kids, two cans, and a piece of string leading from one room to another.

8. *Daydream.* Allowing your mind to wander when it wants to is as natural as breathing, never a waste of time, and the only time you may ever have in a busy day to let your brain relax

enough so that your subconscious can help you find creative solutions to problems you didn't even know you had.

9. *Play strategy games such as chess, backgammon, checkers, or bridge.* Strategy games keep the mind active, sharp, and— like your car's battery that needs to be used frequently— ready to meet everyday problems in a creative way.

10. *Learn a foreign language.* Taking up French, Russian, or Japanese, say, torques the mind just enough so that you begin thinking in new patterns. Never mind that a second or third language is a handy tool that can open business and social doors, speaking in someone else's tongue often puts an entirely different slant on an issue you only think you understood.

11. *If you're right-handed, try using your left hand to do things, and vice versa.* No great life changes will likely come from this little exercise, but you may be surprised to discover how just approaching a problem from a reverse perspective can help you think creatively.

12. *Balance your checkbook without using a calculator.* It's amazing how this small task alone can reveal how much of our brainpower we've given over to machines. Besides keeping our minds active, this exercise typically forces us to pay closer attention to where the money is going.

13. *Read 3/4 of a novel, stop, and write your own ending.* You may not actually have time to write it out, but just thinking like a novelist—mentally playing with elements of plot, subplot, character, and description against the fabric of a real novel— can't help but sharpen your latent creative skills.

14. *Stand on your head—literally—and get the blood flowing to your brain.* This is an ancient exercise intended to improve

mental function, and it works. The brain loves blood and oxygen. Yoga practitioners believe regular gravity reversal is good for body, mind, spirit, and soul.

15. *Do jigsaw and crossword puzzles*. Both exercises are stimulating yet relaxing. Crossword puzzle devotees say crosswords are stimulating, challenging, fun, and not only improve vocabularies but help boost brainpower.

four

How to Unleash Your Creative Powers:

The Ten Gateways to Wealth, Success, and Skyrocketing Productivity

A room full of engineers tried to come up with new ideas for home security alarm systems but got nowhere—until Bryan Mattimore led them through a "mindstorming" session. In a matter of minutes the engineers had produced not one or two, but a half dozen ideas for new devices.

When the marketing people of a food company wanted to name a new ice cream, they got their answer through "picture prompts," another Mattimore learning tool.

When the Krazy Glue people wanted to create line extensions, Mattimore had them close their eyes and take mental excursions through various departments of an imaginary department store. The result: a whole bag of new ideas. These are just three of the many ways Mattimore helps individuals to max their creative potential, and companies to sell more products and services.

Mattimore believes that we are all capable of astonishing flights of invention, ingenuity, and even occasional brilliance. All we need, he says, is a little help unlocking what only comes naturally.

"The instinct to create is very strong in each of us," he says. "The trick is to help draw it out." To draw it out, Mattimore asks people to think and see in ways that are very different from what they are used to.

For example, in the "mindstorming" session with the engineers, Mattimore asked participants to write down as many ideas as they could think of, no matter how whacky or bizarre.

"The first five or so are usually old ideas," he says. "The next five are a little more interesting, more adventurous; but the next ten after that are the really new ideas. That's the far-out territory that we like to explore.

"In the case of this group, the best idea turned out to be a combination of number 5 and number 11 from the same person."

To come up with original ice cream flavor names for an upscale market, Mattimore had a group of managers flip through a stack of magazines putting together images, words, and phrases in search of tantalizing combinations. A photograph of a symphony orchestra yielded Raspberry Rhapsody. A comic book and *Popular Mechanics* produced Cookie Dough Dynamo. Other images inspired Midnight Brownie Crunch.

The Krazy Glue "visit" to the imagined department store generated a raft of new products. Each player was assigned a particular part of the store to "tour." From the jewelry department came special Krazy Glue repair kits. Water proof Krazy Glue emerged out of the boat department. From the automotive department came heat-resistant Krazy Glue. And huge containers of Krazy Glue for construction and home repair were the result of the "visit" to the hardware department.

When Ernst & Young wanted help naming a new online consulting service they turned to Mattimore. The idea was to have customers call in with questions such as, "What's the best telephone system in Mexico?" or "What's the best accounting procedure to value a company?" Ernst & Young would provide the answer within twenty-four hours. So Mattimore imagined *himself* as the computer, getting questions, generating answers. Before long, the name "Ernie" began to percolate in his head. The more he imagined, the more he became "Ernie."

"This computer really wanted to be called Ernie," Mattimore recalled. He submitted the name, and Ernst & Young loved it.

Another client asked Mattimore for help in trying to fix chronic maintenance problems in the company's manufacturing plants. Mattimore had no idea how to fix those problems himself, but he knew where the answers were. So he suggested that management place white boards in the middle of the plants and ask the workers themselves for ideas on how to fix the problems. The white boards went out on a Thursday and by the following Monday, management had not one but two proposals, both later patented, that solved the maintenance problems once and for all.

"White boards are great for getting people to start thinking creatively," Mattimore said. "For one thing, once the white board is up people get their antennas up and the buzz starts going around. Things begin appearing on the board. People start thinking. They have continual access to the board day in and day out. They start adding their own ideas. Or maybe they'll think about

> "White boards are great for getting people to start thinking creatively. Once the white board is up people get their antennas up and the buzz starts going around. Things begin appearing on the board. People start thinking."
> —Bryan Mattimore

their uncle Jim at NASA, and give him a call, see if uncle Jim has any ideas. Over time, more and more people make a connection with the board and the idea train starts to roll."

Participating in one of Mattimore's workshops can be like lighting an afterburner in your brain. With Mattimore leading the session, you can be sure of a productive meeting. But anyone can use Mattimore's methods to make magic (the definition of magic here is great, new, creative ideas). Here are a few of the acclaimed Mattimore Methods.

Brainwriting

Participants are seated around a room with one common goal: ignite the creative spark and generate new ideas. Each participant writes down an idea he or she would like the group to consider. That piece of paper is passed to the next person, who uses the original idea to "jump up" to an enhanced version of the original, or trigger an entirely new idea. Everyone writes down their thoughts until all the sheets have been passed around and each "idea sheet" eventually winds up back in the hands of its original owner. Everyone then evaluates the now much larger idea pool. The best ideas are plucked from the pool and transferred into action.

> With everyone standing, and ideas posted around the room for everyone to see, natural group dynamics tend to kick in.

Brainwalking

In this exercise, participants stand (they don't sit) and write their ideas on flip chart paper hung on the walls. There's one sheet of paper for each player and participants move from one sheet to the next. With everyone standing, and ideas posted around the room for everyone to see, natural group dynamics tend to kick in. Energy is typically high as players interact about each other's ideas from one page to the next, then build on the posted results throughout the day.

Mattimore says brainwalking and brainwriting are "the most powerful techniques we know of for getting a lot of ideas out very quickly. Each person generates at least one—possibly several ideas—on each sheet. If you have 10 people who 'visit' a sheet 10 times in as little as 15 minutes, the group has generated more than 100 ideas."

The Worst Idea Technique

The notion here is to come up with "a really awful, occasionally disgusting, sometimes repulsive idea," according to Mattimore. "For example, think of the worst possible idea you can for soup. How about a soup with rocks in it? How about a soup that has green slime...eye of newt, or even snot in it? How about throw-up soup?"

> With brainwalking and brainwriting, 10 people can generate 100 ideas in 15 minutes.

This curious approach is handy when a group clutches and locks into what Mattimore calls "creative performance anxiety" (pushing hard for a great idea but coming up dry).

"It's impossible to fail at this technique," he explains, "because who's going to say, 'Your idea wasn't bad enough?'"

According to Mattimore, to get a great idea we often have to be willing to have a lot of bad ideas first. Paradoxically, it's often the bad ideas, he says, which get us to look at a problem "in an entirely new, often unconventional, way..., and ultimately lead to a breakthrough concept."

Idea Hooks

Word associations are the key in this technique, which uses metaphors as a launching pad to discover new ideas. For example, if a company is trying to think of new ways to improve company communication, associations such as "smoke signals," "body language" and "love" would open the door.

> Imagine yourself experiencing a typical day in the life of a target market consumer—a customer in a hardware store, for example—and the results can be amazing.

"You can easily find metaphors, associations and examples of key themes in Idea Fisher® software," Mattimore says. "Concrete nouns are best. We usually find them in the people, animals and things and places sub-categories of Idea Fisher®.

"Once you've got a list of twenty or more associations, just write those associations on flip chart paper. Let people pick any Idea Hook they like, then have them write down whatever they associate with this Idea Hook."

Mind Excursions

Participants imagine themselves experiencing a typical day in the life of a target market consumer. Results of this exercise are sometimes "amazing," according to Mattimore. "We find that anyone can generate a wealth of information—facts, feelings, problems, needs, or whatever—with this method. We then take that information and try to create new products and services."

Great Thinkers

In this exercise, each player adopts the role of a great thinker such as Einstein, Disney, Mozart, or Ansel Adams. Players are asked to imagine themselves as a great thinker and to try to approach a concept, theory, problem, or assignment from the point of view of the great mind.

A variation on this approach is what Mattimore calls the superhero technique. Each participant adopts the role of a superhero such as Superman, Spiderman, Batman, or Wonder Woman, for example. "In this world, anything is possible and the resulting 'super' ideas can often be really out-of-the-box stuff," Mattimore said.

> The idea is to combine words to create brand new concepts.

Yet another version is what Mattimore calls the hero technique. In this format, teams of two or more players try to mentally position themselves as idols of a specific target market. For example, Madonna, David Letterman, and Howard Stern might represent the college market. The resulting hip and youthful products and services are hatched from the stars' imagined points of view.

Idea Naming

The group generates a list of key words that relate to a particular creative challenge, then assembles those words into categories: nouns, verbs, adjectives. The idea is to combine words from each category to create brand new concepts.

For example, suppose you're trying to invent a new customer service program. Associated words might look like this:

verb: moving (fast)
nouns: telephone, survey
adjective: automated

The resulting combination of "fast-moving, automated, telephone (or survey)" might suggest a service that uses voice recognition computers to get immediate customer feedback.

Picture Prompts

"We have found that the variety and richness of beautifully rendered drawings can stimulate creative thinking in ways that no other exercise can," Mattimore revealed.

> The variety and richness of beautifully rendered drawings can stimulate creative thinking in ways that no other exercise can.

Each player is given a visually compelling picture (not a photograph—Mattimore says drawings such as ads, artistic, or creative designs work better), then is asked to come up with three ideas from each picture.

"We've found this method generates some very exciting out-of-the-ordinary thinking," Mattimore told me. "At first, people are sometimes understandably reluctant, because they might feel self-conscious. But once they start getting into it, you never know what they're going to come up with. The results are often spectacular."

Mindmapping

Invented by Englishman Tony Buzan in the 1960s, mindmapping uses key words, diagramming, and symbols to trigger creative thinking. It works something like this:

Write a key word that represents the problem or assignment in the center of a page and circle it. Then "free-associate" off that circled word, writing down every new key word that comes to mind. Connect related thoughts with lines. Then connect the related thoughts back to the center like the branches of a tree. Keep going until you've filled up the whole page. Then to add a little zest and help you remember and organize what you've got, add symbols to the mindmap.

"At this point you've got your rough draft," Mattimore said. "Now it's time to step back and consider the mind map as a whole. What are the most important ideas you've come up with? What thoughts seem to be related? What are the most fertile areas for new product development? What other ideas does the mindmap suggest?"

> Consider the mind map as a whole. What are the most important ideas you've come up with? What thoughts seem to be related? What are the most fertile areas for new product development? What other ideas does the mindmap suggest?"

Cut and Paste (Collaging)

This approach is particularly useful for developing germs of ideas into full-blown concepts, according to Mattimore. As the name implies, players cut and paste magazine images, words, or phrases relevant to the assignment they're working on.

Begin by passing out a variety of visually stimulating magazines such as *House and Garden*, *Sports Illustrated*, *Architectural Digest*, or *OMNI*. Everybody gets scissors and glue. Then cut everybody loose (individually or in small teams) to try to tell a story using photos, text, drawings, headlines, and advertisements. It's okay for the players to add their own handwritten phrases, words, or drawings. When the collage is finished, participants present it to the group, which will then add further idea suggestions to the original creation.

"This is a powerful and fun exercise," Mattimore said. "It's mentally stimulating and consistently productive."

Listening to Mattimore, I couldn't help being reminded of Arthur C. Clarke and the development of the communications satellite.

> The communications satellite, which we now take for granted, was once as wild an idea as walking on the moon.

The communications satellite, which we now take for granted, was once as wild an idea as walking on the moon. The communications satellite is the brainstorm of an inspired futurist, who provided a kind of "picture prompt" for other scientists to carry the ball forward and turn science fiction into reality.

In 1945, when he was twenty-seven, Clarke, author of *2001: A Space Odyssey*, virtually invented the communications satellite in a scientific paper. The idea caught the imagination of a number of engineers. Carrying a kind of snapshot of the new idea around in their heads, they eventually built a machine that wound up in orbit doing exactly what Clarke said it could do—beaming TV, radio, and telephone signals all over the world.

A physicist by training, Arthur C. Clarke created the world's most famous fictional computer, HAL, featured in *2001*. Today, computer scientists—inspired by Clarke—are working to create artificial intelligence that can think, talk, and even have a personality like HAL. Clarke's new book, *3001: The Final Odyssey*, is likely to help launch yet another generation of would-be scientists.

Bryan Mattimore spends his time helping the Arthur C. Clarkes of industry and commerce find themselves. He believes that we each have a little Arthur C. Clarke inside, and that the same passionate curiosity and imagination that inspires Clarke can inspire anyone willing to ask the question, "What if?"

The Miracle of Intuition:

The Creative Connection Between
the Hunch and the Home Run

If creativity is the sun that can light up lives, intuition is the moon that can bathe us in magic. Together, like yin and yang, they complement each other marvelously. In fact, it could be said that in business a creative mind that is also powerfully intuitive can be virtually unstoppable.

Hotel tycoon Conrad Hilton was in the process of bidding on a hotel in Chicago early in his career when a flash of insight suddenly came to him. "My first bid hastily made, was $165,000. Then somehow that didn't feel right," he recalled. "Another figure kept coming—$180,000. It satisfied me. It seemed fair. I changed my mind on that hunch. When they were opened, the closest bid to mine was $179,800." Hilton got his hotel.

> In business a creative mind that is also powerfully intuitive can be virtually unstoppable.

McDonald's founder Ray Kroc was just a milkshake mixer salesman when, while delivering eight machines to the McDonald brothers restaurant in 1952, he suddenly saw the light. He saw without any doubt in his mind that the wave of the future in the United States was fast-food hamburgers. That's when he made his bid to buy out the McDonald brothers—and the rest is history.

Sony chairman Akito Morita listened to legions of his marketing and sales people warn him that the Walkman would be a big flop, but then acted on his own instincts and launched the Walkman, anyway. The Walkman was a monster hit.

Edwin Land was taking pictures with his little girl at the beach one day when she suddenly turned to him and said, "Daddy, wouldn't it be nice if we had a picture right now?" Land got the picture right away. Thus was born the Polaroid Land camera, a landmark in photographic history.

Grant Tinker, former head of NBC, has long believed in the value of intuition. "Sometimes the boss has just got to go by his gut, hold his nose, and jump," Tinker says. Tinker led NBC to many a splash ratings hit.

Former Chrysler Chairman Lee Iacocca, who likes to think of himself as the father of the Mustang, the minivan, and the modern American muscle car, has always listened to what his heart was trying to tell him. "To a certain extent," he says, "I've always operated by gut feeling." Iacocca married aggressive creativity with sly intuition and helped steer the car business in a new direction.

> Former Chrysler Chairman Lee Iacocca has always listened to what his heart was trying to tell him.

Taki Kyrakides, a onetime immigrant business success story and now head of the Internet Stock Market, says that for him intuition, "is like playing the piano without reading the notes." He believes that intuition, like mastery of a musical instrument, can be developed and per-fected—and he credits his own intuition for guiding him to success.

Jon Chait, president of computer games company Reality Bytes, a big believer in solid business principles, is nevertheless convinced that hunches are as important as analysis. "All senior managers, and especially entrepreneurs, must bank on their intuition," he says. "When you are driving into new areas, you are constantly chal-lenged to rely on gut feeling to make decisions."

And research would appear to back up Chait's assertion.

Weston Agor, Ph.D., a former professor and later head of a con-sulting research group, provided intuition tests to more than 10,000 executives and came up with surprising results.

"The findings are unequivocal," he reported. "The higher the level of manage-ment, the higher the raw ability to intuit solu-tions, and the more reliance is placed on intuition."

"The higher the level of management, the higher the raw ability to intuit solutions, and the more reliance is placed on intuition."

In fact, intuition may be a much more important factor in successful business ven-tures than most corporate people are willing to admit.

"I talk to a lot of executives who give me technical reasons why they make their decisions," observes Dr. Sandy Weinberg, professor of entrepreneurship at Muhlenberg Col-lege. "A lot of executives make decisions based on intuition and then go back and find technical reasons to justify those decisions."

Success magazine looked into the characteristics of intuition and came up with the following list of ways that experts say anyone can develop their "sixth sense."

1. *Devour information.* Some experts believe intuition generates from the proposition that the brain is like a powerful Internet database, which can hold countless gigabytes of information subconsciously. "I marinate myself in information, bombard myself with news, different ideas, perceptions, facts—any information I can get a hold of," says Virginia Littlejohn, president of Global Enterprise Group, a consulting firm. Then she draws on the resulting vast reservoir of information to produce knowledge, which in turn helps her make correct—and creative—decisions.

> Experts believe intuition generates from the proposition that the brain is like a powerful Internet database, which can hold countless gigabytes of information subconsciously.

2. *Study beyond your discipline.* John Ferrara, Gold Mine Software cofounder, recalls that he started his company in 1989 with $3,000 and "a big leap of intuition." "I had lots of industry knowledge. But I think that just as important was my exposure to Eastern philosophy and yoga, and the reading I did—books like *Siddhartha* and *Autobiography of a Yogi*—that had nothing whatsoever to do with business or computers." Blend ancient wisdom with modern science, allow intuition to occur, and suddenly you're sitting on top of a gold mine.

3. *Drain your brain.* "Say you have until tomorrow to dream up the perfect name for your company's new wrinkle cream," says Marsh Fisher, cofounder of Century 21 Real Estate and CEO of a computer software company. "Begin by asking yourself what word or concepts you associate with wrinkles. Old. What's the next word? Young. What does young signify? Fitness. That leads to health, vitality. Wear yourself out.

Make a long list. Then start working on associations with the word cream. Now take these two lists and start rearranging words. That's how you will intuit your new product name, idea, or solution."

4. *Flip a coin.* Literally. Have a tough decision? Flip a coin. Note how you feel about the results. Interestingly, if you are pleased, the coin toss is reinforcement. But if you're somehow not happy, you've just gained new insight into your powers of intuition. Your intuition is at work, revealed through the coin toss, and it's trying to tell you something important.

5. *Listen to your body.* People who often experience flashes of intuition also sometimes report that they sense what feels almost like a mild surge of electricity at the moment of discovery or recognition. Maybe it's just a flush or a flutter or a curious little tingle. But it's something. Maybe it's a sign. And maybe you ought to step back and pay attention.

> People who often experience flashes of intuition also sometimes report that they sense what feels almost like a mild surge of electricity at the moment of discovery or recognition.

6. *Get physical.* Some researchers believe that the simple act of exercise frees the mind to wander in the subconscious. "Any sort of physical activity is good for quieting down your mind," says Richard Contino, author of *Trust Your Gut! Practical Ways to Develop and Use Your Intuition for Business Success.* "If you jog, for example, or work out in a gym, you channel off nervous energy that blocks the intuitive thought process."

We used to call this clearing your head. Virtually everyone knows that it's only when you've cleared your head that the right answers—and the right questions—can start coming in.

7. *Be still.* Veteran stock picker Bill Staton, chairman of Staton Investment Management, says he owes much of his success to simply sitting quietly and closing his eyes. "It never fails me," he says. "The answer I'm looking for will come to me. I'll see it like a bright neon sign that says YES BUY or NO DON'T BUY." To see how well this simple approach actually works, Staton recommends that people interested in building their powers of intuition pick a mock portfolio and demonstrate to themselves the power of silence and meditation by watching hits accumulate.

> It's true what they say about showers. The mind unwinds. We relax. Things start popping into our heads.

8. *Get into the shower.* It's true what they say about showers. We think a lot in the shower. The mind unwinds. We relax. Things start popping into our heads. A senior executive friend of mine had a shower put in his office for just that reason. The shower cost $25,000, but he claims it's been worth millions to the company.

9. *Trust your inner voice—then act.* "I was reading the *Wall Street Journal* one day and came across a word I didn't know," recalls Taki Kyrakides. "I had a calculator with me and said to myself, 'Wouldn't it be something if this thing could translate words?'" The result was Lexicon, the first handheld electronic translator. A few years later, Kyrakides, head of the Internet Stock Market, listened to another inner voice and produced the world's first optical scanner. And on yet another burst of intuition, he bought a sunken cruise ship for $900,000, raised it, refurbished it, and started

Regency Cruise Line, which four years later was the sixth-largest cruise line in the world.

10. *Look before you leap.* Just to make sure your intuitive brainstorm isn't a fizzle, take the time to do a little research. Cynthia Ekberg Thai had an idea to launch Health Expo in New York City. "I was reading a paper and saw that Comdex, the big Las Vegas computer show had been sold to the Japanese for $800 million. A light bulb went off in my head," she recalls. "Why not a similar show for the health care industry?" The next day Thai was in the library doing her homework. First, she confirmed that nothing like Health Expo existed. Then she educated herself about the health care industry, the world of big consumer shows, and what it would take to market a project like Health Expo. She launched the business in 1995 and drew 20,000 visitors—a huge number for a first-time event.

11. *Find a suitable partner.* Every intuitive person needs a methodical, analytical type to keep an eye on details and watch the numbers while the intuitive is constantly thinking Big Picture.

"If you are an intuitive person, make certain you have analytical people as part of your team," cautions consultant Weston Agor. "They often see things you don't. Listen to what they have to say."

> Every intuitive person needs a methodical, analytical type to keep an eye on details and watch the numbers while the intuitive is constantly thinking Big Picture.

These are the ways experts believe we can profit from our own intuitive potential.

So ask yourself: Are you creative? Do you try to see things differently, act boldly, think in new ways? Even if the answer is no, it's enough that you are at least asking the question.

Are you intuitive? The true answer may be an answer of degree. Just the willingness to allow yourself to think like an intuitive person may be the beginning of a new chapter for you and your business. Put them together and combine a creative approach with an intuitive bent and you may be surprised by what this powerhouse combo can deliver.

six

The New Pioneers:

How Entrepreneurs Are Building the Next Economy

A refugee from a big pharmaceutical company, sick of inertia and bureaucracy, buys a tiny storefront in a needy Philadelphia neighborhood and sets up his own drugstore. Just a few years later, Richard Ost had reinvented not only the drugstore business, maybe forever, but also became an important force for the good in his adopted community. He ended up doing four times more business than the average American drugstore, and teaching the big boys how it's done.

Five-foot tall Charlene Pedrolie takes over a furniture factory in western Virginia, turns the whole place on its ear, and proves that conventional corporate wisdom, traditional manufacturing processes and business school hotshots put together can't hold a candle to the

> Charlene Pedrolie proves that conventional corporate wisdom, traditional manufacturing processes and business school hotshots put together can't hold a candle to the creative energy of ordinary people unleashed to figure things out for themselves.

creative energy of ordinary people unleashed to figure things out for themselves.

A plant manager at a California factory making truck undercarriages for Toyota has to find ways to meet contractual yearly price cuts without slashing working salaries or sacrificing quality. So he constantly finds creative new ways to improve and winds up blazing new territory almost every day.

> Business is not what we have always believed it to be, a Newtonian machine of mechanical laws that works like a clock, but rather an organism that functions like a living thing.

These and other stories from the front lines of job evolution are related in *The New Pioneers: Men and Women Who Are Transforming the Workplace and Marketplace* by Thomas Petzinger Jr. Petzinger argues that America is experiencing a revolution that's changing the face of business. Essentially, the book says that business is not what we have always believed it to be, a Newtonian machine of mechanical laws that works like a clock, but rather an organism that functions like a living thing. Business, it says, is about adoption, invention, flexibility, and fewer rules and regulations based on industrial models that don't convert well into the age of service, information, and technology.

The next economy, according to Petzinger, started in earnest after the Gulf War, when companies the world over stopped spending. A dismal recession set in and two things started happening that had not happened in memory: first, companies began laying people off by the thousands—with no intention of ever taking them back again; and second, the people being let go were largely middle managers, many of them at the height of their careers and at the top of their form.

The same hand that shook all these men and women out of the corporate tree is the same hand that loosed these same seeds of creativity upon the land in the greatest diaspora of talent America had ever seen. So it can't be surprising that these displaced energies eventually took root in a million new entrepreneurial businesses that have already started to make the world a more interesting and exciting place.

So it's never been a better time to be a stone.

For pharmacist Richard Ost, as with so many of the other new entrepreneurs Petzinger writes about, the key to success lies more in on-the-job creativity and ingenuity than long-accepted business practices. For example, when Ost saw that his business depended on a winning commercial relationship with his largely Hispanic and African-American clientele, he immediately translated his computerized database of 1,000 or so regimen instructions to Spanish. With that one thoughtful act, business exploded, and he had to expand into a parts store next door. Ost also knew that his business depended on customer loyalty, so he hired people from the community, dressed them up in local team jackets, then added family medical benefits (almost unheard of among inner-city employers), profit sharing, a stake in the sale of every item, and control of every cost. He held fortnightly staff meetings to review financial results and discuss ways to become even more profitable.

Soon his business had blossomed to three stores, and Ost had attracted enough attention to start a second career as an industry consultant, teaching others in the industry how to get closer to employees and customers alike. By the time he sold out to Rite Aid (giving his former employees bonuses and other payments in the process), his original $10,000 investment was generating $5 million a year.

When Charlene Pedrolie walked into her new job as plant manager for the Rowe Furniture Company, she knew right away she had a tough assignment. Rowe research had revealed customers had become impatient and impulsive. Customers wanted custom furniture and they wanted it now. So Rowe set up computer touch screens to let customers design their own furniture right in the store. Then Rowe sent Charlene out to the 500-employee factory to make it happen.

Charlene saw that the old assembly-line way of making furniture just wasn't going to cut it, so she simply threw out the rule book and started from scratch.

What happened next was so revolutionary and so chaotic that for awhile Charlene wasn't sure she was going to be able to pull it off. First of all, she eliminated most supervisory positions. Then she put everybody on the plant through a crash course learning everybody else's job, told them to organize themselves into clusters—or "cells" as she called them—and told each cell that from now on they would be responsible for a particular line of furniture. There followed a period of confusion, frustration and mistakes. But after a few weeks, with the factory floor looking more like pandemonium than precision, something amazing happened. The pieces started to fall into place and before long the factory was delivering custom orders in just 30 days, and in 10 days just a couple of months after that—in an industry accustomed to working on lead times of up to six months.

According to Petzinger, the Rowe story is just another testament to what he calls the creative power of human interaction. It suggests, he says, that efficiency is intrinsic; that people are naturally productive; and that "when inspired with vision, equipped with the right tools, and guided with information about their own performance, people will build on each other's actions to a more efficient result than any single brain could design."

Then he offers the story of Dana Corporation manager Mark Schmink who got the job of first building, then running a factory in Stockton, California, to make a single product: truck undercarriages for Toyota. Schmink, too, understood that the success of the enterprise demanded new ideas. Because not only did he have to get the whole thing up and running, he also had to make sure he met the annual price cuts called for in the contract with Toyota. And he had to do it without sacrificing either salaries or quality. It was the toughest assignment of Schmink's life. And he knew that to make it work, he would have to continuously improve his operation, year after year, with no letup.

"When inspired with vision, equipped with the right tools, and guided with information about their own performance, people will build on each other's actions to a more efficient result than any single brain could design."

—THOMAS PETZINGER

Schmink began by hiring welders who had never welded before (he didn't want old habits to cloud creative thinking) and as many qualified people from varying backgrounds as he could find (he wanted fresh approaches from many different points of view), and wound up with 19 different nationalities in the first 300 people he hired. He created a plant library full of research materials and periodicals, and even provided bestsellers on tape to get people's minds moving on the way to work. He required that every employee submit two productivity ideas in writing every month (some of which included improving working conditions, but Schmink knew that that, too, affected productivity). He personally responded to every written suggestion and flashed minute-by-minute productivity figures on big electronic scoreboards in the factory. And every time his team hit another milestone, he celebrated with an event like a barbeque or a day of free sodas.

With Toyota happy, Dana happy and his people happy, Schmink was revealing what most of us already know: Take a creative self-starter with new ideas and the resolve to do what it takes to get the job done, then give him the job and get out of the way.

Petzinger also talks about Jerry Whitlock, the self-styled "Seal Man" of Stockton, Georgia, an independent distributor of seals and gaskets. Just when the experts were saying that high-tech would drive the middleman from the economy, Whitlock and thousands more like him were not only proving the experts wrong, but were themselves using the very technology that was supposed to wipe them out to actually build their businesses.

As Petzinger put it, never was a gasket salesman so wired. Like a twenty-first century communications Rambo, Whitlock armed himself with two cell phones, lashed a beeper to his belt, set up e-mail and a "blast fax" system to target scores of prospects at a shot, launched a Web site, and even mounted a laptop on the gear hump in the cab of his truck. With his crackling array of electronic gadgetry in full swing, the "Seal Man" was able to compete with even the biggest of the big— General Electric and General Motors to name just two—and today he and his wife routinely fill orders from places as far away as Dublin, Singapore, Sweden, Trinidad,

> With his crackling array of electronic gadgetry in full swing, the "Seal Man" was able to compete with even the biggest of the big—General Electric and General Motors to name just two—and today he and his wife routinely fill orders from places as far away as Dublin, Singapore, Sweden, Trinidad, Chile, and Mexico.

Chile, and Mexico, while buying from vendors in Germany, Venezuela, Ireland, Australia and Austria.

Rather than eliminate Jerry Whitlock and others like him, technology helped shape Whitlock into the ultimate middleman, and one of the growing army of new pioneers.

Meanwhile, over at Sohio in Cleveland, an enterprising scientist by the name of Carol Latham was working in the lab when the order came down to find a way to use ceramics to cool electronic devices like computer chips. Ceramics were good heat insulators, but they were also brittle and hard to shape. Carol pondered the problem and one day the flashbulb went off in her head. Why not combine ceramics with plastics?

Which is exactly what Carol Latham did, coming up with what can only be described as a perfect product. But to her surprise and frustration, none of the Ph.D.'s and lab managers seemed to care in the least. And it didn't help she was a woman.

"I couldn't get anywhere," Carol recalled. "So one day I just resigned."

It was the best move she ever made.

Carol began by setting up shop on her living room table, turning low-value commodities into high-value substances that improve the performance of electronic equipment.

It wasn't long before she was renting a small corner of a local commercial plant. She named her new company Thermagon (as in "heat be gone"), started making sales calls and hired a West Coast representative.

Her first order was from IBM. Then followed Silicon Graphics, Aavid Engineering, and many more. Intel recommended her products to companies building laptops with Pentium processors.

By the end of the 1990s, Carol had moved into a former knitting mill. With 18 employees, including two of her sons, she was doing $10 million in business a year and growing at a rate of 200 percent annually. And that was just the beginning.

By the end of the 1990s, Carol had moved into a former knitting mill. With 18 employees, including two of her sons, she was doing $10 million in business a year and growing at a rate of 200 percent annually. And that was just the beginning.

Enterprising people like Carol Latham are popping up all over, often enabled by technology. Take the case of college professor Morris Shepherd who found his niche sipping a latte and reading the *New York Times*. Shepherd spotted a little item about a new Xerox machine that could quickly and cheaply turn out entire handbooks.

Bingo! Right away Shepherd knew he was looking at his future, because he had a way to finally solve the problems academics have in trying to pull together far-flung publications for students.

In *The New Pioneers,* Petzinger tells how Moe Shepherd set up his new business, called Book Tech. He installed scanners and systems to standardize page size, then began custom printing books and shipping them to whatever student co-op or bookstore the customer required. Word quickly got around the academic community. So many orders started pouring in, Shepherd put in an Oracle database to let customers design their own books. Soon even Barnes & Noble was outsourcing its custom copying business through Book Tech, and the professor was solidly into his new career.

Giving people what they want—exactly what they want—can be the competitive edge in small entrepreneurial ventures. For example, Bill Dudleston began building stereo speakers in his father-in-law's Ohio garage in the early 1980s. He found out what hard-core audio connoisseurs wanted by placing ads in audiophile magazines, then seeing what drew the most responses. He built his speakers to match what people demanded, then began receiving a ton of mail from new customers with suggestions on how to further refine and improve the product. So

> Giving people what they want—exactly what they want—can be the competitive edge in small entrepreneurial ventures.

each piece of new intelligence played a role in the creation of the next generation of speakers. Dudleston's designs began getting rave reviews in the audiophile press and he wound up with a loyal cult following, especially in Japan.

In San Jose, California, Mike Sinyard founded a company called Specialized Bicycle Components which helped launch the mountain-bike craze. Sinyard began building seriously cool mountain bikes back in the 1980s. He put together a crack sales team that pushed the product into stores. But it wasn't long before the big players like Schwinn caught on and pretty much locked up the mountain bike market in volume stores like Kmart. So Sinyard concentrated even harder on his core market, the small specialty bike shop. He assured himself a place in the sun by setting up a board of shop owners who provided nonstop feedback, which in turn guaranteed that the bike shops' fussy customers could count on getting exactly what they wanted from Mike Sinyard. The result: Specialized products never stop changing and the company never stops improving. At last check, Specialized was on its way to $200 million in annual sales.

Sometimes the key is simply to buck the trend. In Boulder, Colorado, Steve Bosley built the tiny Bank of Boulder into a regional powerhouse by expanding drive-through service with live tellers 24

In Boulder, Colorado, Steve Bosley built the tiny Bank of Boulder into a regional powerhouse by expanding drive-through service with live tellers 24 hours a day—just when other banks were cutting back and installing ATMs.

hours a day—just when other banks were cutting back and installing ATMs. Customers loved it. Then he inaugurated a 10-kilometer run called Bolder Boulder, which became one of the most popular in the world, and put the bank on the map. On top of that, he offered an extra quarter-point in interest on certain certificates of deposit when the University of Colorado won a big game, drawing a wave of deposits. The payoff: Bank of Boulder wound up being named the most profitable community bank in America.

Another way to propel your company to the top is simply to turn it inside out. That's what Ron Rosenzweig did with his firm, Anadigics Incorporated. Anadigics makes gallium arsenide chips, which handle high-frequency radio signals better than silicon chips. During the Reagan years, Rosenzweig hitched his star to "Star Wars," the Strategic Defense Initiative. When "Star Wars" went bust, Anadigics almost did, too; and Rosenzweig suddenly found himself back in the cable TV switching gear business and having to think fast to keep the company afloat.

So he took a bold step. Essentially, he stripped away the marketing and sales people from his organization and told his engineers that from now on they were the marketing and sales people. In other words, he put the techie scientist/engineers in the lab in direct contact with his potential customers.

"People with a fundamental engineering skill set are best suited to solving the customer's problem," Rosenzweig explained. "We give them this responsibility and tell them, 'It's your job to satisfy the customer in the time he wants. You are not limited by any budget or travel allowance. Just do what you have to do'." So one engineer, Ron Michael, took off immediately and traveled the country visiting trade shows, conventions, customers, and retailers. He looked inside every switching box he could get his hands on, then popped the question to potential customers: "How much would it be worth to you to substitute all these parts for a single chip?"

The response was overwhelming and Anadigics was back in business.

"If you have the solution," Michaels says, "it sells itself."

Clever solutions from creative minds mean business.

As Nietzsche said, *what doesn't kill me makes me stronger.* Cemex, the giant Mexican cement company, was being killed by the chaos and hopeless traffic of Mexico City. With trucks often unable to reach customers on time, loads of cement were spoiling, orders were getting cancelled, customers were screaming, revenues were threatened, and business was slowly grinding to a halt. So Cemex executives, knowing the problems of Mexico City were never going away, decided to somehow try to embrace the chaos rather than fall victim to it.

To learn how to deal with chaos, management took an eye-opening trip to the FedEx hub in Memphis. They were awed by the stunning efficiencies of the FedEx information, processing, handling, and distribution systems. They watched in amazement as tons of letters, parcels and packages flooded in and out, from anywhere to anywhere, 24-hours a day, every day, almost without a hitch. But they were even more impressed by the FedEx slogan, *It's on time or it's on us.* It was hard to imagine making the same promise back in Mexico City.

The next stop was the 911 dispatch center of the Houston Fire Department. As Tom Petzinger related in his book, the visitors sat in rapt attention in the darkened room incredulous at the poise with which dispatchers fielded heart attacks, fires, false alarms, and emergencies of all kinds. What became quickly apparent is that there always seemed to be just enough ambulances and paramedics in just the right places around town to handle all the calls. And that's when the revelation hit.

Back in Mexico City, Cemex's bosses cut loose the delivery trucks from their assigned zones to wander the city as part of one big pool with an artificial intelligence system triangulating them to destinations and mixing plants, all the while taking account of traffic patterns. Business started to pick up.

Next, drivers were enrolled in weekly customer-service classes spanning two years. Management chucked onerous work rules so nothing would get in the way of getting the product to the customer on time. The company launched same-day service and unlimited order changes. And when they introduced a 20-minute delivery guarantee, business really took off. Thanks to creative management and a willingness to learn and change, Cemex was back on track and on its way to greater profitability than it had ever known.

When Paul Graziani quit GE Aerospace with the rights to a satellite software he had developed, he founded his own company, Analytical Graphics, and offered the software which he called "Satellite Tool Kit," for $10,000 a pop—and before he knew it he had a nice little business. But he soon became frustrated when he saw his add-on modulars starting to outsell the core program. With Satellite Tool Kit sales slowing and add-ons speeding up, he saw that he had to get more Tool Kits into the market fast to feed the add-on market. So Graziani made the toughest, most courageous and most difficult decision of his career. He decided to start giving away his core product, like Gillette gave away razors to sell blades, to try to take his little company to the next level.

As Petzinger says in his book, Paul Graziani became a giver. He distributed tens of thousands of free compact disks in satellite trade magazines and his bold bet paid off. Business has never been so good. In fact, at last word investment bankers were falling all over themselves to determine who would eventually take Analytical Graphics public in an IPO.

Paul Graziani was acting radically. But was he acting creatively?

Gillette, Kodak, Netscape, Pointcast, Source Craft and others have given, only to receive more abundantly.

Through generosity, by sharing knowledge, Graziani created new growth and wealth for himself, his company, and his investors. Maybe it's true what the good book says in Proverbs: "One man gives freely yet gains even more. Another withholds unduly, but comes to poverty."

Giving can go far in business, but a willingness to take big risks can take you all the way to the top.

Petzinger also recounts the story of Georg Bauer who, when he took over as head of Mercedes-Benz Credit Corporation in Norwalk, Connecticut, had only one thing on his mind: Grow the business by cutting costs and improving service. But to do that, Bauer knew he'd have to rip the place apart and virtually start all over again. Which is exactly what he did.

Importantly, he had no idea how to remake the organization. Nor did he have any idea what it would look like on the other end. So he decided to turn the whole project over to his own employees.

"Let the people in the organization find the weaknesses in the organization," he told the other bosses. "Let's let it grow from the bottom up."

So the mandate came down: Set up cross-function teams, wipe out waste, and turn this place into a model of great service and efficiency.

Everything was fair game. There were no sacred cows. No idea was too loopy, no job exempt. Wild and radical thinking was openly encouraged, and Bauer passionately urged everybody not to fear risk or failure.

Over and over again Bauer told his people to have no fear.

Right away, teams tore office walls down, lowered cubicle partitions and encased conference rooms in glass so everybody could see who was meeting with whom. New bonus programs compensated teams for performance. They even changed the name of the place from "corporate headquarters" to "North American Support Center." And to top it all off, a gleaming Mobius sculpture was put in the lobby precisely because the look of it seemed to change all the time.

As just one example of the kinds of changes employees created, Margaret Brayden not only eliminated her own job as the company's records-retention coordinator, but also her entire department. Everyone was reassigned and Margaret herself was rewarded with a place on a special team called "change management."

In just two years, the firm nearly tripled its assets to 23 billion dollars, and J. D. Powers & Associates ranked Mercedes-Benz Credit Corporation first in the industry for customer satisfaction.

Talk about credit. The credit goes to Bauer for tearing down walls and obstacles of all kinds and unleashing everybody to work without fear of failure. And to all his employees who pitched in together to solve their own problems and design for themselves a model of productivity and profitability.

Taking risks is one thing, but defying the sacred tenets of a whole industry is another.

The New Pioneers paints an inspiring picture of the little guy beating all the odds in the story of Pete and Laura Wakeman, who went west after graduating from Cornell in the 1970s to set up a bakery in Dillon, Montana.

Pete and Laura were serious about baking. They made their honeywheat bread, for example, by grinding their own whole wheat and greeted every customer at the door with a free steamy slice. Before long people were lined up at opening time, clearing the shelves in just minutes.

It was immediately apparent to the Wakemans that they had hit on something good, but they were reluctant to compromise their nice new life. So they pushed back business hours when they realized that getting up in the middle of the night wasn't for them, and refused to expand because they didn't want to go into debt and have to march to someone else's tune. But when somebody proposed a franchise, that seemed like a good idea, because it meant expansion without a lot more work.

That's when the Wakemans started making history. They began franchising their operation, Great Harvest—but after a compulsory year of training and technical help, the franchisees were free to run their franchises any way they liked.

Compare the Great Harvest approach to the lock-step conformity of most other franchise food operations all over the world:

rigorous rules to insure convention and uniformity. Regular visits of inspectors from the corporate office. Innovation not only discouraged but actually forbidden.

By contrast, at Great Harvest there are no operating restrictions outside of serve it hot and make it whole wheat. Wakeman and his wife are fussy about who operates under the Great Harvest name. They accept just one in a hundred applicants. And who are these model franchisees? Wakeman told a trade group: "People who love learning for the plain fun of it, who see business as an excuse to play, and love all of life for the sheer thrill of a bumpy ride."

The result, as Petzinger notes, is nonstop innovation. Each franchise constantly tweaking, honing, and improving product and service to meet demands of regional and local customers.

The glue that binds the whole thing together is communication. All stores are hooked up electronically through the central office back in Montana. So everybody immediately gets to hear about everybody else's great ideas and best practices.

Take the case of Ed and Lori Kerpurs, who run a Great Harvest outside Philadelphia. After their year's apprenticeship, Ed and Lori added cookies to the menu, then launched a coloring contest for kids. Soon they were getting five thousand entries a month and swarms of kids begging their parents for repeat visits so they could see their entries on display.

While Ed and Lori are sharing their ideas, they are also learning from others in the system. Recently, for example, they traveled to Northfield, Michigan, to study counter-service concepts, checked out new signage ideas in Chapel Hill, North Carolina, and went to Boston to share tips with another couple who, like themselves, were trying to run a bakery with a new child underfoot.

Put it all together and you've got an operation, as Petzinger notes, that operates more like a network than a brand, and more like a community than a corporation.

In fact, Petzinger takes it a step further: "Freed to do their best work and free to test it against others, the people in a group became a single intelligent being, much as billions of neurons become a single brain or millions of intelligent citizens become a single nation," he writes. "Although the people at the top might discover what's good for an organization, contrary to centuries of received wisdom they will never discover what is best. Because nobody, as the saying goes, is as smart as everybody."

Petzinger believes successful companies in the next economy will operate more like organisms naturally developing and growing in cooperation with one another, rather than man-invented hierarchical machines marching to strict work rules—stifling novelty and using employees more as drones and less as creative and intelligent beings in their own right.

> Petzinger believes successful companies in the next economy will operate more like organisms naturally developing and growing in cooperation with one another, rather than man-invented hierarchical machines marching to strict work rules.

The future, he believes, will see working people flourish in the rich soup of businesses "biosystems" that will set loose creativity as never before and spur a new, restless energy that will eventually recreate the marketplace.

The Four Fundamentals of Professional Fulfillment:

Putting Talent and Experience to Good Use

Creativity is not a mystery, nor a religion, nor a secret society off limits to all but the most talented among us. Creativity is as natural as air or water, and like air and water will try to fill emptiness and seek equilibrium. Allowed to flourish, it will lead us to places where we thought we might never go.

The worker on the assembly line who demonstrates creativity will either find a way to improve the process and be recognized and promoted up to another level, or leave the job entirely for something else where his ingenuity will be more useful. Given a chance, he may even arrange to switch to another job within the same organization where he sees an opportunity to put his talents to work without restraint.

For example, a floor worker figures out how to assemble jet engine parts and eliminate a cumbersome middle step simply by changing the order in which the components are pieced together. The

> Creativity is not a mystery, nor a religion, nor a secret society off limits to all but the most talented.

result is a 20 percent productivity improvement. The worker is promoted to team leader and soon after comes up with an even better idea that speeds the process another 10 percent. Management promotes the team leader to shop foreman. But the creative process doesn't stop there (because the creative process never stops). As shop foreman, he sees that the entire assembly process is flawed and reconfigures the plant floor, realigns the teams, and creates an entirely new format to benchmark quality control before the engines go out the door. Eventually, the company promotes the shop foreman to plant manager, and then to vice president, and so it goes.

But the scenario could take a different yet equally rewarding path. Our shop foreman may find his ideas fall on deaf ears and feel his talents are wasted. So he quits and joins a small supplier. In this uncrowded environment his ingenuity is appreciated, and he rises rapidly. But soon he feels he has learned enough about the business to quit yet again and begin his own parts operation, which he does. Starting from scratch in the new operation, he uses everything he has learned during his apprenticeship to eclipse the competition in cost, quality, distribution, speed, service, and customer satisfaction. Now his powers of creativity are at full throttle. He has never felt so alive. The business grows rapidly on the strength of his continuing innovations, and just a few years later he sells his parts business to his original employer for more than $50 million.

An all-American story, and all thanks to the natural human inclination towards creativity.

But what exactly is creativity, and how does creativity figure into the human drama and every person's desire to find fulfillment?

An acquaintance recently confided that he was feeling frustrated, out-of-sorts, not at all himself—and he had no idea why. Business was good. Life was never better. He was a millionaire many times over—capping out a career that was by any measure a roaring success.

Things had been going this way for years.

So what was wrong? What could possibly be wrong when you're on top of your game, enjoying the admiration of your fellow man, rich, and well-positioned for the rest of your life?

That's a good question that some very successful people are asking themselves, and whether we've hit the heights or not, we all owe it to ourselves to find an answer.

In the case of my acquaintance the answer was not only elusive, but surprising. And strangely, it all began with Sylvester Stallone. It turned out that my friend had seen a portion of a TV interview in which Sly was talking about how he had hit a kind of a wall. Flush with career success and more money than he could ever hope to spend, Sly found himself privately wrestling with a curious ennui. A nagging hint of emptiness started to deflate his comfortable, near-perfect world of fame and fortune.

Shortly before the TV interview, Sly and his wife had had a baby girl who was diagnosed with a malfunctioning heart that needed surgery. The infant pulled through. But the experience shook Stallone, forcing him to take a hard look at his priorities and reassess his life. The result was a pledge. In the wake of his daughter's crisis, Sylvester Stallone vowed to greet each new day as an opportunity to somehow make the world a better place. He wasn't quite sure how he would do that. But as an example, he talked about finding a way, every day, to improve himself.

In the wake of his daughter's crisis, Sylvester Stallone vowed to greet each new day as an opportunity to somehow make the world a better place. As an example, he talked about finding a way, every day, to improve himself.

This got my friend to thinking. In his years he had done a lot of things, but he had never even thought about trying to make the world a better place. He had thought a great deal about his career and family, and lately he'd been thinking a lot about re-engineering and growth and shareholder value. But he couldn't say he'd spent much time trying to figure out how to improve the world. On the other hand, he had thought about improving himself. He'd worked hard on his golf game, took some lessons in wine and cigar appreciation, collected a little art, and even had a plastic surgeon play around with his double chin and sagging eyelids. He had done all that, but in all honesty he couldn't say that any of it had made him any happier.

> What makes for a good life? Is it success? Not necessarily. Is it money? Not necessarily. Is it freedom to come and go as you choose? Not necessarily.

So he wasn't sure that Sly's approach of trying to do something every day to improve himself was the answer. And that's when my friend and I started to figure out, from the perspective of our combined 100 or so years, just exactly what makes for a good life. We had to ask some obvious questions.

Is it success?

Not necessarily.

Is it money?

Not necessarily.

Is it freedom to come and go as you choose?

Not necessarily.

Is it family and friends? (We're getting warmer here. But the answer is still: not necessarily.)

Is it luxury?

Not necessarily.

Is it parties and beautiful people and a steady diet of sex, caviar and champagne?

Probably not.

Is it a special talent like a singing voice, artistic bent, athletic skill?

Not necessarily.

So if it is not necessarily any of these things by themselves, is it all of them or any combination? Very possible, but again, not necessarily.

Then we got to the most sobering question of all, certainly the toughest.

How about God, we asked. Could the answer be God? Well, the answer *could* be God if you're talking about trying to connect with the divine. Connecting with the divine is fulfilling—has been since before recorded history. In fact, you could say that somehow, touching God might be not only the objective of every earthly life, but also the highest attainable state in the human condition. So God is a definite "very possibly." But if you are talking about religion—manmade, brokered, organized religion be it Christian, Jewish, Muslim, it doesn't matter—a lot of people will tell you the answer is an equally emphatic "probably not."

> Connecting with the divine is fulfilling. In fact, you could say that somehow, touching God might be not only the objective of every earthly life, but also the highest attainable state in the human condition.

What if you were to substitute "love" for "God?" For the sake of argument, let's say love and God are interchangeable. But the answer is still the same. All of which led us to a very difficult conclusion. If the solution to our quest did not lie in earthly pleasures or the admiration of our fellow man, or even in the purely spiritual, what could possibly be the correct answer?

To find the answer, we were forced, ultimately, to look inward. And with a little bit of poking and probing the elusive little rascal finally came out. We realized that the answer to the good life was actually not one but several things, which, when put together, wound up as a little acronym:

CHIM. As in, "Keep your chim up":
    C create
    H help
    I improve
    M make it happen

You will note that this acronym does not include matters of the heart (we'll call this spirituality). But spirituality is a given—not only because it is arguably true that we are all seekers of the spirit (even the toughest of the tough and the baddest of the bad are seekers of the spirit), but more importantly because these four components are all in themselves aspects of the spirit.

Of the four, the two most important parts of day-to-day spiritual practice are the aspects of creation and help. When we really began exploring the subject, my friend and I agreed that the fuel that feeds the furnace is creativity. Stop being creative and you begin to flame out. Help—that is, serving others in

> The two most important parts of day-to-day spiritual practice are the aspects of creation and help. Stop being creative and you begin to flame out. Help—that is, serving others in some way – is the other part of the equation that seems to make life worthwhile.

some way—is the other part of the equation that seems to make life worthwhile.

For all of recorded history, the great sages have told us, serve ourselves and we find emptiness. Help, teach, and give to others and we find fulfillment. (So paradoxically we end up only helping ourselves after all.) Even in times of cynicism and materialism, this is a lesson we are all taught from birth but which most of us choose to ignore. (Dreams of a villa on the Riviera are understandably more compelling than the thought of teaching in an inner-city school, or schlepping for a relief agency in some godforsaken, ravaged corner of the world.)

Let's look at CHIM.

Create. Turn the TV off. Try writing a poem, or painting a picture, or working in clay, or taking photographs. Anything to ignite that little flame that you hope might grow into a roaring fire at the office and in life itself. Anything to take you back to that primitive, precious part of all of us that somehow has to be let out, that thing that—like romantic love—can restore our faith in life, give us a startling sense of completeness, let us fly.

At work, approach your job in a new way. Think of interesting ways to make the work more fulfilling. Approach the process of creativity at work as you might approach a game or a sport, looking to master the skills vital to success. Discover new and better ways to play the game. Productivity blocked? Try learning new computer technologies. Morale flat? Set up a new plan to cut the workers in on some of the equity. Creativity stifled? Arrange brainstorming sessions to come up with new ideas. Team spirit down? Set up a company soccer or softball team—and while you're at it, treat your top producers to a long weekend in Paris (go ahead, spend money, you'll get it back three times over).

We have all heard of the great inventors, writers, artists, composers, engineers, mathematicians, theorists, philosophers, and others who roared through life with a singular sense of purpose and ambition, flew over setbacks and disappointments that may have stopped others, and worked and created well into a highly productive ripe old age. And when the body no longer cooperates, the mind presses on. Think of Stephen Hawking, mentioned in another chapter, perhaps the greatest theoretical genius since Einstein, confined to a wheelchair, unable even to speak, but leading the world out of the darkness of subatomic and quantum physics and into the light with the astonishing power of his mind alone. Think of Carl Sagan, philosopher and astronomer, who was brainstorming with NASA officials on the design of the international space station right up until just a few days before he finally succumbed to cancer.

Larry Ellison, the quixotic billionaire chairman of Oracle Corp., keeps himself tuned for peak performance by living his life as a work of art in progress. He's an accomplished surfer and martial arts enthusiast who surfs and practices Zen Buddhism to relax. His California estate is a study in Oriental architecture, painting, and sculpture. Ellison learned long ago that there is no elixir like an active, aesthetic, and meditative approach to put life back into life—not unlike restoring blood to a choking heart.

> Larry Ellison, the quixotic billionaire chairman of Oracle Corp., learned long ago that there is no elixir like an active, aesthetic and meditative approach to put life back into life – not unlike restoring blood to a choking heart.

Help. The greatest gift any of us can offer is to enrich other people's lives with our own. And among the greatest ways to enrich other people's lives is to teach. Become a teacher and you fulfill your own destiny. But you need not be an educator to teach. When you are old enough to know something well, teach it. Curiously, some of our greatest learning comes from teaching (we've all heard the teacher say that she learned more from the students than the students learned from her). Teaching is a natural extension of ourselves. Everybody teaches—even if they don't know it. Mentors teach on the job. Doctors teach. Lawyers teach. Consultants teach. Executives teach.

> When you are old enough to know something well, teach it. Everybody teaches – even if they don't know it. Mentors teach on the job. Doctors teach. Lawyers teach. Consultants teach. Executives teach.

For example, Bill Mayer, the former president of Credit Suisse First Boston, went on to serve as dean and visiting lecturer at two business schools. Every year, retired senior executives from around the country move into graduate and undergraduate teaching positions. Thousands of others volunteer their knowledge and expertise, and still others farm themselves out as consultants to help remake old companies and start new ones.

But if you feel that teaching is not your bag, then give something else. Give encouragement. Give advice. Give guidance. Give your time, maybe even your money. Give something, because if you give nothing (it's true what they say in the Bible) you will very likely get next to nothing in return.

A woman friend of mine confided that her career did not take off until a mentor—her boss's boss—finally took notice of her and started giving her more responsibility. The immediate boss, unhappily, wound up out of a job when it became clear that he had felt threatened by the woman and her talent and had been deliberately stifling her progress within the firm. Today the woman is vice president of a large cosmetics company and rumored to be next in line for the top job. Her mentor is retired but remains a close personal friend and confidant.

> We add value to any equation if we make a process work better, redesign something so that it doesn't break, or simply leave a place better than when we found it.

Improve. We add value to any equation if we make a process work better, redesign something so that it doesn't break, or simply leave a place better than when we found it.

I spoke with an aircraft engineer who said the happiest days of his professional life were spent redesigning a jet engine that delivered twice the thrust with half the noise using a third less fuel.

The boss of a midsized company told me he went away on vacation only to return to find that his new executive assistant had come up with a bold new proposal for product distribution that wound up saving the company over a million dollars a year. Sometimes we improve things by helping people help themselves (making them accountable, but forgiving them their mistakes), or being part of a relief organization that, for example, feeds children who might otherwise not eat. The wisest among us have long since learned that the fullest lives are led by people who not only take satisfaction from helping other people, but also take pleasure in trying to improve, if only in some small way, whatever surrounds them.

Make it happen. Creativity, help, and improvement will all falter if we cannot somehow put them together to make things happen. The creative mind seeking to help and improve is itself a potent combination. But launch them all in the same direction behind a single objective and doors suddenly fly open.

That's why, with few exceptions, action is more desirable than inaction. Most of the successful people you know are in the habit of making things happen. That's how they became successful. Sometimes they wouldn't take no for an answer. Sometimes they had to leap over ineptitude or incompetence to get something done. Sometimes they had to take back ownership of their own ideas so those ideas would not die in other people's hands. Sometimes they had to stay up a little later, work a little harder, perform a little better than the next guy. Sometimes they had to just say no. Sometimes they had to just do it—when everybody else said it couldn't or shouldn't be done. You know these people. You may even be one of them yourself.

> Creativity, help and improvement will all falter if we cannot somehow put them together to make things happen. That's why action is more desirable than inaction. Most of the successful people you know are in the habit of making things happen. That's how they became successful.

part two

The Players:
How the Game Is Won

eight

The World's Greatest Business Magician:

How Steve Jobs Keeps Pulling Rabbits Out of Hats

D o you believe in magic?

Business, like other walks of life, has its magicians. And if there is a Houdini of business, it would have to be Steve Jobs, who retook center stage of his creation, Apple, just in time to perform arguably the greatest trick of his versatile career.

Just when critics and naysayers were about to bring down the final curtain on Apple's failing operetta, Jobs pulled a very big rabbit out of a hat.

In 1998 Jobs agreed to serve as interim CEO at the pioneering computer company he had founded, and from which he had been bounced as chairman in 1985. In the intervening years he started two new ventures: Next—a top-end, high performance computer manufacturer—and Pixar—the world's finest digital animation firm. Together, they have further fattened Jobs's personal fortune by hundreds of millions of dollars.

> The Apple story is an example of what can happen when you yank the creative leadership and visionary fire out of any company, and then just as suddenly throw it back in.

The Apple story is an example of what can happen when you yank the creative leadership and visionary fire out of any company, and then just as suddenly throw it back in.

After Jobs's forced departure, Apple went from being a technology leader and a cultural trendsetter to just another boring computer company that lost its way, but eventually even forgot who it was. A string of CEOs flailed away in a vain effort to put the company back on track, but nothing worked until the board persuaded the master himself to come home and work his inspired magic.

And it wasn't until then that things finally started to turn around for Apple.

Jobs took one look at what was going on and he could hardly believe his eyes. Right away, he slashed product lines from eighteen to four, reorganized the company to make departments more efficient, hired a new marketing chief, altered distribution to sell Macs only through resellers and stores committed to Apple, cut inventory to the bone to save costs, launched a vital software development program with Microsoft, swiftly mended a faltering software relationship with Adobe Systems, launched an employee equity plan to help encourage everybody to pull extra hard on the same oar, and helped spearhead Apple's first wildly successful product in years, the iMac. (Whew!)

What are the secrets to Jobs' success?

The answers are myriad and elusive, but if you listen to Jobs talk, you begin to recognize the constant that seems to saturate so many quirkily creative people: a joyous refusal to think like a grownup. Jobs may be a CEO several times over, but at heart he's still just a very bright teenager on an endless quest for excellence. In a *Fortune* interview shortly after returning to power at Apple, Jobs tried to explain where the magic comes from.

Fortune: You're 43. You've already made it big in business, yet you're not on the downward slope of your life yet. Have your motivations changed as a middle-ager?

Jobs: Somebody told me when I was 17 to live each day as if it were my last—and that one day I'd be right. . . I've never really cared about money that much. I guess what I'm trying to say is that I feel the same way now as when I was 17.

Fortune: Do you ever think you may be getting a little conservative?

Jobs: One of my role models is Bob Dylan. As I grew up, I learned the lyrics to all his songs and watched him never stand still. If you look at the artists, if they get really good, it always occurs to them at some point that they can do this one thing for the rest of their lives, and they can be really successful to the outside world, but not really be successful to themselves. That's the moment that an artist really decides who he or she is. If artists keep on risking failure, they're still artists. Dylan and Picasso were always risking failure.

This Apple thing is that way for me. . . even though I didn't know how bad things really were. . . I decided that I didn't really care, because this is what I want to do. If I try my best and fail, well, I tried my best.

What makes you become conservative is realizing that you have

> "One of my role models is Bob Dylan. As I grew up, I learned the lyrics to all his songs and watched him never stand still. If artists keep on risking failure, they're still artists. Dylan and Picasso were always risking failure."
>
> – STEPHEN JOBS

something to lose. Remember *The Whole Earth Catalog?* The last edition had a photo on the back cover of a remote country road... It was a beautiful shot and it had a caption that really grabbed me. It said, 'Stay hungry. Stay foolish.' It wasn't an ad for anything— just one of [*Whole Earth Catalog* founder] Stewart Brand's profound statements. It's wisdom. 'Stay hungry. Stay foolish.'

> Remember *The Whole Earth Catalog?* The last edition had a photo on the back cover of a remote country road. It said, 'Stay hungry. Stay foolish.' It's wisdom. 'Stay hungry. Stay foolish.'"
> — STEPHEN JOBS

Fortune: No regrets about business decisions?

Jobs: Sure, there are a zillion things I wish I'd done differently. But I think the things you most regret in life are things you didn't do. What you really regret was never asking that girl to dance.

In business, if I knew earlier what I know now, I'd have probably done some things a lot better... but so what? It's more important to be engaged in the present.

I'll give you a perfect example... I was reading this book by [physicist and Nobel laureate] Richard Feynmann. He had cancer, you know. In this book he was describing one of his last operations before he died. The doctor said to him, 'Look, Richard, I'm not sure you're going to make it.' And Feynmann made the doctor promise that if it became clear that he wasn't going to survive, to take away the anesthetic... Feynmann said to him, 'I want to feel what it's like to turn off.' That's a good way to put yourself in the present—to look at what's affecting you right now and be curious about it even if it's bad.

Fortune: People you've worked with say the word that best describes your management style is persistent. Where did you get your persistence?

Jobs: I don't think of it as persistence at all. When I was growing up, a guy across the street had a Volkswagen Bug. He really wanted to make it into a Porsche. He spent all his spare money and time accessorizing this VW, making it look and sound loud. By the time he was done, he did not have a Porsche. He had a loud, ugly VW.

You've got to be careful choosing what you're going to do. Once you pick something you really care about, and it's a worthwhile thing to do, then you can kind of forget about it and just work at it. The dedication comes naturally.

Fortune: You seem to enjoy building companies as much as you enjoy building products.

Jobs: The only purpose for me in building a company is so that it can make products. Of course, building a very strong company and a foundation of talent and culture is essential over the long run to keep making great products . . .

> "When I was growing up, a guy across the street had a Volkswagen Bug. He really wanted to make it into a Porsche. He spent all his spare money and time accessorizing this VW, making it look and sound loud. By the time he was done, he did not have a Porsche. He had a loud, ugly VW."
> — STEPHEN JOBS

Fortune: Still if you look at your first tenure at Apple, part of your goal was to build a new kind of company. You had much the same goal at Pixar.

Jobs: . . . I was lucky to get into computers when it was a very young and idealistic industry. . . no one was really in it for the money.

My heroes—Dave Packard, for example, left all his money to his foundation. Bob Noyce [the late cofounder of Intel] was another. . . I met Andy Grove when I was 21. I called him and told him I'd heard he was really good at operations and asked if I could take him out to lunch. I did that with others, too.

These guys were all company builders . . . There are people around here who start companies just to make money, but the great companies, well, that's not what they're about . . .

At Pixar one of the most satisfying things is that there are a lot of folks who don't really care about getting rich but who care a lot about the art or technology. Yet they will never have to worry about money for the rest of their lives. Their families can live in a nice house, and they can concentrate on what they really love to do. It's wonderful.

Fortune: Now that you've stabilized the ship, will Apple start pioneering again?

Jobs: The iMac is a pretty good indication of where we're headed. The whole strategy for Apple now is, if you will, to be the Sony of the computer business.

"I don't really believe that televisions and computers are going to merge. You go to your TV when you want to turn your brain off. You go to your computer when you want to turn your brain on . . ."

I don't really believe that televisions and computers are going to merge. I've spent enough time in entertainment to know that storytelling is . . . not interactive. You go to your TV when you want to turn your brain off. You go to your computer when you want to turn your brain on. . . .

There's this whole [computer] consumer market which hardly anybody with the right skills is focusing on. . . . Apple's the only PC company left that makes the whole widget—hardware and software. That means that Apple can decide that it will make a system dramatically easier to use, which is a great asset when you're going after consumers.

The technology isn't the hard part. The hard part is, What's the product? Or, Who's the customer? How are they going to buy it? How do you tell them about it? So besides having the ideas and the technology and the manufacturing, you have to have good marketing to reach the consumer.

Fortune: Can we expect Apple to move into related consumer electronics businesses?

Jobs: If Mercedes made a bicycle or a hamburger or a computer, I don't think there'd be much advantage in having its logo on it . . . There's nothing wrong with just being in the computer business . .

People focus too much on entirely new ideas . . . Most good products really are extensions of previous products.

For example, computers are still awful. They're too complicated and don't do what you really want them to do—or don't do those things as well as they could. We have a long way to go. People are still making automobiles after nearly 100 years. Telephones have been around a long time, but even so the cellular revolution was pretty exciting. That's why I think the computer revolution is still in its early stages. There's a lot of room for doing new and exciting things with the same basic product.

And as Jobs speaks and performs his magic, the whole backstage troupe of Apple scientific and design shamans is feverishly at work concocting the next-level iMac. It's just the kind of fertile creative tropical zone Jobs loves and lives for.

> "Computers are still awful. They're too complicated and don't do what you really want them to do. Telephones have been around a long time, but even so the cellular revolution was pretty exciting. That's why I think the computer revolution is still in its early stages."
>
> – STEPHEN JOBS

"The Mac is the expression of Steve's creativity, and Apple as a whole is an expression of Steve," Oracle chairman and close friend Larry Ellison told *Fortune*. "That's why, despite the 'interim' in his title, he'll stay at Apple a long time."

Adds Intel chairman Grove, a longtime Jobs admirer, "Steve will always be Steve. The only thing that will change is that he'll lose his hair."

nine

Shake and Make:

How Some of the Most Creative People in Business Perform Miracles

P robably the first person to identify the link between creativity and leadership was an obscure academic by the name of Dr. Abraham Maslow, who started writing about management back in the early 1960s before the Beatles were big and when the Corvair was a hot new car.

In 1962, Maslow, a Brandeis professor, took a summer sabbatical in a southern California electronics plant. The result of that visit was a small journal that would someday have a profound effect on later management giants like Peter Drucker.

The plant happened to be one of the first in America to deploy teams on the assembly line. Maslow saw that the system was good for morale and productivity. He began to write down his observations, and what he wrote was thirty years ahead of its time.

Way before personnel became human resources and before business books were popular, Maslow started talking about what he called "self actualization" and "continuous improvement." He coined the term, "enlightened management," and wrote about the benefits of "synergy." Put people in teams, let them figure things out themselves, recognize their good works, and creativity would begin to flow, he said.

"The more influence and power you give to someone else in the team situation, the more you have yourself. Generosity can increase wealth rather than decrease it."

> "The more influence and power you give to someone else in the team situation, the more you have yourself. Generosity can increase wealth rather than decrease it."
> —MODERN MANAGEMENT PIONEER DR. ABRAHAM MASLOW.

The right way to run a business is not through a chain reaction of cause and effect, but rather as a kind of "web" in which "every part is related to every other part," he wrote. Maslow even recognized that a fixation on short-term results was often at the expense of long-term growth. He actually foresaw the day when companies would include human capital and customer goodwill in financial statements. And it's interesting to note that before he died in 1970—and twenty years before the collapse of the Soviet Union—Maslow predicted a "post Marxian" workplace, a triumph of democracy and good business practices "as revolutionary as the ideas of Galileo, Darwin, or Freud."

Maslow was a pioneer and deserves the lion's share of credit for the forces of good that are changing the way we will work in the twenty-first century. But you need not be a visionary to notice a relationship between creativity and leadership. It's arguably true that a leader devoid of creativity is no leader at all, and that creative business people are either comfortable in leadership roles or lead by example.

You may even go so far as to say that creativity and leadership are two sides to the same coin.

Way before Tom Peters and his landmark book, *In Search of Excellence*, Konosuke Matsushita was writing the book on leadership, risk-taking and new ways to go to market. He didn't spend a lot of time making art, but he unleashed all his creative talent in a tsunami of inspiration that built a startup into Panasonic, the world's largest consumer products firm, and paved the way for generations of enlightened managers to come.

> As far back as the 1930s, Konosuke Matsushita was already preaching his gospel—a set of management aphorisms inspired by a trip to a Japanese temple complex where he was surprised to find people happily working for no money.

As far back as the 1930s, Konosuke Matsushita was already preaching his gospel—a set of management aphorisms inspired by a trip to a Japanese temple complex where he was surprised to find people happily working for no money. The eye-opening lesson he gleaned from that experience was that if people feel they are performing meaningful work, they will be happier and more productive.

Revelations followed:

- Treat people you do business with as if they were family.
- Service, not the sale, creates permanent customers.
- Being conscientious on the job is never enough: always think of yourself as completely in charge of your job and responsible for your work.
- If you can't make a profit with society's money, people, and resources, you are committing a crime against society.

But while he saw profit as a very good thing, his business philosophy came down to nothing less than a liberating proclamation for all mankind: "The mission of a manufacturer should be to overcome poverty, to relieve society as a whole from misery, and bring it wealth."

Matsushita's vision may have been a little ambitious, but his legend lives on at Panasonic where even today workers still sing the company anthem and recite Matsushita's business principles.

Another Japanese pioneer, Toyota founder Kiichiro Toyoda, took one look at American supermarkets and knew he'd found a better way to build cars. Toyota noticed that American supermarkets order what they need almost on a daily basis—because if food sits too long on shelves it rots, and because most markets can't afford the added space and costs for storage. Toyota applied this "just in time" approach to his production lines. The result: no more parts warehousing, better coordination of production, higher efficiencies all around, and impressive cost savings. Today, "just in time" is the standard for car makers in the United States and Europe and a way of life for hundreds of other industries all over the world.

> Toyota founder Kiichiro Toyoda noticed that American supermarkets order what they need almost on a daily basis – because if food sits too long on shelves it rots, and because most markets can't afford the added space and costs for storage. Toyota applied this "just in time" approach to his production lines.

If you want to see an almost perfect marriage of business and creativity, look no further than Bill Gates, about whom enough has been written to fill a library. Suffice it to say that Gates almost single-handedly launched the PC revolution, then a few years later turned his massive company around on a dime to chase the Web, then altered the future of TV by artfully steering television towards the day (not far distant) when it will be more like a PC than a TV, then led the charge to capture the corporate intranet business. We're talking here about a man who is central to historical technology revolutions that will forever change the way we live.

If you're lucky enough to recognize your creative potential at an early age, it's probably safe to say that you'll stay a creative soul all your days. Such is the case with Joseph Engelberger, the father of the industrial robot, who at age seventy-one was trying to earn a new moniker: father of the home robot. "Common sense tells you home robots have got to end up a bigger market than factory robots," says Engelberger, who, on the way to realizing his dream, has designed hospital robots that deliver meals, medications, X-rays, and patients' records—freeing up doctors and nurses for more important tasks. At last report, he was looking for a financial backer to help him finally move into the home.

> If you're lucky enough to recognize your creative potential at an early age, it's probably safe to say that you'll stay a creative soul all your days.

Engelberger knows that to exercise your creativity you've got to be prepared to try whatever works. So does eccentric trading whiz Victor Niederhoffer, one of Wall Street's high priests of economic voodoo, who admits that the *National Enquirer* is "the only newspaper I ever read." Niederhoffer, a onetime Harvard squash champ, uses the tabloid as a research tool. To get a handle on commodities, Niederhoffer patterns his trades on fluctuations in Beethoven's musical scores such as the "Moonlight Sonata." And to spot easy pickings, Niederhoffer relies on what he calls "Lo Bagola," a trading pattern named after an African writer who noticed that rampaging elephants almost always exit a village the same way they come in—like panicky speculators in fast-moving markets.

If Niederhoffer is crazy, he's crazy like a fox. He makes money—sometimes a lot of money—on three of every four trades.

Ever seen an elephant jump? It's unlikely you ever will. But that's exactly what Chase Manhattan, America's biggest bank, had to do to launch itself into the future. Chase Vice Chairman William B. Harrison Jr. saw a hole and drove his entire team right through it. On the other side, he found himself in a whole new ball game. Chase was the first major U.S. retail bank to go head-to-head with Wall Street in underwriting U.S. equities. Says Harrison: "If you want to play with the big boys and offer a wide range of products all over the world, public equity is something you have to have." Even better, have it first.

> To spot easy pickings, eccentric trading whiz Victor Niederhoffer relies on what he calls "Lo Bagola," a trading pattern named after an African writer who noticed that rampaging elephants almost always exit a village the same way they come in—like panicky speculators in fast-moving markets.

Mergers and acquisitions super lawyer Stephen Volk's unusual talent is that he's a patient listener who moves with lightning speed when he's heard enough to know what he's got to do. Unlike the hostile bid takeover artists of yesteryear who thrived on confrontation, soft-spoken Volk seeks common ground with a real talent for untangling knotty legal issues, soothing enormous egos, and closing tough deals. A few of those deals: Morgan Stanley and Dean, Witter; Sandoz and Ciba-Geigy; British Telecommunications and MCI.

Volk is used to tangling with the Masters of the Universe who conduct business in the savage metaphors of Wall Street, where you often hear people talking about hunters and skinners— as in "Bob is a hunter," or "Tom is a skinner." No doubt, you flash to images of men in camouflage stalking stags in the forest or flaying and gutting hanging carcasses with sharp knives dripping gore.

I confess I did. When I heard traders and brokers and investment bankers talking about hunters and skinners, I couldn't help but imagine all the carnage. The language itself seems appropriate for a profession that has been known to glory in predation and conquest. When one speaks of being "killed," "shot," or "ambushed" on Wall Street, one is not talking about war and death but about careers and jobs. "Take no prisoners" is simply another way to describe transactions, as are "heart shot," "flesh wound," "walking wounded," "execution," and "kill or be killed." On Wall Street, you don't just rip your client off, you "rip the client's face off."

Yet even here in this world of men figuratively killing other men (and women) and women figuratively killing other women (and men), hunters and skinners embrace in a creative dance that keeps the money pouring in. The hunter makes things happen: finds the deal, bags it, secures the transaction, brings home the bacon. The hunter generates revenue, creates the magic that makes bonuses a happy reality.

Once the deal is secured, the hunter dumps the "carcass" back at the "camp" (the office) and steps out on the hunt again—leaving the skinners to strip the hide and cut the kill into manageable pieces. The skinners are all the professionals who labor day in, day out at the

> Masters of the Universe conduct business in the savage metaphors of Wall Street, where you often hear people talking about hunters and skinners – as in, "Bob is a hunter," or "Tom is a skinner." Hunters can't be hunters without skinners, and skinners wouldn't have anything to do without hunters.

business of moving tons of paper and "dressing the carcass" for distribution and consumption. It's like an assembly line and it has worked well for generations. Hunters can't be hunters without skinners, and skinners wouldn't have anything to do without hunters. But of the two categories, it is said—never publicly—that the hunter is far and away the most vital to the business.

Yet curiously, both the hunter and the skinner have to demonstrate creativity just to survive. In the highly compact and competitive world of investment banking, it takes a hunter's instincts and ingenuity to recognize opportunity and seize it; to position the deal, strike quickly, woo other parties, close the transaction. Back at the office, it takes yet another kind of creativity to divide the spoils, get top dollar for the players, spin off possible second-tier transactions, and find ways to generate new products from what's left on the table.

Clearly, then, a creative approach is a winning approach. But common sense will tell you that hunters are usually best working alone, and that for every ten or so skinners you're only going to need one hunter. Problems arise at the big banks when the ratio of skinners to hunters begins to look more like twenty to one. At that point, all the creativity in the world isn't going to carry the day, because there very likely won't be much of a day to carry.

In the high-stakes world of bigtime advertising, the greatest creative challenge is not the quick kill but the shortest line with the widest impact. That means writing for the ear, not the eye. Write for the ear and the eye will follow. No one knows this better than ad people who over the years have come up with some

In the high-stakes world of bigtime advertising, the greatest creative challenge is the shortest line with the widest impact. Write for the ear and the eye will follow.

memorably catchy slogans. Here are just a few:

> One-time presidential contender and full time media baron Steve Forbes boiled his world view down to two words: *flat tax.*

> Just do it (Nike)
> Coke is it (Coca Cola)
> Be all you can be (The U.S. Army)
> Where do you want to go today? (Microsoft)
> Not your father's automobile (Oldsmobile)
> Where's the beef? (Burger King)
> We want to be your airline (TWA)
> Got milk? (The Dairy Council)

Then there's onetime presidential contender and full-time media baron Steve Forbes, who boiled his worldview down to two words: *flat tax.* The most creative writing— and, like haiku, the most admired—is invariably the simplest.

Running an insurance business requires the same artful economies. Just ask Kaj Ahlmann, former CEO of Employer's Reinsurance, which generates 25 percent of GE's powerhouse GE Capital division. Ahlmann has the mind of a steel trap but the playful nature of a free spirit. One day at headquarters in Kansas City, he decided it was time for an adventure, so he packed a bunch of junior people into his big, red Chevy Suburban and set out over the plains on a spot check of satellite offices. By the time the Danish-born Ahlmann and his merry band made it back to the office a couple of days later, their seemingly madcap escapade had produced five brand-new financial services products that added several million dollars to corporate profits.

Robert Shillman, CEO of Cognex, puts on a Three Stooges routine to welcome new hires. To keep morale and motivation on a roll, he's been known to chuck $10,000 cash bonuses from a Brinks truck, and reward 15-year veterans with trips to exotic places.

"We had a lot of fun," Ahlmann said later. "And of course we talked business—because that's the only thing we all had in common. We were all together on a little journey in a very small space. The result was we got more done on that one outing than in a whole month of meetings."

Getting the best out of people is usually no laughing matter. But Robert Shillman, CEO of Cognex, goes for the yuks every time. Shillman, a former MIT professor, even goes so far as to personally puts on a Three Stooges routine to welcome new hires. He calls his people "Cognoids" and likes to lead the entire company in the corporate anthem, accompanied by an employee rock band. To keep morale and motivation on a roll, he's been known to chuck $10,000 cash bonuses from a Brinks truck and reward fifteen-year veterans with trips to exotic places.

"Our antics break down barriers between managers and workers," Shillman explains. He must be doing something right. Cognex was recently ranked fifty-second in a *Fortune* magazine list of the fastest-growing companies.

The creative mind sees expansion in offbeat places. Take the curious case of Cuba, Castro, and the Canadians.

Just about every imaginative capitalist nation except the United States sees Cuba as an economic wet dream just waiting to happen. For example, while America views Cuba as an obstacle, Canada looks at Cuba as an opportunity. While America postures and makes a lot of political noise about Castro, Canada rushes in and sets up a beachhead for the spectacular economic invasion that is sure to follow. Leading the charge is far-thinking Canadian Ian Delaney, chairman of Sheritt International Corp., an energy and mining company that has the biggest western presence in Cuba. Delaney wooed Castro like a wolf on the make and wound up in bed with the Red. If it's true that first to market gets the market, Sheritt has already eclipsed any like-minded ambitions from U.S. corporations on the island.

> Just about every imaginative capitalist nation except the U.S. sees Cuba as an economic wet dream just waiting to happen. While America postures and makes a lot of political noise about Castro, Canada rushes in and sets up a beachhead for the spectacular economic invasion that is sure to follow.

"Cuba is the best investment opportunity in the world," Delaney declares flatly. If he's right, his contrarian willingness to court Castro, take risks, and buck the United States will pay off perhaps even beyond his wildest dreams.

Meanwhile, closer to home, creative marketers are figuring out that the middle class is shrinking, while the upper and lower classes are growing. So they've invented something called two-tier marketing. For example, Banana Republic sells tony jeans for $48, while its Old Navy stores sell a similar version for $22. Both chains are doing a bang-up business. General Motor's Saturn sells new cars to the monied folk, and "pre-owned" Saturns to less prosperous customers. Phone companies offer so-called phone arcades for the economically challenged and glitzy high-end cellular bells and whistles to the affluent. (Motorola launched a $3,000 satellite phone for globetrotting execs.) Even food is seeing a revolution. "The $4 meal is doing all right," notes one consultant of cuisine, "and the $50 meal is doing all right. It's the $20 meal that's in trouble."

As the middle class continues to deteriorate and the gap between the haves and have-nots looms ever larger, and as both ends of the spectrum start splintering into market-ripe factions, clever marketing people will be there to make sure nothing stays on the shelves for very long.

Sometimes creativity means just being able to see things as they really are.

American Express president Kenneth Chenault suffers no illusions about why his company found itself out of favor with a lot of commercial clients.

"We've said in the past that the company was arrogant and not realistic about the competitive environment," he said. Translation: we were charging merchants too much for every transaction. "Over the last four years we've become very externally focused." Translation: we're cozying up to the people we've alienated and offering to charge less.

The word on Main Street and Wall Street is that American Express is finally waking up from a long orgy of obnoxious self-indulgence that left a lot of people, especially small business owners, shopkeepers, and restaurants, feeling like American Express had been taking advantage for too long. With its new user-friendly approach, it's now possible that Amex will generate enough good will to win back old friends.

Jim Oates, president of the Leo Burnett advertising company, derives his ferocious work ethic, management style, and a big part of his creative drive from famed coach Woody Hayes. The ad man remembers several Hayes anecdotes that helped shape his career:

"I remember Hayes telling the story about the farm kid who asked his coach how he could become physically stronger. Coach told him that the way to get stronger was to go out every single day and lift a calf. By the end of the summer, the coach told the kid he'd be very strong. For me the message was I had to learn something new every day— and even today I still try to learn something new every day.

> You don't make a touchdown on every single play. You deal with it in pieces. Break it down into sections that are manageable. One step at a time all the way to the goal line.

"Another Hayes principle that influenced me is that you don't make a touchdown on every single play. You deal with it in pieces. Break it down into sections that are manageable. So today I treat big projects and big problems the same way: One step at a time all the way to the goal line.

"The third thing Hayes taught me—he even wrote a book about it—is that you win with people. It's people, their quality, their drive, their discipline, that makes any organization successful. It worked for Woody and it's worked for me."

In the combative computer arena, it's tough to wrestle such sumo heavyweights as Compaq, IBM, Hewlett-Packard, Apple, and Digital. But Dell Computer founder Michael Dell found a way to not only stay out of the ring, but perhaps even beat the giants at their own game—and become a giant himself.

Early on, Dell saw a hole in the market and drove a truck right through it.

Unlike its competitors, Dell doesn't develop dazzling new hardware technology. Dell simply assembles and sells dependable computers, then bypasses the industry network of manufacturers, distributors, and resellers to sell directly to the customers. In fact, Dell doesn't build a computer until it gets an order.

When the Web came along it made a good business even better. In addition to a constant flood of phone orders, Dell was now getting thousands more daily on the Net.

"The only thing better would be mental telepathy," says Dell, who expects his business to keep right on moving, and then outpace the industry via the Internet.

British entrepreneur Felix Dennis loosed his creativity—and made a fortune—by staying slightly ahead of the wave.

"I have one talent," says Dennis, "and that's figuring out what people want about two minutes before they know it themselves."

Back in the 1970s, Dennis came up with the idea of producing collectors magazines for some of the biggest movie blockbusters of all time, including *Star Wars* and *E.T.* In the '80s, just as Apple's Macintosh was taking off, he launched *MacUser*, Europe's first Macintosh magazine. Later, he sold the American version to Ziff-Davis for $26 million. In the 1990s he made another $83 million by selling his stake in a computer mail-order company he founded. Recently he announced plans to launch a new men's magazine in the United States.

"American men's magazines are boring," Dennis says. "They take themselves so seriously. *GQ* is for men who like socks better than sex." Clearly, Dennis likes sex better than socks. And with his spicy new publication, the shoe may finally be on the other foot in men's magazines.

IBM CEO Lou Gerstner's creative talent is an uncommon aptitude for problem-solving and an uncanny feel for what works. Some people think he did the near impossible when he single-handedly saved IBM from self-immolation, then wrestled the giant back to relatively good health—making painful decisions (for IBM employees, not shareholders) and bucking scornful naysayers all the way.

"Lou revels in complexity, and this is five-dimensional chess," says Larry Ricciardi, an old pal and IBM's top legal beagle.

And when it comes to getting everybody playing the same tune, Gerstner knows how to rally the troops.

> IBM CEO Lou Gerstner's creative talent is an uncommon aptitude for problem-solving and an uncanny feel for what works.

"There is no place to hide in 1997," he told employees in an annual worldwide speech. "This is the year of reckoning for all of us— 1994 was the year we proved we could survive; 1995 was the year we stabilized; 1996 was the year we showed we could grow; 1997 is going to be the year we have to show we can lead. We have no more excuses. We can't say we're still getting our act together."

Straight talk from a straight shooter. The jury is still out on IBM, but had Gerstner not stepped into the top slot in 1993, the case might not have even made it to trial.

When Towers Perrin, the big human resources consulting firm got an assignment from Nissan U.S.A. to set up a workplace diversity program, they missed a chance to strut their stuff and show how good they really are.

According to the *Wall Street Journal*, Towers Perrin's pitch eventually came down to this: We'll study your company in detail and then customize a program to fit your needs.

The Towers Perrin credo: "Prescription without diagnosis is malpractice."

But when Towers Perrin submitted a study four months, 121 pages, and $105,000 later, the Nissan U.S.A. people were less than impressed. The prescription, Nissan said, was "so broad, so generic, we didn't think it reflected what we thought we were going to get . . . it did not seem to be particularly tailored to Nissan."

It wasn't. On the very day it submitted its recommendations to Nissan, Towers Perrin submitted a "strikingly similar" report to Thomson Electronics. In fact, all nine major recommendations made to Thomson matched Nissan's word for word. The same for all fifty-four accompanying "tactics and objectives" and all thirteen elements of a proposed implementation plan.

Further research by the *Wall Street Journal* revealed that the "vast majority" of advice given to seven Towers Perrin clients was "identical."

Now what, we have to ask ourselves, was Towers Perrin's management thinking? Were the boys and girls at Towers Perrin unaware of that old kindergarten adage which basically says that the truth has an embarrassing way of making itself known?

Here's a clear case of a company that ignored its creative potential—only to pay the penalty for that neglect in the form of eventual public humiliation.

GTE Chairman Chuck Lee remembers attending Harvard Business School with a group of assorted corporate geniuses from companies all over the world. One day he wound up in a project team competing in a computer simulation game with talented managers on other teams. Each team, convinced it had the smartest people, was certain of victory. But in the end Chuck's team lost—because every time they met, one of the geniuses on Chuck's team came up with a brand new plan. Moral of the story: Teamwork is critical, and don't keep changing the plan. Further moral: First make sure your plan is a good one, then stick to it. That's Chuck Lee's creative talent: coming up with a good plan, inspiring and motivating the players, then helping drive the plan to a successful conclusion.

Leonard Riggio did for the book business what Home Depot did for the hardware business. Riggio, CEO of bookselling megastore Barnes & Noble, has always thought big. In fact, he says that when he was in college, "If I had gotten a job at a hardware store, I would have been Home Depot today."

> Barnes & Noble CEO Leonard Riggio bought a then sleepy, ailing Manhattan bookstore called Barnes & Noble back in 1971, and the book business hasn't been the same since. Riggio consolidated the industry, virtually single-handedly creating the superstore concept.

Riggio bought a then sleepy, ailing Manhattan bookstore called Barnes & Noble back in 1971, and the book business hasn't been the same since. Riggio consolidated the industry, virtually single-handedly creating the superstore concept. It was Riggio who came up with the sweeping discount idea that drew new customers by the tens of thousands. It was Riggio who opened on Sundays and put in climate-controlled village squares with cappuccino, comfy chairs, cooking demonstrations, even clowns.

"He understands how to make it all work," says bestselling author Nora Ephron, "like everything else in America—as a theme park."

Independent bookstores complain about the theme park approach, which has hoovered away a lot of their business. But Riggio says he's just getting started. He plans to grow the new online division and add 500 more superstores.

The man who gives Barnes & Noble headaches is Amazon.com founder Jeffrey Bezos, who skyrocketed from chump change to billionaire in less time than it took to attend his alma mater, Princeton. The son of a Cuban refugee, Bezos early on began to show signs of the creative fire that would later shape the world's first Internet book order company.

When Amazon.com founder Jeffrey Bezos was still a preschooler, he became so deeply engrossed in tasks that teachers had to pick him up and move him—still in his chair—to his next activity.

When he was still a preschooler, he became so deeply engrossed in tasks that teachers had to pick him up and move him—still in his chair—to his next activity. As a teenager, he tried to design a hovercraft from a vacuum cleaner and turn an umbrella into a solar oven. In high school, he set up what he called the DREAM institute, a summer school program designed to ignite creative thinking in other kids. In college he lunged into computer sciences and soon after that suddenly found himself the youngest-ever senior vice president at investment banker D. E. Shaw & Co., charged with finding cool Net ideas to invest in.

And it wasn't long after that that Bezos saw an opportunity and quit to chase his new dream. He worked up a business plan, found investors, and set up operations in Seattle. Then he named his new baby Amazon, opened up business on the Web, and the rest is history.

Former Israeli Prime Minister Benjamin Netanyahu is a national leader whose creative knack is thinking like a business leader. In an interview with *Business Week*, Netanyahu could have been mistaken for any hard charging CEO. His vision for Israel's economy?

"We're not built for low-knowledge, high-discipline industries; we're made for high-knowledge, low-discipline industries. . . . Changing production, and marketing because of the computer revolution fit the Israeli work-force like a hand in glove . . . Israel is the Silicon Valley of the Eastern Hemisphere. . . The only things holding us back are the concentration in the economy and the anachronistic socialist restraints that have to be discarded."

> Former Israeli Prime Minister Benjamin Netanyahu is a national leader whose creative knack is thinking like a business leader.

How quickly can Israel grow?

"We can double gross domestic product per capita in 10 to 12 years. But that will more than double the economy, because the population will grow because of immigration."

Aren't there limits to growth in such a small land?

Netanyahu's vision of Israel as a prosperous high-tech business machine, and his ability to articulate that vision, may in the end do more for the citizens of Israel than any government program could ever hope to accomplish.

"What we have to do is increase the supply of knowledge workers. Our high-technology industries need an infusion of 15,000 high-quality technologists, programmers and so on."

What hopes does he have for regional economic integration?

"I think you have three economies in the Middle East. The have-nots who have nothing. Then the haves who have oil, basically a single-crop economy, and Israel, which is increasingly a post-industrial economy."

Netanyahu's vision of Israel as a prosperous high-tech business machine, and his ability to articulate that vision, may in the end do more for the citizens of Israel than any government program could ever hope to accomplish.

Intel Chairman Andy Grove's philosophy is simple: Make pricey, sophisticated chips to serve an ever-growing demand for PC's. To that end, he is investing in dozens of industry-related companies, exploring exciting new chip-based technologies, building huge new plants every nine months or so, and creating new laboratories to develop products for the future. Intel engineers and scientists are pushing digital photography, for example, and developing 3-D, multimedia, and virtual reality applications for markets all over the world. Intel is in a creative frenzy, you might say, staying ahead of the game on the theory that all ships rise with the tide.

"Our primary objective is to grow the market for all products, not just Intel products," says Craig Kunrie, director of the Intel

Architecture Labs. Even competitors are pleased: "Anything they do that creates demand for computing power is a good thing," admits Jerry Sanders, CEO of rival AMD. "The whole industry is pulled along by their spending."

Big money, big talent, and lots of brain power are an almost unstoppable formula for success at Intel, which keeps right on blazing new territory and building whole markets in good times and bad.

> Big money, big talent, and lots of brain power are an almost unstoppable formula for success at Intel, which keeps right on blazing new territory and building whole markets in good times and bad.

Being creative can mean being contrarian. The unthinkable became thinkable when labor chieftain Douglas McCarron turned his cozy world upside down and brought corporate slash-and-burn tactics to the United Brotherhood of Carpenters.

"Who says you're entitled to a lifetime job just because you work at a union?" asks McCarron, who fired one third of his staff, eliminated whole departments, and outsourced some functions, such as printing. Howls of protest went up from local leaders when he eliminated some councils and locals. But shock turned to admiration when McCarron's leaner nationwide organization helped councils mount more effective organization drives. In just half a year, the union brought in 1,300 new members.

For McCarron, running a successful union is no different from running a successful business: First you cut costs, then you become more productive, then you grow. As for the naysayers: "People have got to understand," he says, "that we're here to deliver the best possible product for members' dues money."

America's unionized carpenters are likely getting more than they thought they were paying for.

Millions of people struggle to wring the best performance they can out of themselves in whatever they do. But sometimes it's just dumb luck or fate that wins the day. We've all heard, for example, of scientific breakthroughs that happen quite by accident. Such an accident at the University of Maryland may someday prove to be the end of AIDS. A researcher accidentally put female mice in a cage with males who had been injected with cells of Kaposi's sarcoma, an AIDS-related cancer. That mistake should have ruined the experiment. But when the females became pregnant, the researcher was amazed to discover that the pregnant mice were basically immune to Kaposi's sarcoma. It turned out that a hormone in pregnant mice kills Kaposi cells. Even more interesting, an early trial with a handful of cases showed that the same hormone kills the AIDS cancer in humans, too.

Stanley Matthews lived a nightmare but wound up in a dream world of his own making. Matthews is no executive—nor would he want to be—but he can teach us all about how to rebuild a useful, even creative, life from ashes.

Stanley was a London cabbie whose world came down on him—literally—when at age twelve a wall collapsed as he played among ruins. From that day forward, Stanley's life would never be the same. Months later, when he awoke from a coma in a hospital, he could neither remember who he was nor recognize his parents. He drooled, soiled himself, and couldn't eat without help. Doctors declared him a hopeless case and urged that he be committed to an institution for the mentally ill. But Stanley's dad, a lorry driver, wouldn't hear of it. He took the boy home and spent the better part of two years struggling to give Stanley back his life.

But in the end, even the father finally threw in the towel. "Stanley," he said, "you may be an idiot, but you're still my son, so I'm going to teach you how to fend for yourself."

Years later, Stanley recalled: "That's when me dad taught me to steal. He taught me well, he did, but he always told me never to take more than I needed."

So Stanley took up thieving and got by. But sometime around his eighteenth birthday he began to wake up. First, he retaught himself how to read, then write (block letters only), then enrolled in the Army. For the first time in years, he actually looked and felt normal. It wasn't long before he was married, then a father. One of his two sons took up tennis and it was Stanley who, day in and day out, encouraged the boy to be the seventh ranked player in England and to play Wimbledon. Stanley put himself through the five years of study and special training required to obtain a London cabdriver's license and settled into a job that was to last until his sixty-fifth year, in 1998. Then without missing a beat, he set up a workshop in his back yard and plunged into a second career of building toy castles and doll houses.

Characteristically, Stanley Matthews had never built a single toy castle or doll house in his life. It was just something he wanted to do and that was all there was to it. "I knew I could do it," Stanley explained, "because the thing I've learned in this life is that you can do anything you like."

Now any day of the week you can find Stanley Matthews in the shop behind his house in Kent creating the stuff of dreams. He's in his third and possibly final adventure, but he says his heart is full and his soul is content. "I'm doing just what I want to do," he says. "Who could ask for anything more?"

When three entrepreneurial twenty-somethings from famous wine-making families got together to try to attract gen Xers away from martinis and designer beer and back to wine, they set out to change the staid chateaux-and-vineyards image of fine wines and try to make wine way cool. To do that, the Wine Brats, as they call themselves, hold Wine Rave parties in trendy nightspots and put out a hip newsletter, *WINEX*, which pokes fun at stuffy wine jargon and etiquette. *WINEX* runs stories on toothpaste tastings and hangovers, and its seminars are a hoot. In one, for example, they tell how to pair wine with popcorn, Doritos, chips, and salsa while TV sets play reruns of *I Love Lucy* and *Happy Days*. The jury is still out, but the Wine Brats are convinced they're building a future market of loyal wine aficionados who would rather sip a Pouilly-Fuissé than chug a Pilsner.

Hollywood is famous for its creativity, but Hollywood executives have taken creativity to a new level of discipline. They've hired a battle-hardened Marine veteran to put authentic grit, spit, and polish onto the big screen. "Drill Sergeant to the Stars," Captain Dale Dye, who served three tours

Hollywood executives have taken creativity to a new level of discipline. They've hired a battle-hardened Marine veteran to put authentic grit, spit, and polish onto the big screen.

and took three bullets in Vietnam, runs a kind of boot camp for war movies to make sure stars get it right.

"You can't portray a good military man unless you've walked a mile in his boots," says Captain Dye, who helped Oliver Stone make *Platoon*, one of the most wrenchingly realistic war flicks of all time. Later, he worked with Tom Hanks and other actors on Steven Spielberg's powerfully authentic World War II film, *Saving Private Ryan*. Dye forbade the actors to use their real names. His opening address at the *Private Ryan* boot camp set an unmistakable tone: "This may be a short-term job for you, pal, but it's a crusade for me," he growled. "I promise you one little thing, shit-for-brains: You will not be allowed to disgrace or dishonor the people who laid their lives on the line for this country. I will not have it. Once you understand it, you will not have it either."

The cast got the message, then spent a week crawling and sleeping in mud, drilling with bayonets, scouting with a compass, and learning to speak like soldiers spoke sixty years ago.

Does your company need a Captain Dye?

Creativity breeds activity and activity breeds longevity. Earle Jorgensen is 100 years old and still having a blast helping run the California steel company he founded in 1921. And just to make sure the good times continue to roll, Jorgensen, now chairman emeritus, gets up three times a week at 5 A.M. with his wife, now in her eighties, to work out with a personal trainer. Then it's straight to the office.

> Creativity breeds activity and activity breeds longevity.

"I've always worked, see," Jorgensen tells a visitor, "I'm too busy to die."

Jorgensen just loves to go to work, which seems to be a characteristic of people who not only achieve their professional goals but

> A smile and a sparkle in the eye through the good days and the bad, the fat years and the lean, seems to work as well—or better—than any magic potion known to man.

actually live long enough to enjoy the rewards of their achievement. A smile and a sparkle in the eye through the good days and the bad, the fat years and the lean, seems to work as well—or better—than any magic potion known to man. Throw in an active, adventurous mind that treats the whole business of life as one big delightful game and you've got somebody like fifty-one-year-old Dennis Koslowski, CEO of Tyco International, whose creative talent is deal-making. In sheer volume, Dennis may hold some kind of record: Since 1992, he's bought no less than eighty-eight companies—including U.S. Surgical—for $15 billion, and counting.

He's been having such a rocking good time that for five years running he's missed one of his greatest passions, the annual sail race from Newport, Rhode Island, to Bermuda. But he doesn't mind, because Koslowski and creative people generally enjoy whatever journey they happen to be on at a given time, whether it's at the helm of a racing yacht or behind a desk in the executive suite.

Seventy-two-year-old Brewster Kopp is on just such a journey. Kopp is retired from a successful LBO career—but not from life. "It's much more blessed to give than to receive. I'm more sure of that than ever," says Kopp, whose deals are now humanitarian and charity-based. "I'm more of a workaholic now than ever. But now I can choose every day what I get to do. I feel like a kid in a candy store."

Kopp gives 90 percent of his time to charities, including helping run the $20 million International Bible Society investment portfolio, and says he does indeed, feel blessed. He also helps manage the Stewardship Fund, which advises the wealthy on giving. "There's a lot of money floating around," he explains, "I try to help find that money a good home." Every time a big chunk of change finds a good home, Kopp finds peace of mind.

Executives at Aramark created a way to feed a market that's been hungry a long time. They've come up with a fancy menu for upscale fans in the most expensive seats at sporting events. Instead of just beer, hot dogs, and Cracker Jacks, tony fans can now also order chef salads, white wine, and mesquite chicken through vendors carrying hand-held computers. Moments later, the orders are rushed direct from the kitchen to the spectators.

Meanwhile, marketers in the health snacks industry have noticed that green—the color green—is very good for business. When researchers discovered that consumers believe almost any food, even cookies or cheese, is probably good for them as long as it comes in green packaging, they started seeing the color of money. As reported in *Business Week*, top brands Snackwell and Healthy Choice use green packaging, and the makers of Famous Amos Cookies and Hershey chocolate bars now use green wrap for some low-fat products. Green is such a hit, in fact, that the Snackwell people now say they plan to package all their products--even the higher-fat foods—in green.

> Marketers in the health snacks industry have noticed that green—the color green—is very good for business.

IBM, Hewlett-Packard, 3Com, and Intel saw the color of money in another trend—the emerging market for home networks—and stepped in to meet the demand. With more families now having two or more PCs in the house, the digital heavyweights set up an alliance to design products to let home computers talk to one another or share a common printer. Catching the wave before the wave caught them, the digital big boys can now surf the home PC network market all the way to the bank.

Business itself rides on a wave of creativity. In just one week, *Business Week* reported on a tiny turbine engine being developed to power laptops; a new high-tech toy that lets virtual skiers wearing simulation headsets "feel" moguls through weak electrical signals to the scalp; a new micro needle that allows scientists to analyze material one atom at a time; and new fences that can kill millions of mosquitoes by bringing them to sticky deaths in mineral oil through a chemical lure that imitates an old mosquito favorite, buffalo breath. The constant rising tide of new products and new ideas day in and day out help keep the ships of commerce afloat.

> The constant rising tide of new products and new ideas day in and day out help keep the ships of commerce afloat.

One idea that seems to have more buoyancy than others gives the term, "Tennis, anyone?" new meaning. When the Penn Racquet Sports people, America's number one maker of tennis balls, saw tennis ball sales flatten in a decade-long lull in recreational tennis, they decided to throw their business to the dogs. Thus was born R. P. Fetchem's, a "natural fetch toy" for canines, made of felt and sporting a price tag almost double what you'd expect to pay for a can of regular tennis balls. "Ten times more people own pets than play tennis," explains Penn President Gregg R. Weida. Dog owners aren't flinching. In fact, they're biting. With dog toys selling for as much as $26, R. P. Fetchem's look like a bargain and consumers are snapping them up.

All the creative thinking in the world may do you no good if people don't get what you are trying to tell them.

When William Foulke Jr., former chairman of Provident National Bank, left the Navy as a young officer and Admiral's aide after World War II, the last thing the Admiral said as Foulke walked out the door was, "Bill, you've got what it takes. You can go far. But first you've got to fix something. . . First you've go to learn how to speak to people."

> All the creative thinking in the world may do you no good if people don't get what you are trying to tell them.

Foulke took the Admiral's advice and enrolled immediately in a Dale Carnegie course. "It changed my life," Foulke recalled. "I remember two things especially. Carnegie spoke to our class and said, 'The first minute is always the hardest. Once you get through the first minute, almost anyone can be a good speaker.' The second thing I remember he taught us was that if you're not nervous, you're probably not going to do a very good job."

Foulke was an apt student. He overcame his fear of speaking, took a job with a bank, and never looked back. The Admiral was right. Foulke leveraged his natural talent and intellect with his newly found speaking skills and arguably talked his way all the way to the top of his profession.

All these people we've been talking about are creative in any number of different ways. The simple important characteristic creative people share is a proven ability to make things happen. They make things happen through leadership, innovation, ingenuity, and a willingness to take risks. Put all those elements together and you've got a formula for success.

10

ten

Snapshots in Enterprise:
How Some People Create Opportunity

sk Tom Balsley what he does for a living and he'll probably tell you he's a gardener. But in fact, Tom Balsley is one of the world's most sought-after landscape architects with award-winning signature works from New York City to Tokyo. His dance card is filled years in advance, and as his reputation has spread, he has had to turn away work. For his entire career, Tom has owed his success to the disarmingly simple concept that work is art and art is work. Work has no place. Work is in the shower, on a mountain, or in a plane somewhere over the Pacific—wherever Tom is. Creative work, like breathing, is part of life itself, as spontaneous as sex and as ever-present, forever throbbing a micrometer under the skin. Balsley is incapable of separating his work from himself. For him, there is no nine to five. Nor can he leave the office at the office, because he *is* the office.

> Tom Balsley has owed his success to the disarmingly simple concept that work is art, and art, work.

To be sure, landscape architecture is very different, say, than bookkeeping, clerking, hotel housekeeping, office maintenance, garbage collection, janitorial work, managing a business, or owning a big business.

Or is it?

Can pushing a broom have creative virtue or confer any semblance of personal fulfillment? I won't argue the case here, other than to suggest that a Zen master might give even the most passionate detractor a good run for his money. What I would like to propose is that any path in life can be either a dead end or a stepping stone, and the deciding factor might arguably be the degree of imagination and creativity one brings to the job.

> Any path in life can be either a dead end or a stepping stone, and the deciding factor might arguably be the degree of imagination and creativity one brings to the job.

A creative approach would lead naturally to finding better, more interesting ways of doing things (a newly designed broom, more durable floor wax, more productive cleaning process, redesigned work week, better seasonal maintenance programs, for example). This would invariably attract attention, which would lead, in turn, to either (a) a dead end, in which case the enterprising will see the light and take their talents elsewhere (many a Cambodian refugee in the United States might recognize what I'm talking about here); or (b) an earned opportunity, in which enlightened management will know a good thing when it sees it and, in the storied American tradition of cream rising to the top, promote the worthy individual towards his or her greatest potential.

Now, how does Tom Balsley fit into this? Balsley and creative people like him intuitively bring an extra dimension to their work that most of us have to learn. Creative people see challenge where we see drudgery, opportunity where we see monotony, a chance to have fun where we see crushing boredom. For them, solving problems, seeing new angles, improving processes, saving money, introducing aesthetics, and generating ideas or just generally making things work better are for creative people as natural as the sun coming up in the morning. And I would suggest that if you start a Tom Balsley at the bottom of the heap, he will not stay there long and the thing that will propel him on an upward trajectory is the degree to which he is capable of unleashing the creative genie within.

The question of how, exactly, to unleash that genie is a good one, and I suspect there may be many more answers than I am capable of giving. But Balsley has a surprisingly simple answer that's as good as any and seems to work for him every time.

"I think that to create, at least for me, your hands have got to be moving," he told me. "When I'm at the drafting table, designing, my hands are working all the time and the process just seems to flow more freely. When I begin to draw and sketch, the ideas start pouring out."

We can all picture artists painting on canvas, shaping clay, carving marble, welding steel, folding origami. But what about the rest of us? What about the tens of millions of people who don't call themselves artists?

Imagine yourself in the front of a room of business people. You are making a presentation. Now you're at the white board, magic marker in hand, mapping out a

> "When I'm at the drafting table, designing, my hands are working all the time and the process just seems to flow more freely. When I begin to draw and sketch, the ideas start pouring out."
> —LANDSCAPE ARCHITECT TOM BALSLEY

schematic that depicts various components of your business plan. You block out several areas, then begin to draw arrows. Circles appear, and the whole thing begins to come together on the board. The more you draw, the more excited and confident you feel. You are vigorous, alive, all thoughts of self-doubt banished. You are building this thing right before their eyes, and because your enthusiasm is genuine, it catches fire in the audience and begins to fill the room. The robust sense of professional satisfaction you feel is the same satisfaction the shaggy-haired artist feels as he pastes together an eye-popping papier mâché sculpture of a towering nude in Soho.

> You are vigorous, alive, all thoughts of self-doubt banished. You are building this thing right before their eyes, and because your enthusiasm is genuine, it catches fire in the audience and begins to fill the room. The robust sense of professional satisfaction you feel is the same satisfaction the shaggy-haired artist feels as he pastes together an eye-popping papier mâché sculpture of a towering nude in Soho.

Or let's say you're at home with your laptop Sunday afternoon writing a report that's due Monday. You've had some ideas, the pieces are beginning to fit, and the thing is finally coming together. Now you're on a roll. It's like the train is leaving the station, picking up steam, and you're on your way. The ideas are really cranking now and your fingers are dancing across the keyboard. In a final climactic rush you finish the report, flush with a glow of accomplishment, and can't believe four hours have gone by.

It's the power of your own creativity that makes you feel fulfilled.

Or you're an engineer having coffee with a colleague in a cafeteria and the answer to your design problem has just come to you. Excitedly, you start to sketch the pieces of the puzzle in your notebook. The more you draw, the more you sketch, the faster it comes. Now you feel the thrill of discovery as you realize that the solution is even better, more elegant, than you thought. And now your schematics are flying across the page as your hand tries to keep up with your brain. In no time, you have used up half the notebook, but there it is, finally, all on one page, a physical representation of what your subconscious has been helping you assemble in your head for the last two weeks.

Again, it is your own powers of creativity that have seized the initiative and forged an engineering work of art. The overwhelming sense of accomplishment you feel is the same sensation any artist would feel when a work is finally done.

Or you're an investment banker putting together a deal with local partners in Warsaw. You make your initial proposals over dinner. The whole thing is in your head. It feels right. And not surprisingly you find yourself getting excited as you flesh out the main components and map details. But the more you get into it, the more you notice your hands carve the air, slicing, making little circles, drawing lines in space, slashing, jabbing. And the more your hands try to shape your thoughts, the easier your thoughts seem to flow. Fold your hands on your lap and you lose momentum.

> Your hands carve the air, slicing, making little circles, drawing lines in space, slashing, jabbing. And the more your hands try to shape your thoughts, the easier your thoughts seem to flow. Fold your hands on your lap and you lose momentum.

While creativity gives new meaning to work, it can provide a richly rewarding new life to those in retirement as well. We have all heard the story about the hard-charging CEO who retires and drops dead a month later; or the exec who stops working and takes up golf as if golf were a job in itself; or the retiree who gets into the booze and descends into a private hell; or the lost soul who leaves his job only to slide rapidly into dementia; or the affluent but anguished retiree who is unable to find any meaning in life outside the former job, spends too much time alone in darkened rooms, and winds up putting a gun in his mouth.

Most of us find self-worth in work. Take work away and too often you take away our very identify. Stripped of order, routine, a daily schedule, the company of coworkers, and the security of a predictable paycheck, most of us suffer a degree of shock. We feel frightened and vulnerable. We see for the first time, perhaps, the true fragility of our lives. And we look for something to fill the hole left by the job that went away.

> A lucky few are blessed with a backup system that kicks in when the paycheck job disappears. They are drawn to a creative pursuit that fills the void.

A lucky few are blessed with a backup system that kicks in when the paycheck job disappears. They are drawn to a creative pursuit that fills the void. Sometimes that pursuit has been with them as a hobby, like the accomplished watercolor artist I know who became successful as an artist only after retiring from her career job. The progression was altogether seamless. In her case, as in others, the avocation suddenly became the vocation—with happy results. Interestingly, her second "career" as an artist actually eclipsed in achievement her life as a corporate vice president—not only in income, but also in recognition—and provided a sense of well-being she had never known before.

Some brave souls embrace, rather than fear, the sudden inaction of retirement. They find delight, rather than dread, in tranquillity and segue smoothly into a time of reflection, mediation, even prayer. They cast off the yoke of bondage to their former employer and feel almost immediately at home in the strangely unstructured world of leisure. Even contented voyagers must eventually migrate towards the grail of creation.

> Some brave souls embrace, rather than fear, the sudden inaction of retirement.

At some point they must yield to the natural human need to make something entirely new, something of their own invention, to create something interesting or beautiful out of thin air: write that children's book you've always wanted to write, get out the oils and paint flowers in June, start a small business importing hand-carved Indonesian art, build a model ship, or restore the '55 T-bird in the shed out back. To deny these things would be to deny the tide.

Virtually all of us have experienced this powerful force of nature in one way or another. And all want to be useful. We want to think that our lives have value, that we are in some way making a contribution. To believe otherwise would be to greet every new day with a kind of emptiness. The consequences of not feeling useful can be alcohol, drugs, domestic violence, and more. So it is naturally to our advantage to actually *be* useful.

Such is the case with Michael Milken, the disgraced former junk bond king who did jail time, then suffered the further agony of a scary bout with prostate cancer. Banned for life from the securities business, Milken emerged from jail an apparently chastened man with a real need, maybe for the first time in his life, to help other people (and make good money in the bargain). Thus was born Knowledge Universe, which aims to cash in on the knowledge-based economy now in full bloom. Some analysts believe that education of all kinds will emerge as one of the leading investment opportunities in the early part of the twenty-first century, not unlike what health care was to the end of the twentieth. And Milken, along with his brother and Oracle founder Larry Ellison, are so sure it's a good bet that they've slapped down roughly $500 million to try to harvest a large piece of the $665 billion now spent in the education industry. They've focused their attentions on executive education, corporate training, day care, even talking toys to help kids learn faster. And Milken has taken his commitment one step further by throwing a little more of his own money into inner-city learning centers he calls Mike's Math Club. On top of that, Milken regularly shows up to do some of the teaching himself. If you can believe him—and I do—he says the teaching part of his job makes him as happy as he's ever been. It's the youthful rush of joy that signals the man—or woman—who has found a way to make themselves useful.

> It's the youthful rush of joy that signals the man—or woman—who has found a way to make themselves useful.

I am reminded of an executive friend of mine who only reluctantly accepted an invitation from an acquaintance to distribute food to the needy on Christmas Eve. The experience was an epiphany for my friend, who got such unexpected joy from his act of kindness that he's organized his entire company to do the same thing in towns all across North America and Mexico. When he retires, he says he will spend the rest of his days working to feed the poor and destitute.

Sometimes the catalyst is hardship. Don King, the flamboyant American boxing impresario, had to serve half a year in the slammer.

But he put the time to good use by reading nothing but Shakespeare. His command of the Bard later produced an electrifying effect on unsuspecting listeners, often reporters, as in this bizarre exchange after the famous Muhammad Ali-George Foreman fight had been postponed:

Reporter: Will this postponement affect your plans?

King (with a sly grin and suitably dramatic pause): As William Shakespeare said, "Sweet are the uses of adversity, which, like the toad, ugly and venomous, wears yet a precious jewel in its head." (In other words, some good will come out of this delay.)

King floored the reporter, and continues to floor anyone willing to listen to his handy collection of Shakespearean one-liners—even though it's probably safe to conjecture that most people don't have a clue what he's trying to say.

Steven Spielberg, who is arguably as astute a Hollywood executive as he is a filmmaker, draws his creative octane from both the magic and pain of his own childhood, which inspired such all-time Spielberg blockbusters as *E.T.*, *Close Encounters of the Third Kind*, *Raiders of the Lost Ark*, and *Jurassic Park*. Now-famous chilling touches such as a glass of water trembling to distant vibrations and branches rattling on the roof are part of Spielberg's own early view of the world. As the product of

> Steven Spielberg, a lonely child with a penchant for story-telling, sought solace in fantasy, and began writing scripts and shooting movies with his father's 8mm camera before he was a teenager.

divorce and frequent moving in childhood, Spielberg, a lonely child with a penchant for storytelling, sought solace in fantasy and began writing scripts and shooting movies with his father's 8mm camera before he was a teenager.

But it wasn't until his senior year in high school, when his family had just moved to Saratoga, California, that Spielberg experienced a new kind of fear that would forever change him. It was there that Spielberg says he was tormented by anti-Semitic remarks from his classmates, who would sneeze, "Hah-Jew!" when he passed in the halls. Sometimes jocks would beat him up after school. Years later, the anguish of that experience finally found fruition in *Schindler's List*, another Spielberg megahit and one of the most critically acclaimed movies ever.

> Adversity forces us to focus our minds marvelously.

Adversity forces us to focus our minds marvelously. I am reminded of a consultant friend of mine who saw 80 percent of his business evaporate in the recession of the early 1990s, but redirected his energies into writing a book, which launched him onto the speaking circuit where he's making more money than he used to make as a full-time consultant. It never occurred to my friend to panic, or wallow in self-pity, or grow depressed for lack of something useful to do. He simply saw the free time as a gift that he might never have gotten to enjoy had the recession not come along when it did. And he was finally able to give vent to a slew of ideas that had been percolating for years in the back of his mind.

And then there's the curious case of an acquaintance who wound up in the hospital for an extended stay. He is an active man who liked to say he had never been sick a day in his life, and he later told me that next to the pain and discomfort it was the unrelenting boredom that bothered him most. After a couple of days he found television intolerable, and he was either too medicated or feeling too poorly to read more than a chapter of a book at a time. Even his favorite standby, crossword puzzles, lost their appeal as a steady diet. In the end, he found himself having to confront a number of aspects of his life he had never had the time or inclination to seriously consider before.

The thing that seemed to weigh on his mind most heavily (when he took the time to actually think about it) was his law practice. He had been singularly unhappy with the law in recent years. Maybe it was the chaos in the courts, or the abundance of lawyers at every turn, or the frustrating inequities he saw all around him in the justice system, or maybe it was just that he had never really wanted to be a lawyer in the first place. Whatever it was, as he lay in his hospital bed, he suddenly began to see the need for a big change.

> Mary Berner, publisher of *Glamour* magazine, to stay fit and still have time for the children, jogs home every night after work and has her briefcase delivered by messenger.

"I had never had the time to stop and think about it," he told me. "But the hospital experience was a blessing in disguise because it changed my life."

In the end, he wound up selling his law practice, buying the motor-sailer he'd always dreamed about, and moving with his wife to the U.S. Virgin Islands where he runs a successful boat chartering business. He even has time to dabble in photography and write a column for a local paper.

"I'm living the dream," he says. "I'm just sorry it took getting sick to make me see the light."

Sometimes seeing the light simply means figuring out how to have it all—career, marriage, family, and children. Over the years, women have had to be more imaginative in this pursuit than men.

For example, Marsha Gerlin, CEO of United Scrap Metal, ended up the sole breadwinner in her family. To make sure her children bought into the proposition, she took them once a week to public housing in Chicago, "to make the point of what would happen if we didn't have any money. It worked. The requirement on their part was that they had to provide me with grades that were outstanding. They were."

Betsey Johnson, president of The Betsey Johnson designer company, bonded with her daughter Lulu from an early age. "She was in traffic, she was at business meetings, she was going to sleep on the cutting table." Mom and daughter grew up together in the company and at twenty-three, Lulu was not only mom's best friend, but assistant to the president.

Mary Berner, publisher of *Glamour* magazine, was at the height of her career with a working husband and three small kids at home in Manhattan. To stay fit and still have time for the children, she jogs home every night after work and has her briefcase delivered by messenger.

Denise Ilitch, vice chairwoman of Little Caesar Enterprises, wanted to make sure her children were getting the best, so she set up a quality child care center at her own company. The center also serves as a recruiting lure, and employees, both men and women, are more productive according to Ilitch.

> Denise Ilitch, vice chairwoman of Little Caesar Enterprises, wanted to make sure her children were getting the best, so she set up a quality child care center at her own company.

Ellen Knapp, vice chairman and chief knowledge officer at Coopers & Lybrand, decided early on never to work for a startup company "into which I would have to devote every waking moment of my life – and that might not be there the next day." She leveraged her skills as a sought-after technology person to "choose jobs that didn't demand a lot of travel." And when her son was hospitalized with an emergency appendectomy, she lived in his hospital room for a week, working out of her laptop.

An enterprising and flexible approach to life helps all these women enjoy fulfilling lives.

So whether we are working, retired, "in between" jobs, serving in the military, in college or university, or simply independently wealthy, we have access to a power that not only redeems us from our own tendencies towards mediocrity but provides an unexpected jolt of awakening that opens all kinds of doors, some of which may never have been opened before.

Is Your Company Dying?

Advice from a Creative Master to Put Life Back in Your Business

The difference between a company that is healthy and a company that is dying—and may not even know it—is what advertising high priestess Charlotte Beers calls the spirit of creativity.

Beers knows something about creativity. An amazingly creative and insightful thinker herself, she spent an entire career managing creative people and eventually wound up running Ogilvy & Mather, and later J. Walter Thompson Company, two of the world's most successful—and creative—ad agencies.

"If you don't have the spirit of creativity in your company, you're not going to make it," she declares flatly. "It's easy to tell when a company is going stagnant: if creativity is discouraged, if people are not comfortable airing their ideas, if there are 100 reasons

The difference between a company that is healthy and a company that is dying—and may not even know it—is what advertising high priestess Charlotte Beers calls the spirit of creativity.

> "If creativity is discouraged, if people are not comfortable airing their ideas, if there are 100 reasons why something can't be done, if individual excellence is resented, then that company is going to fail."
>
> —CHARLOTTE BEERS

why something can't be done, if individual excellence is resented, then that company is going to fail."

Other signs of a company in rapid decline: very sterile language, rigid control of meetings, and what Beers calls "public hangings."

"If you read a lot of mumbo-jumbo and buzz words in the company's documents, memos, correspondence, and marketing and advertising materials, that's not a good sign. It means the company has lost contact with its creative heart.

"Another bad sign is when the company's meetings are more like military tribunals or court-martials or the reading of a will than forums for airing creative ideas. In that kind of an environment people naturally feel stifled."

But nothing, she says, is more deadening to the creative spirit (and life force) of a company than "to watch a colleague be humiliated and strung up in what amounts to a public hanging. If you talk to successful creative people, you will hear an inspiring litany of setbacks and failures—one mistake after another—all the way to the top. That's how they get to the top, by making mistakes, learning from those mistakes, then pushing confidently ahead."

Most big companies set up systems that close doors, rather than open them, according to Beers.

"The most potent competitive weapon a company can have is a clear vision of what it is about, where it is going, and how it's going to get there," she says. "But while too often the few people at the top may believe in the vision and try to articulate it, people in the middle don't get the message. These are the people who are not only supposed to get the message, but to make it happen. Yet these are the same people who wind up complaining they don't know where the company is headed and don't know what senior management wants."

Her conclusions:
- Make the message clear, then make sure everybody gets the message and understands it.
- It's more important to try and fail than fail to try.
- People in companies should be free to talk up and down and sideways within companies, across all departments and hierarchies, without restriction.
- No idea is stupid.
- Bosses should cultivate creativity as a corporate asset that can produce bottom-line results.
- The least likely people sometimes have the best ideas.
- For a company to be great it must also be creative.

How does your company stack up?

twelve

The Executive as Creator:

How Business People, Like Artists, Can Create Masterpieces

The president of a Wall Street firm was on a roll—and didn't know it. We were in the middle of a conversation. He was painting the air with his hands, caught in a kind of private rhapsody, describing the merger of two competing financial giants. I watched with keen interest as he became almost a different person, talking excitedly about fit and synergy, assets and liabilities, efficiencies and redundancies, projections, relative strengths and weaknesses, ebbs and flows, highs and lows, growth, opportunity. Evaluating, assessing, measuring, carving the air with his hands, trying to show what was going on inside his head.

Turns out he had been talking to one of the merger parties himself a couple of years back. For different reasons he had decided against a marriage at that time.

Get him on his game and he could show you right away—while never intending to draw attention to himself—why he was president. He was able to describe his business in a way that was anything but textbook: colorful, enthusiastic, full of fun and excitement.

Instead of paint, the creative business person works in strategies. Instead of clay or marble, he creates with numbers and ideas that translate into action. Where the architect might design a church, he might design a brand new company.

Not unlike an artist, in fact, arguably as creative in his way as a Picasso or Michaelangelo. Instead of paint, the creative business person works in strategies. Instead of clay or marble, he creates with numbers and ideas that translate into action. Where the architect might design a church, he might design a brand new company all the way from the mail room to the boardroom, or engineer a brilliant merger or acquisition.

This is the same man who later complimented me (I used to dabble in painting), "You're an artist. I wish I could do what you do." When I tried to tell him that he was the real artist, he promptly objected. In spite of my insistence, he could not be persuaded otherwise. He was convinced—and continues to be convinced—that I, and people like me, are the artists and that he is not. This denial amazes me.

"No, no," he says emphatically, waving off my protests. "I've got no talent. I'd just love to be able to paint or write."

But what is important here? I have not created jobs for tens of thousands of people. Nor have I personally designed pioneering financial products that helped create a new industry and generate billions of dollars. Nor can I claim credit for engineering dozens of ingenious and complex transactions that helped make thousands of people millionaires. But tell this man he is a fountainhead of creativity and he will have none of it.

It's not uncommon for real talent to be incapable of recognizing itself, particularly when we are talking about people like my CEO friend who are not self-aggrandizing. Yet the working world is filled with people whose natural creativity helped propel them out of the pack and way beyond their fellow working stiffs. Some creative talents are so robust that they cannot only improve our lot but in some cases even change the world.

The end of the nineteenth century saw an explosion of creativity, innovation and invention that made it possible for us to live the way we do today. Assorted geniuses such as Edison (electric light, phonograph, ticker tape), Bell (telephone), Ford (cars), Carnegie (steel), Firestone (rubber), and a little later the Wright brothers (aviation) virtually created the twentieth century.

The latter part of the twentieth century saw a revolution of innovation growing out of World War II, the space program, and a couple of digital kids in California by the names of Gates and Jobs.

Martha Stewart, perhaps America's most successful woman entrepreneur, not only cobbled a business from scratch but also created an industry. She built a booming, top-end catering enterprise into an empire of bestselling Martha Stewart books on good living, a popular magazine with her picture and name on every cover, a television videotape production company, and lucrative marketing partnerships with Time-Warner, Kmart stores, cable TV channels, the NBC Today Show, and CBS. She attributes her stunning success to a love of hard work ("as long as it's creative"), a driving ambition ("I test myself every day") and the need for

Martha Stewart built a booming, top-end catering enterprise into an empire of best-selling Martha Stewart books on good living, a popular magazine with her picture and name on every cover, a television videotape production company and lucrative marketing partnerships with Time-Warner, Kmart stores, cable TV channels, the NBC Today Show, and CBS.

very little sleep ("I sleep only three or four hours a night, which gives me more time to write and think").

From the beginning, she's played the game according to her own standards of excellence.

"Everything I've done I've tried to do with ethics, honesty, intelligence and especially creativity, she told me. When I was a kid I saw an ad with a punch line that read, '. . . living without boundaries'. I never forgot that line and I tried to live my life without boundaries. But if you exceed the boundaries of honesty and integrity you've gone too far. Look at Leona Helmsley. She had everything, she exceeded the boundaries of honesty and wound up in jail. Look at Stew Leonard. He ran maybe the most successful food store in America. But he got caught heading out of the country with a suitcase of cash and he wound up in jail, too. And don't forget Michael Milken. The idea is to stretch yourself in your business. The more creative you are, the more you grow. But push the envelope of integrity and you're making a mistake."

> "Everything I've done I've tried to do with ethics, honesty, intelligence and especially creativity. When I was a kid I saw an ad with a punch line that read, ' . . . living without boundaries'. I never forgot that line and I tried to live my life without boundaries."
> —MARTHA STEWART

While the right hand is bursting through barriers and the left hand is keeping things inside the parameters of ethics, the rest of Martha is constantly on the march, always thinking, always designing, always creating.

On a trip in France, when she wasn't reading up on local history and doing her homework for the region, Martha Stewart was snapping photos of gardens and sketching ideas for her next book—

while the rest of the party chatted over long meals or napped on the bus. One morning about dawn as the rest of us slept at a small chateau, Martha was up and out feeding the geese and rowing slowly across a small, tranquil lake in the first rays of sunshine "just thinking" and taking photographs in the clean air and crisp light.

Martha's talents run from solid business skills (in addition to being a successful model, she once also had a very profitable career as a stock broker) to serious artistic ability. Her hand and eye are in every book she's every published and on every page of her magazine, *Martha Stewart Living*.

And it didn't take Martha long to figure out that an important part of the future of merchandising will belong to computer programs and masters of the Web. To take her sprawling empire to the next level, she recruited a small army of talent to create her own personal organization software.

What you can expect to see in the next century is Martha Stewart on the Web and Martha Stewart software selling Martha Stewart merchandise and giving endless Martha Stewart advice and design and entertaining ideas to millions of Martha Stewart fans and customers, tens of millions of Martha Stewart potential new customers, and countless millions more worldwide who perhaps never even heard her name before.

That's how Martha uses sheer artistic and business talent in combination with technology to succeed beyond even her own dreams of success.

But not every business star can claim artistic talent. Many highly visible and successful people probably couldn't draw a circle or paint the side of a house. But they get the same genuine creative thrill as any real artist when they do what they do best: put together the beautiful deal. Donald Trump's book, *The Art of the Deal*, attempts to try to define the curious link between business transactions and aesthetics.

> Many successful people probably couldn't draw a circle or paint the side of a house. But they get the same genuine creative thrill as any real artist when they do what they do best: put together the beautiful deal.

The venerable Estée Lauder, a pioneer who had a big hand in creating the high-end cosmetics industry worldwide, got off to a shaky start. Like so many other visionaries, in the beginning she had only a dream and a solid belief in herself and her products. Estée's story began during the Depression in a humble home in Queens, New York, where she concocted her version of folk skin potions from the old country. She built her business from scratch, literally door-to-door. But after awhile the elixirs started to catch on and Estée's little business began to grow.

Virtually every great American success story is an epic journey of the dauntless entrepreneur struggling against seemingly hopeless odds, and Estée's experience is no different. Every step of the way she ran into scoffers, nay-sayers and detractors. Early on, she realized she had to rely on sheer ingenuity to keep the fledging enterprise afloat.

Estée Lauder was one of the first to realize that she wasn't selling skin cream; she was selling beauty and eternal youth. So, in the early days when she ran into sale or price resistance, she let her naturally creative mind find ways to pry open locked doors.

For example, she remembers the time in San Antonio, Texas, in the late '40s when the biggest department store in town told her, in effect, to get lost and take her stuff with her.

Undeterred, Estée demanded to speak with the store manager. When she was able finally to get his attention and sit him down, she positioned herself as a partner who could help the store prosper. When the store manager objected that a few jars of skin cream had no place in his strategic plan and politely but firmly suggested she was wasting his time, Estée had a sudden flash of insight.

"I've got it!" she cried. "Start the New Year with a New Face! That's the slogan. New Year. New face. I am sure this will bring customers into the store."

The store manager liked the ring of it and decided to take a chance on this bold newcomer from New York and her boxes of homemade skin emollients. Of course, Estée was right. She wasn't selling skin cream. She was selling a whole new look, and a new face. The customers loved it and bought out the store.

Later, in another establishment in another city, a store magnate complained bitterly that business was so bad he couldn't sell the merchandise he already had on the shelves. The last thing he needed, he said, was more cosmetics.

Estée's counter took him back. "Business bad?" she asked, incredulous. "Bad? I *started* my business in the *Depression*, when there *was* no business."

The executive sat up and listened. Suddenly he was impressed with this gutsy little lady. Before he knew it, Lauder was inundating him with exciting new marketing and sales ideas that she said could move her cosmetics off the shelves faster than he could stock them.

He finally said yes and they shook hands. Again, Estée was right. The Estée Lauder products sold out.

Even in the 1990s when she was in her nineties, Estée was still doing what she always did best—selling herself and her products in a characteristically upbeat and creative way that made people want to buy her magic potions.

Estée Lauder's march to fame and fortune went on like that, from store to store, state to state, and finally spread all over the world. Even in the 1990s when she was in her nineties, Estée was still doing what she always did best—selling herself and her products in a characteristically upbeat and creative way that made people want to buy her magic potions.

At a store opening in Budapest, for example, a TV reporter shoved a mike in her face, snapped on the hot lights, and asked the elegant old lady what message she had for the women of Hungary, her ancestral home. Estée didn't miss a beat.

"Every woman looks beautiful the day she gets married," Estée responded. "The women of Hungary should think of how they felt, and how they looked the day they got married." The implication being, of course, think Estée Lauder and Estée Lauder cosmetics. The next day, the store was so jammed with customers that management had to hold people back at the door.

Estée Lauder never claimed to be an artist in the strict sense of the word, but in the end she wound up creating a masterpiece. You need not be an artist to create a masterpiece, but observers have long noticed a demonstrable connection between mathematics and music. People like money managers and math teachers who deal in numbers frequently have a natural affinity for music. I have been told that a disproportionately large number of people in financial services are actually talented musicians. One fund manager tried to describe the link between numbers and music as waves—wave after wave of numbers providing a deep analysis of a proposed merger or acquisition, say, or wave after wave of tens of thousands of notes producing a symphony.

Anyone listening to this description of music as a melodic partner to financial analysis cannot fail to recognize the mystical power of creative energy to not only influence business but also give colorful depth to our everyday lives.

Take art out of the equation and good things still happen.

Put yourself in a room with like-minded people seeking a common goal and it's amazing what can happen. Dozens of companies today help make things happen with a no-holds-barred productivity device first introduced by GE. the workout session. I've seen problems defined then solved on the spot ("drilling down" through one obstacle after another). I've seen otherwise undemonstrative people reach a level of excitement that might come as a surprise to them if they could see themselves in action caught up in the brainstorming and feeling the intellectual temperature of the room soaring around them. One good idea feeds on another and another, all coming together like an arrowhead to drop the dragon dead in its tracks.

> Put yourself in a room with like-minded people seeking a common goal and it's amazing what can happen.

Some of the most successful people in business share two characteristics: they are creative by nature (and not afraid to show it), and also have fun. Richard Branson, the genial former flower child who heads Virgin Airways and Virgin Atlantic Records, comes to mind, as does Time-Warner chairman and CNN founder Ted Turner. Controversial and perhaps not loved by all both men have nevertheless built huge fortunes on the strength of their imaginations alone, relishing rather than shrinking from risk, shrugging off nay-sayers, never doubting for a moment that the sky was the limit.

George Soros, the financial whiz, will gladly admit that he finds his rainbow of investments "fun." Even more so now that he can turn to the one thing he says he enjoys even more than making money: giving it away. As a philanthropist, Soros is almost a class by himself. And the same creative fire that helped bring the cash in is now happily engaged in shoveling it back out to where Soros feels it can do the most good.

The sky really can be the limit for anyone prepared to approach life as a six-year-old. Pablo Picasso said it took him his whole life to paint as a child. At six, we had it all: a sense of adventure, a desire to explore, a need to create. Too young to fear opportunity, we leapt at a hundred challenges a day and kept coming back for more. We came home bruised and bloodied from our fingers to our knees but went out the next morning wanting to lick the world.

Remember? Try to remember, because that six-year-old is still scratching around inside somewhere, still undaunted, and just dying to come out to play.

> Pablo Picasso said it took him his whole life to paint as a child. At six, we had it all: a sense of adventure, a desire to explore, a need to create. Too young to fear opportunity, we leapt at a hundred challenges a day and kept coming back for more.

thirteen

Business Creativity All-Stars—
And How They Got There

Enterprise, like sports, has its winners and losers, but if you're talking about business creativity, the all-star players are the relative few who can take an idea and turn it into an industry. And if you had to point to just one characteristic that seems to embrace all these pioneers, it's a single-minded focus—and talent—for creating wealth.

Normal Pearlstein, Time Inc. editor-in-chief and former managing editor of the *Wall Street Journal*, selected twenty titans who built empires from nothing. Each is a uniquely American success story. Here are some of *Time*'s top picks.

> The all-star players are the relative few who can take an idea and turn it into an industry.

John D. Rockefeller. Rockefeller created the world's first multinational corporation, Standard Oil. By 1913, when he was seventy-four, Rockefeller had amassed a personal fortune of some $900 million, or roughly $190 billion in today's dollars and about three times the net worth of Microsoft's Bill Gates.

Andrew Carnegie. Carnegie founded the powerhouse steel industry that helped propel the United States into the twentieth century. "Put all your eggs into one basket," he advised, "and then watch that basket." Fiercely competitive, obsessed with innovation and efficiency, Carnegie was the archetypal forefather of today's robust crop of bold entrepreneurs. Yet with his contemporary, Rockefeller, he gave away most of his $350 million fortune, in the process building 2,800 free libraries worldwide and declaring that "the man who dies rich dies disgraced." (The better part of a century later, his grandson was waiting tables at the exclusive Palm Beach Bath and Tennis Club in Florida, probably wishing granddad hadn't been quite so convinced of the moral blight of prodigious wealth.)

> Andrew Carnegie gave away most of his $350 million fortune, in the process building 2,800 free libraries worldwide, and declaring that "the man who dies rich dies disgraced."

J. P. Morgan. If Rockefeller and Carnegie built the industrial age, Morgan financed it. Morgan issued stocks and bonds for exciting new railroad companies (not unlike today's software start-ups), brokered deals among them, sat on their boards, and wound up controlling a sixth of American's entire railway system. Later, he created U.S. Steel, the first billion-dollar corporation. For decades he wielded almost unimaginable power by today's standards, acting almost single-handedly as America's central bank, an ominously imperial role that eventually prompted legislators to vote in the Federal Reserve Act of 1913.

Henry Ford. Ford pioneered mass production, and subsequently, mass consumption. He introduced a new product (cars) in such volume that he changed the landscape and the economy of America forever—paving the way for the world's most affluent middle class and the bedrock of the world economy for years to come. Decades before the first Big Mac, Ford invented the dealer-franchise system to sell and service automobiles. As early as 1912, there were already 7,000 Ford dealerships across the country, and America would never be the same again.

> Henry Ford paved the way for the world's most affluent middle class and the bedrock of the world economy for years to come.

David Sarnoff. Sarnoff did for communications what Henry Ford did for transportation. Sarnoff was the shepherd who ushered radio, and then television, into virtually every home in America. Born in Russia, Sarnoff arrived in the United States in 1900 at the dawn of a brave new century rife with optimism and a sense of unbounded possibilities. At fifteen he bought a telegraph key, learned Morse code, got a job with the Marconi Wireless Telegraph Company, and as fate would have it, was on duty the night *The Titanic* went down in 1912. The story goes that Sarnoff stayed at his post for seventy-two hours to bring the shocking details of the disaster to the world.

It was Sarnoff who three years later came up with the first commercial idea for radio, a "radio music box," to bring music into the home. Shortly after, General Electric bought Marconi in 1919 to form RCA. Sarnoff became general manager of the new company and began to turn his idea into a reality. Right away he saw that for RCA to sell radios, first it had to have programming—radio news and sports. So in 1921 he set up the first sports broadcast, a prize fight between Jack Dempsey and Georges Carpentier. Radio sales took off. Then, he quickly set up the world's first network—a string of broadcast stations across the country. He called it the National Broadcasting Company.

With radio launched, Sarnoff next turned his sights to a wacky new idea called television. Introduced as a novelty at the 1939 World's Fair in New York City, television exploded as a commercial success after World War II. Under Sarnoff's leadership, NBC had the first videotape broadcast and first made-for-TV movie. By the time he died in 1971, the world was a very different place than the one he had been born into, due largely to the changes wrought by his own vision.

A. P. Giannini. Founder of San Francisco's Bank of America, which grew to become the biggest bank in the United States, Giannini almost single-handedly pioneered many of the banking services we take for granted today, including home mortgages, auto loans, installment credit, and the first widely used bank card, which we today know as Visa. Giannini provided loans to jump-start the fledgling California wine industry, then helped launch United Artists Studios in Hollywood. His life's work, he said, was to provide the same kind of credit and services to working people that the rich had been enjoying for centuries. "I have worked without thinking of myself," he said. "This is the largest factor in whatever success I have attained." Like Carnegie, he disdained great wealth. For years he accepted virtually no pay. Once when his board granted him a surprise $1.5 million bonus, he promptly gave it all to the University of California. By the time he died, at seventy-nine, his net worth was less than $500,000.

Bank of America founder, A. P. Giannini, almost single-handedly pioneered many of the banking services we take for granted today, including home mortgages, auto loans, installment credit, and the first widely-used bank card, which we today know as Visa.

Charles Merrill. Like Giannini, Merrill saw opportunity in the common man. Merrill believed the small investor could be the foundation of the stock market and set out to prove it. Vowing to bring "Wall Street to Main Street," in 1940 Merrill founded the company now known as Merrill Lynch. At the time of his death in 1956, his firm already had 115 offices, and Merrill's dream of making America the shareholder nation was well on its way to becoming a reality.

Andrew Mellon. Mellon had a big hand in financing America's industrial boom. Through Pittsburgh's Mellon bank, Mellon was the driving force behind Alcoa, Gulf, and other corporate giants. He's also credited with fueling the robust prosperity of the 1920s as secretary of the treasury.

Michael Milken. His pioneering use of high-yield bonds helped launch the 1980s takeover mania by financing corporate raiders.

Arthur Rock. An early backer of high-tech firms such as Apple, Teledyne, and Fairchild Semiconductor, Rock led a new generation of venture capitalists that, according to *Time*, "is driving the greatest creation of wealth in history."

Willis Carrier. Carrier pioneered air-conditioning systems that made possible the Sunbelt boom.

Stephen Bechtel. Bechtel founded the company that built some of the world's largest engineering projects including Hoover Dam, the San Francisco-Oakland Bay Bridge, and the Trans-Arabian pipeline. Bechtel's monumental works showed the world the magnitude of American industrial muscle.

Walt Disney. A pervasive influence in American culture, Disney created Mickey Mouse, produced the first full-length animated movie, invented the theme park, and originated the modern multimedia corporation. Disney was the first Hollywood mogul to embrace television.

Lucky Luciano. Luciano turned organized crime into a business big enough to compete with some of the world's largest corporations.

Juan Trippe. As founder of Pan American World Airways, Trippe ushered in the modern jet age. It was Trippe who introduced "tourist class," making it possible for millions of people to fly for the first time. Early in his career, Trippe pioneered the first Atlantic and Pacific global routes, was first to introduce jet service across the Atlantic with the Boeing 707 in the late 1950s and even helped design the first 747. (Trippe to his friend Bill Allen, boss of Boeing: "If you build it, I'll buy it." Allen to Trippe: "If you buy it, I'll build it.") Trippe actually persuaded Allen to put the cockpit of the 747 on an upper deck, thus creating the 747's signature bulge, because he thought supersonic travel was the mass air travel wave of the future and that the 747 would ultimately wind up being a cargo carrier. Both Trippe and Pan Am are gone, but their legacies linger on.

William Levitt virtually created the modern American suburbia.

William Levitt. William Levitt virtually created the modern American suburbia by building tens of thousands of affordable homes for America's emerging middle class after WW II. Levitt was the first to use assembly-line processes to build homes.

Walter Reuther. Reuther pioneered the labor benefits packages that millions of union workers today take for granted, including pension plans, a guaranteed annual wage, and unemployment benefits. His groundbreaking union work led to health care programs, profit sharing, life insurance, and much more, paving the way for a standard of living that helped define the American dream.

Leo Burnett. As "The Sultan of Sell," Burnett helped distribute the American dream by creating an advertising style that unleashed an assault on our senses and helped prove that eye-catching imagery, not words, are the secret to successful ad campaigns.

Thomas Watson Jr. Watson helped launch the information age by building IBM into a computer powerhouse that led the industry for generations, and even today is the sixth largest company in the United States.

McDonald's founder, Ray Kroc, changed how we eat.

Ray Kroc. McDonald's founder, Ray Kroc, changed how we eat, because he understood that most Americans don't dine—we eat and run. Kroc gave birth to the fast food industry that not only fits a culture constantly on the move, but like McDonald's itself has spread to almost every corner of the world.

Pete Rozelle. Rozelle hooked Americans on pro football as world class show biz, and invested Sundays—and Mondays—with a new, almost religious, significance. Rozelle turned the NFL into big business when he merged the NFL with the AFL, forged huge TV contracts, created Monday Night Football, and presided over the first Super Bowl.

Akio Morita. Sony founder Akio Morita made Sony the most trusted name in consumer electronics, not only in the United States but around the world. In fact, a 1999 Harris poll found that Americans rate Sony the number one brand name—even ahead of Coca Cola, Marlboro, and General Electric. Sony created a new market in small pocket radios (the first company to use transistors in mass-produced consumer products) and went on to make more new markets in pocket-sized cassette players (the Walkman), miniature TVs, CD players, top quality TVs, and broadcast studio equipment. Morita was so convinced that the United States was the key to Sony's eventual global success that he moved his entire family to New York City in 1963 to better understand American culture, customs, and regulations. The move paid off. The Sony brand was a hit in the United

States and went a long way toward changing the image of "Made in Japan" from one of cheap imitations to an enduring concept of superior quality.

Sam Walton. The Wal-Mart founder not only brought low prices to small cities but actually changed the way big business is run. Just as Henry Ford changed America's work and recreation habits, Sam Walton's single-minded pursuit of discounting and higher volume altered forever America's spending habits. As Wal-Mart stores spread across the land, so did a revolution in business philosophy: a shift of power from manufacturer to consumer that continues to this day across scores of industries. In the 1960s, Walton was one of the first to harness the power of the computer to drive Wal-Mart's rapid expansion, which paved the way for a whole new breed of "category killer" retailers, including Home Depot, Barnes & Noble, and Blockbuster. By the time he died in 1992, the Walton family's net worth approached $25 billion and Wal-Mart was number four in the Fortune 500, behind only General Motors, Ford, and Exxon.

> Just as Henry Ford changed America's work and recreation habits, Sam Walton's single-minded pursuit of discounting and higher volume altered forever America's spending habits.

part three

The Rewards:
Reaping the Harvest

fourteen

The Rewards of Creativity:
How Creative Leaders Think

The fruits of creativity are products and services, but the harvest is wealth and prosperity. Turn on the creative engine, open the pipeline, and out the other end come things that people will buy. The more creative, the more imaginative the product or service, the greater the harvest.

Some companies have a culture that almost breathes creativity. Take 3M, which launched 500 products in just one year. Or Pfizer, which a *Fortune* survey found eclipsed Merck as the most innovative drug powerhouse. Or Intel, which feeds the widening maw of growing worldwide computer demand with a spectacular banquet of digital chips.

> Turn on the creative engine, open the pipeline, and out the other end come things that people will buy.

The survey found that Enron, a natural gas company, Mirage Resorts, and even Coca-Cola, which built a priceless franchise on just one product, also rate high in the creativity equals productivity sweepstakes. Not surprisingly, it is often the CEO, department head, or chief strategist who sounds the alarm for innovation when profits start to slip. The mandate comes down: Bust out of ordinary day-to-day business and go for the breakthrough product.

According to *Fortune*, Pfizer's CEO Edward Steere sets the tone for the entire company by encouraging his scientists to stretch their sights and start focusing on unfamiliar areas of research such as genetics. To make sure that he and other bosses at headquarters in New York don't get in the way of serious progress, Steere located Pfizer's research and development labs far away in England, where creativity can flourish unfettered.

Enron CEO Kenneth Lay turned the staid natural gas industry upside down with a radical approach: new products, new services, new kinds of contracts, new ways of pricing. Lay built spot markets for natural gas, created several new public companies under the Enron emblem and wound up slashing the cost of gas for some utilities by 50 percent, according to the survey.

Mirage Resorts CEO Steve Wynn rocked the sleepy gaming industry with a disarmingly simple idea: give people great service, superb food, and the kind of eye-popping entertainment they can't get back home. To make sure his own people consistently deliver the kind of friendly, enthusiastic service his customers expect, Wynn came up with an ingenious morale-boosting idea: He made the employee cafeterias more attractive than his hotels' coffee shops and decorated back corridors the employees use the same as guest quarters.

> Mirage Resorts CEO Steve Wynn rocked the sleepy gaming industry with a disarmingly simple idea: give people great service, superb food, and the kind of eye-popping entertainment they can't get back home.

At the same time, Wynn saw flattening revenues ahead for the maturing gaming industry, so he set out to literally recreate Las Vegas in a brand new image. To lure upscale visitors—not necessarily just gamblers—he concocted Bellagio, a $1 billion luxury superhotel extravaganza, stocked it with $1.5 million in museum-class art, and hired five of the world's finest chefs to preside over his five new five-star restaurants.

For a man who is almost legally blind, Wynn has the kind of vision that leads change.

Paradoxically, Coca-Cola suddenly discovered the real meaning of innovation only on the heels of its greatest-ever product disaster. When New Coke bombed in the 1980s, demand for Coke Classic surged. This surprising turn of events was an eye opener to Coke's late CEO Roberto Goizueta. "New Coke made us realize that Coca-Cola was more than a flavor or a bottle," he said. "It was a mental attitude."

Inspired, Coke launched a brilliant brand image campaign, which the *Fortune* study found to be "one of the most imaginative, pervasive and successful" in any industry. In fact, in its relentless drive to push a single product, Coke's senior executives believe they have rewritten the very definition of what it means to be creative.

> In its relentless drive to push a single product, Coke's senior executives believe they have rewritten the very definition of what it means to be creative.

"Everybody falls into the trap of looking at the latest gadget," Coke chief operating officer Douglas Ivester told *Fortune*. "Or they think that creativity has to be in the arts or sciences. But you've got to encourage creativity in staffing, strategy, branding, and business processes, too."

Chrysler execs met with one objective in mind: throw out old car-making rules and start again from scratch. The result: Chrysler was the first to form teams that included people from engineering, marketing, and manufacturing brainstorming together to design new cars.

Chrysler knows something about this kind of back-office creativity. In the early 1990s, once again teetering at the brink of bankruptcy, desperate Chrysler execs met with one objective in mind: throw out old car-making rules and start again from scratch. The result: Chrysler was the first to form teams that included people from engineering, marketing, and manufacturing brainstorming together to design new cars. At the same time, Chrysler worked fast to improve relations with suppliers in a new way of doing business that made both sides happy and served as a model for the rest of the industry. Chrysler even went so far as to encourage suppliers to come up with solutions to design problems—with happy results.

In just a few years, Chrysler was well back from the brink and getting imaginative new models to market faster than any other of the Big Three automakers. On top of that, Chrysler soon had the highest profits per vehicle and best-performing stock of any U.S. automaker.

The lesson to be learned from all this is that simply thinking in new ways can translate into growth, speed and fatter profits, increased market share, higher stock price, better returns for shareholders, happy customers, suppliers, and employees, and a work environment that's stimulating and fun.

Some people work to live. But the lucky few live to work. If their work evolves into a creative source of fulfillment there can be no better way to live.

fifteen

15

Creating Wealth:
How Good Ideas Really Do Pay Off

The most keenly admired art in our time has come to be the creation of wealth. When it comes to making money, a handful of visionaries stand out. Of course, they've all got brains, talent, drive, intuition, and guts. But when you throw in unbridled business creativity, you get a magic potion for success straight out of a fairy tale. *Fortune* magazine spotlighted five of the brightest.

Take the case of bearded and shaded Nike CEO Phil Knight, a rebel with a cause if ever there was one. Back in the 1960s, Knight kicked the stuffing out of the sleepy footwear industry by betting that joggers would be willing to pay out the toes for high-quality running shoes. He bet right.

When the snappy sneaker market started getting a little crowded in the 1980s, Knight resoled his successful athletic shoe company, transforming Nike

> Nike CEO Phil Knight kicked the stuffing out of the sleepy footwear industry by betting that joggers would be willing to pay out the toes for high-quality running shoes.

into a marketing machine that filled the airways with ground-breaking commercials that spotlighted emotion rather than product.

Today, he's retreading yet again, shaping Nike into a marketing giant that manages sport events while peddling Nike gear.

"We decided we're a sports company, not just a shoe company," says Knight, who wants to see the now-famous Nike "swoosh" logo on every shirt, shoe, and hat in every televised sporting event in the world. "If you watch Arizona play basketball on television, you see their shoes only about 10% of the time, but the uniform logo is visible about 75% of the time."

> "We decided we're a sports company, not just a shoe company."
> —NIKE CEO PHIL KNIGHT

From signing up superstar athletes like Michael Jordan, it wasn't such a big jump to signing deals with college teams, the Dallas Cowboys, and Brazil's national soccer team. Now it's on to producing Nike events from golf tournaments to soccer matches.

That's a long jog from the days of the simple running shoes.

"Today we promote our athletes and the brand while at the same time making money on the event," Knight told *Fortune*. "It's pretty nice synergy."

Nike is Phil Knight's Sistine Chapel.

When Richard Teerlink slid into the saddle as Harley-Davidson's CEO in 1989, he realized he was driving more than just a motorcycle company. He saw fanatically loyal customers who equate Harley-Davidson with a yearning for freedom and independence. So Teerlink began selling nostalgia. To win new customers and secure old ones, he opened Harley stores and cafes coast to coast, selling Harley apparel and bringing Harley enthusiasts together under one roof. At the same time, he launched a serious quality control program and encouraged all 5,000 employees to get involved by offering incentives for good ideas on how to improve Harley-Davidson motorcycles.

On top of that, Teerlink began asking Harley-Davidson customers themselves how they thought the company could do a better job. He created Harley Owners Groups (HOG), which now numbers 360,000 fanatical members. Local chapters organize frequent road rallies, which Teerlink and other executives attend as often as possible. When customers speak, Teerlink listens: he carries a pad and pencil to write down suggestions and new ideas.

> Harley-Davidson CEO Richard Teerlink realized he was driving more than just a motorcycle company. He saw fanatically loyal customers who equate Harley-Davidson with a yearning for freedom, and independence.

Harley-Davidson is on a roll because one man recognized profits in nostalgia and created wealth from brand loyalty.

Amgen, the big pharmaceuticals firm, is different from other drug companies in one very important way. Amgen stresses lab research, not market research. Rather than start with the disease and work back to the science, Amgen does exactly the opposite—in the belief that companies should take brilliant science and find applications for it. For example, the company's immune booster also helps keep the side effects of chemotherapy from killing cancer patients.

The maverick behind this inspired (and profitable) approach is Amgen CEO Gordon Binder, who not only invests in the lab but also has collaborative arrangements with about 200 colleges and universities that are primed with hundreds of millions of federal research grants every year. "That kind of money will produce a lot of interesting things," he says.

And so it does. Recently, a Rockefeller University professor came up with a new gene that may help make fat people lose weight. This could be big news in markets where people spend $30 billion a year trying to shed pounds. It's not surprising that for a decade Amgen has been number one in average annual return (68 percent) of the Fortune 1,000. That's the kind of medicine investors love.

Champion Enterprises CEO Walter Young helped reinvent the housing industry by taking a creative approach to a dying business. When he took over in 1990, Champion was going nowhere selling inexpensive, factory-built houses.

"People thought we were in the trailer park business," he recalled. "It was a real perception problem, and it was all of our own making."

Young perceived an opportunity. He had a hunch that millions of families who couldn't afford to build a home of their own would be delighted to have a factory-built home trucked right to a lot.

> Champion Enterprises CEO Walter Young had a hunch that millions of families who couldn't afford to build a home of their own would be delighted to have a factory-built home trucked right to a lot.

"Most people wait a year to get their house built," he said. "In three days we can build a house that's equal in quality but less expensive."

At the same time, Young began courting traditional developers, who are normally his competitors.

"Most developers don't earn their cost of capital because they're hanging on to all this land while they wait to get the house built," he explained. Pretty soon both customers and developers began seeing a good thing, and business started to take off. In the late '90s, almost one-third of all housing in the United States was manufactured. Young's goal was to build that number to one-half.

Other companies are turning on the creative juices by changing the rules to make new markets. Boston Market and Starbucks Coffee changed the face of the fast-food business forever: Boston Market by peddling "home-cooked" food to people too busy to cook for themselves; and Starbucks by offering a sleepy supermarket commodity, coffee, in trendy stores in a hundred different varieties.

The auto retailing business is being turned upside down by megadealers such as CarMax and Auto-By Tel, AutoNation USA, and Driver's Mart, who plan to offer more brands and models at a better price and with a minimum of hassle than today's traditional dealer network (kind of like the auto marketing and distribution versions of fast-food restaurants).

Teamwork in business is great. But it takes a bold leader to coach and inspire a successful team, and it takes runaway creativity to inspire the leader.

And you need only open the newspapers almost any day of the week to read about yet another twenty-six-year-old Webnoid genius who has just catapulted himself overnight into the near-billionaire hall of fame by launching a public offering of a new Internet technology or product that has not yet generated even a penny of revenue.

> You need only open the newspapers almost any day of the week to read about yet another twenty-six-year-old Webnoid genius who has just catapulted himself overnight into the near-billionaire hall of fame.

sixteen

The Warrior Monk

A New Class of Leader for the Next Century?

One of the toughest, most successful—and eccentric—men I ever knew was also one of the nicest. He liked to hunt and fish, climb mountains in winter, run the occasional marathon into his early fifties, and not only finished two triathlons but actually did quite well. In college he was an all-American linebacker who loved to charge into opposing players and drop them in their tracks. In the Marines, he earned a number of medals for gallantry in action, then went on to become a hard-driving executive who wound up running a large financial services company.

In business he quickly built a reputation as a gung-ho competitor and iron-handed boss who brooked no nonsense, expected the best from his troops, and never took his eye off the bottom line. He demanded loyalty, gave as good as he got, constantly sought ways to improve his operation and never hesitated to take harsh action, if necessary, to cut costs. At the same time, he believed in innovation and was never content unless the stock was heading north and the company growing.

It wasn't until he was almost fifty that we first met. By then, his reputation had been solidly established. In the press, he was portrayed as a talented and charismatic—if enigmatic—gladiator in the blood and thunder arena of Wall Street.

I was thoroughly unprepared for what common sense told me I should expect. Imagine my surprise when I was greeted by a soft-spoken, genial, warm-eyed gent whom I quickly discovered was quick to laugh, self-effacing, and not entirely comfortable talking about himself. He seemed interested in what others had to say and proved to be a good listener.

As we got to know one another, he began to reveal more. He turned out to be an enormously generous man. For example, in casual conversation, I happened to mention a tricky medical problem a member of my family was experiencing. Without missing a beat, and just as casually, he mentioned that at a word from me he would personally arrange to make available the full resources and finest physicians from a major New York teaching hospital where he served as board chairman. (I subsequently learned that he not only routinely extended this kindness, but followed up.)

He served selflessly on many charities, I was to discover, and quietly gave large amounts of money to working causes and the less fortunate. He donated a library to his alma mater, a pavilion to a hospital, and a gym to an inner-city school that had never known sports. But his name never appeared on any of his gifts. I heard that he had once provided college tuition to a Harlem boy whose father was murdered during a robbery attempt, and provided a trip to Disney World for a dying child he had read about in the papers.

This was all very interesting, but there was one final, totally unexpected surprise.

One day while we were having a little talk over a couple of beers on a terrace overlooking a wide, descending lawn and fading sun, he revealed his most astonishing secret. I had known of his kindnesses and good heart, his generosity and thoughtfulness, but I did not know of his deep spirituality.

Deep but simple. He told me that while in Vietnam he had developed an interest in Eastern religions. Back in the states, he had read all the literature he could find on an Indian holy man by the name of Sri Sai Satya Baba. He also sampled various strains of Buddhism, became largely a vegetarian, and began to practice yoga, which helped him look years younger than his actual age.

What he talked about was a concept he called beezel. He said "beezel" with a straight face, so I was instantly curious. Beezel?

Beezel, he said, was his own private shorthand for Beauty, Service, and Love. B-S-L. Beezel. If you had beezel, he said, you had everything. A nice thought, I was thinking, but somehow I could not make a connection between this flower power homily from the '60s and the tough guy in front of me who had killed other human beings in combat.

Love is necessary to generate right thinking and right action, he said. If you have love you will always do the right thing. Service is the most important product of love, the only legitimate reason for work, he said. Beauty, as in beauty of nature or art, was the sanctuary of the soul and the home of love and regeneration. All three are necessary for a complete life, he said. I still couldn't believe what I was hearing.

Finally, I ventured, how about health? Shouldn't health come first?

If you've got beezel, health will follow, he said matter-of-factly.

How about God? Now I was pushing, maybe too far.

> Love is necessary to generate right thinking. Service is the only legitimate reason for work. Beauty is the sanctuary of the soul. All three are necessary for a complete life.

If you've got beezel, you've got God. How about reconciling beezel with the no-nonsense corporate life: ambition, greed, infighting, all the rest?

No problem. If you've got beezel, ambition becomes another form of service, greed becomes an instrument to amass wealth for the greater good, and infighting is simply a fight for the right. Like the good guy against the bad guys? Something like that, he said.

We went on like that for awhile. In the end I could see there was nothing artificial in anything he was saying—he meant every word—and it all began to make sense.

I tell you all this not because beezel is necessarily the answer for everyone, but rather because without beezel my friend would never have found the true key to his success: his own considerable powers of creativity. It was his discovery of beezel—a selfless, positive approach to life—that allowed him to open the doors of his mind. Innovation and imagination flew out that door with frightening speed, letting him experience a kind of enlightenment, command his own destiny, and forever change the lives of others caught up in the wake of his vision.

Even as a youngster, he'd been wise beyond his years, it turned out.

"When I was still a boy I began to feel an emptiness and frustration. I didn't know what it was, and I didn't like it," he recalled. "When I was a teenager I began to read the great philosophers and study some of the world's religions. Nothing was too weird or far out," he said. "Then I enlisted in the Marines. I got back from

Vietnam a changed man, in many ways. In college I majored in economics but I read history until I couldn't keep my eyes open."

He seemed at peace in the afterglow of a sun now sunk beyond the tree line. I felt a little like an eavesdropper, yet somehow privileged, to be a party to all this remarkable disclosure. Could this be the same ruthless magnate and power broker I had always heard so much about?

Eventually, he talked about Vietnam and the unspeakable horrors there. Numbed and sickened, wounded twice, he returned home to general malaise, public venom, and a rapidly changing world—none of which so much as turned his head.

"I just kept pressing ahead," he said. "I never looked back. For me the war was over."

I could not help but wonder if he had been wounded in other ways by the war. If he was, he didn't say, and I did not ask.

After two years in the management training program of a Wall Street firm, he put himself through business school then struck out on his own, and the rest is history.

"Without beezel you can't know yourself, and if you don't know yourself it's difficult to help anyone else," he said. He thought about that, then forged on: "What I mean by that is, if you learn to have love, and use that love to get things done and make things happen, then you can be useful. If you're not being useful—not making things grow or creating new things, for example—then you're not being of service. You're not contributing, you're not fulfilling what you were put here to do."

What were we put here to do?

"We were put here to help other people. That's the whole of it right there."

By the time the sun went down and we had given up the terrace to the mosquitoes and lightning bugs, I was wiser for having listened. I was also a little ashamed—because I knew I could never be all he implied I should be.

That was the last serious conversation we ever had, and the only time he chose to open up to me. We saw one another briefly from time to time, but I never forgot beezel. Then one day I heard he'd been killed in a helicopter accident. I was stunned. My mind raced back to that afternoon on the terrace, and I could see him again, sipping his beer in the setting sun, telling me—a relative stranger—the secrets of his success, telling me about this thing he called beezel.

Does beezel work for everyone?

If it worked for my warrior/philosopher friend—a most unlikely candidate by any measure—then why would it not work for the rest of us? Can beauty, love and service, fully embraced, actually turbocharge the mind's creative engines, giving us power, new life, and expression?

We've each got to find out for ourselves.

seventeen

The Hole in the Ground Theory:

Balancing the Heart with the Head

I s it better to go with your heart, to listen to your gut instincts and hot flashes of intuition, or abide by the calmer, cooler voices of logic and reason?

Psychologist Robert K. Cooper came up with an interesting idea he calls EQ, or emotional intelligence quotient. EQ says that people who rely on their natural intuition and gut feelings are more likely to be successful in business.

For example, he says that if business owners make a pitch to potential investors based on EQ, they will appear more "sincere" and "passionate," which racks up more points "than coldly explaining the balance sheet."

Emotions, it could be argued, are inseparable from creativity. In fact, creativity without emotion—without heart, caring, or passion—is not

> If business owners make a pitch to potential investors based on EQ, they will appear more "sincere" and "passionate," which racks up more points "than coldly explaining the balance sheet."

creativity at all but rather some passive, chilly thing that simply watches, waits, and eventually dies.

If we can agree that creativity and passion together constitute a potent force for the good, then we've got to rethink our traditional approach to the workplace and marketplace. Cooper goes so far as to say that a leader's EQ can ultimately determine a firm's success. And he's convinced we should all switch to a new standard, as in the following:

- Traditionalists say emotions distract them.
- High performers say emotions motivate them.

- Traditionalists say emotions increase vulnerability.
- High performers say emotions increase confidence.

- Traditionalists say emotions cloud judgment.
- High performers say emotions speed analysis.

- Traditionalists say emotions must be controlled.
- High performers say emotions build trust.

- Traditionalists say emotions inhibit data flow.
- High performers say emotions provide vital feedback.

> Traditionalists say emotions distract and cloud judgment. High performers say emotions motivate and increase confidence.

Passion by itself will not determine whether you make it. But allowing your gut instincts to speak to you—if only in a whisper—can stoke your creative embers and even on occasion save you from grief.

For example, I was once party to a sure-fire bonanza that promised to make everyone privy to the insider scoop an instant millionaire.

The play went something like this: a number of people in a small company where I once worked had invested most of their net worth in a start-up Australian minerals oper-

> Allowing your gut instincts to speak to you can save you from grief.

ation. A big Australian private investor and famous British billion-aire were backing the project. I was told I'd be crazy not to get in on this amazing deal before it went public. I listened with interest while they described untapped treasure beyond imagining: gold, dia monds, emeralds, opals, rubies, and more. I could picture a kind of Solomon's mine bursting with fabulous wealth. I could see buckets of glittering gems and gold coming up out of the earth, faster and faster, like a geysering rainbow of cash. My associates seemed gen-uinely interested in helping me. I felt my own excitement build as they described the significance of this unique opportunity, the potential for huge returns, the sure-fire growth, killer profits, on and on. All I had to do was kick in. I'd be in like Flynn and on my way to early retirement.

After all, serious players thought the transaction looked good. Australia was full of unmined riches. The world demand for min-erals was exploding. And we were fortunate to be in on a deal that would make us so rich we'd never have to work again. Thoughts of Rio, Tahiti, Monaco, and the Caribbean started dancing in my head.

And that's when I must have heard the little voice. I don't recall the actual moment or hearing anything in particular. But I do remember saying that I wanted to ask just two questions: (1) Was there a hole in the ground? and (2) If so, was there a road or a train or some way of getting the minerals from the hole in the ground to market?

Curious how the simplest questions can sometimes draw the blankest stares. The answer to number one was either "I don't know," or "we're not sure." The answer to number two was more empty looks, more I-don't-knows.

Don't know? Don't know if there's an actual hole in the ground? Don't know if there's a road or a train track? You gave these people almost every penny you've got and you don't know?

We don't know.

We've read the prospectus, they said. The numbers look good.

Now some uneasy looks, back and forth.

The fact is, this sure-fire transaction sounded too good to be true. And of course, it was. Turned out that for whatever reason—I can't recall—the deal fell through and my friends lost all their money.

There was no hole in the ground.

There was no road, no track.

Some bad guys had made off with the money and now my friends (one money manager and one financial analyst among them) were feeling embarrassed, angry, frustrated, violated.

I, on the other hand, was feeling very lucky. The main source of my good fortune in this particular instance was not smarts. I didn't know enough about minerals investing to make an intelligent decision. And I certainly did not have the money, in any event.

The source of my good luck is what I have come to call the Hole in the Ground theory. The Hole in the Ground theory holds that the dumbest question may well turn out to be the smartest question, and that if you listen carefully the necessary question will come to you just when you need it.

The dark side of creativity is that the wrong things (greed, covetousness, lust, anger, selfishness) can motivate us all and put our talents—and vulnerabilities—to the test.

So before you dig into your pocket, drill down into the issues to make sure you uncover the hole(s) in the argument. The questions to ask are: What is the hole in the ground here? (What's the flaw in this proposal?) Or, *is* there a hole in the ground? (Is there any substance to this proposal?)

The dark side of creativity is that the wrong things can motivate us all and put our talents—and vulnerabilities—to the test.

If you remember the Hole in the Ground theory you may dodge a bullet—and not wind up looking like you've got a hole in the head.

e i g h t e e n

Up and Out:

Taking Your Career to a New Level

" I don't know how to make money . . . . I don't have any idea how to make money . . . . I just keep doing the same old thing and I'm not making any money . . . ."

I overheard this brief but poignant lament on a busy street corner in New York City as a professional-looking young woman confided this source of constant worry to her companion, a man in a business suit who looked distracted and not particularly sympathetic.

They walked across the intersection with the green light and melted into the crowd. But the woman's words left me wondering how many millions of other people are meeting at crossroads their whole lives long, pondering their earthly conditions in ways large and small, then moving on—perhaps never even knowing they are at a crossroads.

In the case of the young woman, the issue was money. But it might have been status or success or love or prestige or yearning of any kind: the desire to improve one's lot, the desire to have more, to

171

live better, to do more, to reach ever higher, to succeed at something—anything—perhaps to actually *be somebody*.

For a moment, I almost wanted to whisper to her just one word: Targets. Seek targets.

Want something? Give yourself something to work for, to live for. Then make the dream real. Make that something happen. Just go there.

I wanted to say, "You want money? Then you have to begin thinking in new ways. You have to begin acting in new ways. Life is short and the world is full of opportunity."

Maybe you've got to jump up and get out. Up and out. You've got to go up and out, I wanted to say. Job going nowhere? Up and out. Your daily routine a bore? Up and out. Feeling flat and unfulfilled? Up and out. Leave the job. Upset the routine. Change your life. I wanted to say that if life is dictating your life, you're not living. But if you ever expect to be able to run your own life, you've got to know what you want. Once you know what you want, you need only go there. But you've got to be willing to put yourself in enough jeopardy to trigger the creative experience, which is born partially of the need to survive and partially of the need to try to harness the sometimes cruel winds of fortune. In the end, creativity is a function of being willing to blow the whole thing, to have fun, to let it all hang out. Legendary business mavericks who win and lose fortunes but always seem to wind up on top are exactly the kind of people I'm talking about.

> You've got to be willing to put yourself in enough jeopardy to trigger the creative experience, which is born partially of the need to survive and partially of the need to try to harness the sometimes cruel winds of fortune. In the end, creativity is a function of being willing to blow the whole thing, to have fun, to let it all hang out.

So it's up and out. Forget the status quo. Way up and way out. Find some other way to go. You can't go anywhere if your feet are stuck, I wanted to say to the young woman. That's why you need something to shoot for, something new, something to rock your socks.

How do you know if your feet are stuck? You know your feet are stuck when:

> Forget the status quo. Find some other way to go.

- The job isn't fun any more.
- It's tough to get up in the morning.
- You drag during the day.
- You watch the clock a lot.
- You seem to be grumpy most of the time.
- You sleep too little.
- You sleep too much.
- You can't think of anything to look forward to.
- Nothing seems to turn you on any more.

If you apply this brief test to your career and recognize the symptoms, then it's time for a change.

Cardinal Health CEO Bob Walter climbed out of a box to get to the top. After college, he got a job with Rockwell International but ran into what he saw as a stifling wall of bureaucracy and quit after just six months. He went to Harvard Business School, started buying up small drug wholesalers, and a quarter of a century later was running a $200 million company with sales of $11 billion and growing.

> You know you're in a rut when it's tough to get up in the morning and the job isn't fun any more.

Generoso Pope, onetime owner of the *National Enquirer*, graduated from

MIT with a degree in air conditioning engineering. It didn't take Pope long after graduation to figure out that air conditioning left him cold. One day he saw a crowd of people gaping at a car accident in New York City and a little bell went off. Pope decided it was time for a change. If people wanted to see accidents, he would show them accidents. So he set out to find a newspaper and ended up buying an obscure horse racing sheet, the *Enquirer*, for $25,000, which he renamed the *National Enquirer*. The rest is history. When he saw people were able to stomach only so much gore, Pope cleaned up his act and started selling the *National Enquirer* as a family publication in supermarkets. After his death in 1988, Pope's $25,000 investment sold for $600 million.

> One day Generoso Pope saw a crowd of people gaping at a car accident in New York City and a little bell went off.

Some of the great unsung success stories of all time are driven by radical, dramatic change—change imposed by cruel fate: the great athlete crippled by an accident who winds up inspiring others on the lecture circuit; the child who spends his early years as a shut-in suffering from asthma who, forced to spend his days indoors reading books, grows up to be a Pulitzer Prize-winning author; the shy, tormented kid who secretly skips school to find comfort and magic in the private world of the movies and eventually becomes one of the most successful producers and directors ever; the person who is fired from a badly needed job only to go on to become a successful entrepreneur worth millions, or better yet, comes back and buys the company that fired him. These and thousands of others are examples of a phenomenon in nature we can call compensation. None of these life setbacks is by choice, but most "victims" seem to agree that their "tragic" experience was "the best thing that ever happened to me."

Potent testimony to the power of harsh change to affect our lives for the good.

What we're talking about here is another kind of change—wrenching change imposed like a hammer blow from the outside. This is what happens when life forces us—in spite of ourselves—to confront our true selves, our greatest potentialities, our destinies. This is life's jarring wake-up call, and it gets our attention like a gun up the nose.

In a surreal heartbeat, Christopher Reeve, Hollywood's "Superman," saw the charmed life he knew come to an abrupt halt and a new life as a quadriplegic begin. Paralyzed below the neck, hooked up to a breathing machine, and confined, probably for life, to a wheelchair, Reeve had to begin again. His new reality thrust him into the forefront of lobbying for medical research and serving as a source of inspiration and magnet of attention for others who have suffered similar devastating injuries. In a TV interview, he allowed that his accident lets him fulfill the most meaningful role of his life.

> Sometimes life forces us—in spite of ourselves—to confront our true selves, our greatest potentialities, our destinies.

That's why I wanted to tell the young woman on the corner: Find your own destiny before fate finds you. Is your goal money? Then money can be the carrot that will lead you to your heart. Just go there.

Down and out? Time to get up and out.

For the briefest moment there on the corner I had a whimsical vision. I imagined the young woman hurling a kind of hook into the night sky. I imagined the hook capturing a star or a comet and I imagined her pulling herself off the path she'd been on, pulling herself up and out.

nineteen

If You Had It to Do Over:

The Importance of Passion

Creativity in business is a state of mind. Creativity flows from the office to the home to the road and back to the office, a constant awareness of innovation and change looking for expression at work and play.

Creativity is born in the individual but takes root in the group, manifesting as joy and spreading like laughter.

When creativity is set loose in any organization—a condition not uncommon in the cyberlabs of Silicon Valley, for example—productivity is launched to a new level.

I remember reading the story of the champion gymnast who had a tough coach and trainer in a Zen Buddhist master. One day in practice, it all came together for the young gymnast. As the coach watched, the boy performed flawlessly on the rings and parallel bars, then nailed his final routine with a picture-perfect twisting, spinning dismount. He stood breathing hard and flush in the

> When creativity is set loose, productivity is launched to a new level.

glorious afterglow of what he knew was his best performance ever, fully expecting the praise he so richly deserved.

Instead, the coach gave his young student a lukewarm reception, allowing as the routines were good, but . . .

But what? the boy wanted to know.

"You have finally mastered the skills you need," the master told the boy. "But you are not yet ready to be champion."

The boy was crushed. What else, he wanted to know, did he need?

The master explained that while the boy's talents burned brightly during the performance itself, the boy had failed to lend the same concentration and quality to what transpired *between* performances, which was most of the time. The mental discipline, the economy of motion, the desire for excellence, the extreme artistry he had demonstrated "in flight," so to speak, he had forgotten to apply to the long stretches of time when his feet were on the ground.

And therein, according to the master, lay the true test of excellence. It is not good enough to be the best only part of the time. A true champion, a true leader, a true artist is at his or her best *all* the time.

Legendary NFL coach Vince Lombardi understood better than most people that being champion can never be a part-time job. And he never missed a chance to spread his gospel of winning.

> "Winning is not a sometime thing—it's an all-the-time thing."
>
> —VINCE LOMBARDI

"You've got to pay the price," he said. "Winning is not a sometime thing—it's an all-the-time thing. You don't win once in a while . . . you don't do things right once in a while . . . you do them right all the time."

Lombardi liked to say that "running a football team is no different from any other kind of organization—an army, a political party, a business. The principles are the same. The object is to win."

Vince Lombardi's creative genius manifested as a talent for motivation, inspiration and leadership that still serves as a model to business people today.

For Lombardi, the instrument of personal fulfillment, the key to the meaning of life itself, was total victory. His creative genius manifested as a talent for motivation, inspiration, and leadership that still serves as a model for business people today.

For another great leader, President Theodore Roosevelt, the meaning of life emerged out of struggle. Struggle was the ruddy color of Roosevelt's creative fire. Struggle was everything. You can imagine Teddy, standing at the back of a campaign train, slashing the air with his fists as he extolled his famous "bully pulpit," preaching the glories of the hard life:

"The credit belongs to the man who is actually in the arena," he roars to the spellbound crowd. " . . . the man whose face is marred by sweat and blood . . . who strives valiantly . . . who errs and comes short again and again . . . who knows the great enthusiasms, the great devotions, and spends himself in a worthy cause . . . who at the best, knows the triumph of high achievement, and who, at the worst, if he fails, at least fails while daring greatly, so that this place shall never be those cold and timid souls who know neither victory nor defeat."

Teddy Roosevelt's creative passion was a kind of furious energy that thrust him to stunning success as a soldier, sportsman, author, lecturer, Navy secretary, governor, and finally president.

For President Theodore Roosevelt, the meaning of life emerged out of struggle.

Most people can only dream of soaring to such heights in their lifetime.

> *"If I had my life to live over, I'd try to make more mistakes next time. I would relax, I would limber up, I would be crazier than I've been on this trip."*
> —ANONYMOUS

But millions more frankly don't care—and are content to measure success in an altogether different way. For the more gently inclined, the path to self-realization is an almost romantic approach to the secrets of life. Yet sadly, the vast majority of us never come to be acquainted with even those tranquil but potent pleasures. In other words, most of us realize only too late that we've allowed the fun of life to pass us by. Witness this moving reminiscence from a dying eighty-two-year-old man, as reported in the *Journal of Humanistic Psychology*:

> *If I had my life to live over, I'd try to make more mistakes next time. I would relax, I would limber up, I would be crazier than I've been on this trip.*
>
> *I know very few things I'd take seriously any more. I would take more chances. I would take more trips, I would scale more mountains, I would swim more rivers, and I would eat more ice cream and fewer beans.*
>
> *I've been one of those people who never went anywhere without a thermometer, a hot water bottle, a gargle, a raincoat, and a parachute.*
>
> *If I had it to do all over again, I'd travel lighter, much lighter than I have.*
>
> *I would start barefoot earlier in the spring. and I would ride more merry-go-rounds, and catch more golden rings, and greet more people, and pick more flowers, and dance more often. If I had it to do all over again. But you see, I don't.*

Too late, perhaps, for this gent who found himself when his life was over. But for anyone reading this book it's certainly not too late. One way to vent creative energy is to think about life and work as a daily adventure. Adopting a fresh, playful approach guarantees nothing. But it can wake us up and make life and work more livable—maybe even fun. In the end, it can access, perhaps stimulate, the vital, hidden part of us that may still want to fly.

What's Next?

I t's hard to say, given clashing cultures, political chaos in the Third World, overpopulation bordering on the unmanageable, global anxiety levels running on overdrive, and countless other complications and distractions. But it's even harder to imagine a future not somehow awash in, and redeemed by, a universe of technology so enabling that it will open up new dimensions to millions.

Computers that run not only our businesses, but our houses, as well. Computers that answer to voice commands. Computers that actually talk. Virtual reality so convincing and powerful we can be "transported" to other places and other worlds. Computers that answer almost every need.

But with all this, a questioning person might watch the digital glitter unfold in the years ahead and begin to wonder: Wonder if it is, after all, a wise thing to turn over our lives so completely to electrons and gigabytes; wonder if our boundless infatuation with marvelous gadgets and all things technical might, while enabling, also subtly deprive; wonder if in some strange way we can't foresee there may be a kind of darkness at the end of this brightly-lit tunnel; wonder if in the end the consequences might even come to outweigh the benefits.

After all, if the world can threaten to come to a complete halt, and nuclear weapons be accidentally unleashed simply because no one thought to program the year 2000 into any program anywhere, what does it profit us to be technically advanced?

A questioning person, someone who has lived long enough to understand cause and effect and the natural laws of balance and moderation, might worry a little about these things.

Give a family a television and they might stop reading. Give a student a calculator and he might stop adding and subtracting. Computerize the entire planet and our machines have the potential to eventually perform virtually all the tasks, physical and mental, that we once had to do ourselves.

The good news: machines unlock secrets and make life easier, even better, for a lot of people. The bad news: we stop participating in our own lives, become physically soft and mentally lazy.

Anything that can dampen our natural aptitude for creativity can't be all good.

In the future, in a world so technically evolved that almost everything is computerized, the most creatively fulfilled among us might well be only those who design the software, those who use technology to create better products or services, and the holdout rebels who resist temptation to rely on anything more than the future equivalent of a Palm Pilot.

The rest of us—the vast majority—may find ourselves merely servants to our creations, endlessly punching keys and blinking at screens, unable to resist the temptation to let the machines do it all. The magnetic attraction of the ever-burgeoning Web and cyber-space, like a noxious charmer, cries out to embrace and woo us ever deeper into what may turn out to be a long sleep of our own making.

Even today, computers can write our poems, create our art, design the architecture and infrastructure that surrounds our lives, provide all we ever thought we needed to know, and like the most trusted of friends be there for us day and night, from first breath to last.

Anyone daring to look even slightly askance at this rosy future might well expect to be accused of seeing the glass half empty. Setting aside for a moment the giddy delights, such a person may ask —in the midst of the blessings—what's to become of our pride of self-sufficiency and independence, our sense of self worth, our character, our passion? What is to become of our true grit, our God-given raw talent to create and make things right out of our own gut, our soul? These are the fundamental parts of our heritage we've never mined, hardly even noticed, because we've had them always and always taken them for granted. And like everything else in life, we may not begin to miss them until they eventually start to fade away.

As the song mentions, where has Joe DiMaggio gone? We might also ask, where have you gone Wolfgang and Johannes, Pablo, Walt, Ansel, Alexander, Thomas, and Albert—all of whom, and many more, walked through their creative lives without digital crutches.

At the very heart of our creative nature lies an ancient need to rely on ourselves. God bless the Web and may it always serve us well. But God bless also the spirit of humankind that gives us the power to surpass even our most magical creations. True creativity requires silence, meditation, sometimes even prayer. Creativity first demands an implosion into the self before the process of nuclear fission can begin and great explosions occur. While the Web can give us riches of knowledge and perhaps even contribute to the process, it can in no way actually be us or do the job for us. Here's the thing: At some point it will always be necessary to switch off the machine and step into the shower or take a nice, long walk in the woods.

Index